LONDON'S
LATE NIGHT
Scandal

By Anabelle Bryant

London's Late Night Scandal

London's Best Kept Secret

London's Wicked Affair

Published by Kensington Publishing Corporation

LONDON'S
LATE NIGHT
Scandal

ANABELLE BRYANT

ZEBRA BOOKS
KENSINGTON PUBLISHING CORP.
www.kensingtonbooks.com

ZEBRA BOOKS are published by

Kensington Publishing Corp.
119 West 40th Street
New York, NY 10018

All Kensington titles, imprints, and distributed lines are available at special quantity discounts for bulk purchases for sales promotion, premiums, fund-raising, educational, or institutional use.

Special book excerpts or customized printings can also be created to fit specific needs. For details, write or phone the office of the Kensington Sales Manager: Attn.: Sales Department. Kensington Publishing Corp., 119 West 40th Street, New York, NY 10018. Phone: 1-800-221-2647.

Zebra and the Z logo Reg. U.S. Pat. & TM Off.

First Printing: October 2019
ISBN-13: 978-1-4201-4647-9
ISBN-10: 1-4201-4647-5

ISBN-13: 978-1-4201-4648-6 (eBook)
ISBN-10: 1-4201-4648-3 (eBook)

10 9 8 7 6 5 4 3 2 1

Printed in the United States of America

This book is dedicated to romance readers everywhere.
Your belief in hope, love,
and happily-ever-after is a precious gift.
Your unfailing optimism and loyalty brighten the world,
and I thank you.

For David and Nicholas, always in my heart.

ACKNOWLEDGMENTS

I have a heart full of gratitude for my brilliant editor, Esi Sogah, who has the power to produce my smile whenever I see an email from her in my inbox. Thank you for your clever guidance and thoughtful support. I truly appreciate you.

My sincere thanks to Kensington Publishing and the fabulous people who work skillfully to enable my story to reach readers. What better kind of magic is there than to share imagination?

Last and most especially, for anyone who has waited for Matthew's story with skepticism and curiosity, you'll find he's changed his ways and intends to change your mind. Thank you for reading!

Chapter One

London, 1817

Lord Matthew Strathmore, Earl of Whittingham, slapped the leather reins and urged the four dappled grays into a faster gallop.

"You're concerned about the weather."

"Astute observation, Coggs." Whittingham heaved a breath of impatience. "Not only are you an excellent man-of-all-things, but a master of insight and circumstance." He flicked his eyes from the unending roadway to the servant seated beside him. Coggs was more friend than valet; still, the man possessed the ability to irritate at times, and this was one of those times.

The weather threatened with increasing fortitude the farther they journeyed from London, and during the last few miles, the air had transformed from chilling cold to the sharp edge of frigid, until each puff of breath that evaporated before their faces reminded them that too long spent outdoors would promise a brittle end.

Worse, they were far and away from any familiar thoroughfare where another stubborn, albeit foolish, traveler might discover their frozen corpses once the cold claimed its victory. Thus, the only hope of reaching their destination before nightfall relied on Whittingham pushing his well-bred stallions to full speed.

"You would be warmer inside the carriage. You haven't a hat or muffler, and the wind has a nasty bite this late in the afternoon."

"If your only purpose upon this seat is to act the nurse-maid, I suggest you climb back inside and keep George company." At the last coaching inn, Whittingham had in-sisted on taking the straps from his young driver. Not only would the lad hesitate in pushing the horses as hard as needed, but there was no purpose in having George suffer the brunt of fierce weather and ill-advised impromptu travel when Whittingham was the one who had insisted they take to the road with haste.

Besides, one more minute trapped inside the interior with his legs folded at an uncomfortable angle would pro-voke a fouler mood than he already possessed. His left leg throbbed like the devil—no matter that the gunshot wound that caused his difficulty occurred a decade ago, the injury needed no provocation to cause pain. The cramped con-fines of the coach, poor roadway conditions, and brutal, uncompromised temperature guaranteed he'd pay for his decision in spades. Hopefully, not the kind that dug graves.

"I'd rather sit beside you in case I'm needed."

Abandoning his grim thoughts, Whittingham resumed the conversation and offered Coggs a nod of appreciation. His mood was blacker than the storm clouds riding the horizon, but snarling at his valet when the man championed the cold to offer support was not in Whittingham's usually congenial nature. "Are you certain? No doubt George has a wool blanket across his lap and a heated brick at his feet."

Saying the words drew an enticing image he'd rather not

consider. He flexed the muscles in his bad leg and glanced at the sky. If the snow held, they would make it to Leighton House before dark. Becoming cold was an inconvenience. Becoming cold and wet was an invitation to death. "You should ride inside. I'll rap on the roof to signal you if the situation warrants assistance."

The valet looked upward and shook his head. "How much farther can it be?"

In a ruse Whittingham knew well, Coggs deflected the uncomfortable subject of limitations, unforgiving injuries, and common sense. His valet deserved a better employer. "At least another hour if the roads remain clear. Leighton House is situated on a sprawling plot of acreage near the western border of Oxfordshire."

"It was hospitable of the master of the house to invite you on such short notice."

"Agreed." Whittingham tossed a too long lock of hair from his forehead. He'd neglected a haircut much like he ignored other ordinary tasks, his time spent within the pages of a book instead. "My studies are of the utmost importance."

"I know that well."

"Do I detect a note of censure in your reply?" Whittingham slowed the team to a lively trot as the road dipped, marred with stony ruts and misshapen holes the perfect size to catch a horse's hoof and damage his leg for a lifetime. The similarity of situation was not lost on him, and once the road smoothed out, he jerked his wrist and jolted the carriage forward to resume their breakneck travel.

"Nothing of the sort," Coggs managed, though he pulled his woolen collar more tightly around his neck to combat the wind that whipped between them. "I hardly wonder why you need to address the issue. You're an impatient scholar. No sooner do you form a hypothesis than you seek the solution with relentless fervor. Why would this endeavor follow a different path?"

"It's reassuring the last eight years of your service haven't gone wasted," Whittingham replied. "You do know me well, although you should make up your mind upon the matter. You've often suggested I live life more fully, embrace new experiences and step away from the solitude of my studies, and now that I'm doing so, you seemed displeased."

Nothing was said for a time after that. Whittingham owned the fact that his work habits were intrusive, if not obsessive at times. He pursued a course of academia once he realized his impairment, a debilitating wound to the knee, would never allow him the gallant luxuries other gentlemen managed with ease. Riding a horse was bearable, but hardly enjoyable. Dancing was out of the question. On most days, the pain remained a whisper, no more than an aching memory of a poorly made decision from his past.

Other days, this being one, the muscles of his left leg cramped and twisted as if a relentless reminder of his limitations, all too quick to persuade him to go home, sit quietly in an overstuffed chair near the fireplace fender, and politely die of boredom.

He would have no part of surrender, and therefore endured the sharpest spike of pain without complaint. He wouldn't be compromised by circumstances he couldn't change.

No sooner did he repeat this silent vow than a westing gust of wind hurried past with a burst of icy air that could only be God's laughter at the earl's ignorance.

True enough, tomorrow he would pay a deep price for his travels today.

"I sincerely hope you acquire the answers to your questions. As your loyal servant, I do as I am told, but as a simple man on this driver's seat, near frozen and somewhat hungry, I pray this trip into nowhere proves worth the effort."

"I have no doubt it will, Coggs." Whittingham smiled, though his mouth was tight from the harsh temperature. "One cannot publish a journal article in *Philosophical Transactions of the Royal Society* without the correct proof of knowledge, and I intend to investigate and repudiate the claims made, if for no other reason than to defend the truth. While Lord Talbot may know his way around scientific theory, his lack of detail leaves me curious and more than a little suspicious. The hypothesis presented in the article failed to contain the precise proof expected with Talbot's notable reputation. The earl hadn't the decency to answer my inquiries through post but has now unexpectedly agreed to meet. That's an adequate start, which I intend to see to a satisfactory end. I couldn't wait around London, at risk Talbot might change his mind. His invitation was surprising but fortuitous. And so, there you have it. Despite the ill weather and the spontaneity of our travel, I had little choice but to act immediately once I received his correspondence."

"Indeed."

"It could be my own perspicuity that raised false suspicions, though Talbot hasn't lectured in London or sought attention for any of the evidences proposed in his series of articles, and it's been several years since his breakthrough experiments have warranted news. Most leaders of academia strive to share knowledge, not hoard it. No one at the Society for the Intellectually Advanced can unriddle his reclusive behavior. A commitment to speak to the most elite intellectual organization in all of England would be a rare and gratifying opportunity, most especially if I brought it forward as chief officer." He flicked his eyes toward the sky and then to the roadway just as quickly. "And as the members of the Society continue to question the validity of the claims made, verifying the article and engaging the earl to speak in London, or likewise exposing him for fraud, will accredit my newly gained position."

"So, with this jaunt into nowhere you have an agenda of multipurpose." Coggs turned toward him, his brows lowered in question.

"Don't I always?" Whittingham answered. "Science is truth. Thanks to my sister's interference, my succession into the position of chief officer was less than smooth. Ferreting out faulty, half-baked experimental reporting will prove with conviction I'm qualified for the position, knowledgeable, and otherwise worthy."

"I see." Coggs nodded.

"That said, putting past publication aside, Talbot might now be nothing more than a charlatan. A dreamer. A man who knows nothing about scientific philosophy other than how to manipulate syntax to thread together a credible suggestion and bamboozle trusting souls. Wouldn't that be an interesting turn?" He looked toward Coggs with a knowing stare. "Either way, I intend to find out."

Theodosia Leighton, granddaughter of the Earl of Talbot, stood before her workstation and stared intently at a glass beaker filled halfway with a mixture of agitative liquids. She checked her grandfather's notations scribbled on the page of the open journal, in reference to the measurements. Something should have happened by now, but the clear liquid inside the glass remained unchanged. She blew a breath of exasperation and stepped away.

"I don't know what went wrong, Nicolaus." She didn't expect an answer as he was accustomed to her thinking aloud, and she paced to the hearth and back again as a way to expend energy while she waited. Curious now, Nicolaus approached the beaker, leaned in, sniffed the liquid inside, and withdrew right after.

"I know." She understood his displeasure. "The formula smells horrible and Grandfather hasn't a notation anywhere to explain the chemical change. With the remaining pages of his journal missing and only half an accounting, I'm at a loss to reproduce the outcome."

Disinterested in disappointment or any recitation of complaint, Nicolaus silently left the room. Theodosia watched him go and could hardly blame his reaction. She'd re-created the experiment several times without success, and yet her grandfather was the most knowledgeable and meticulous scientist Oxfordshire had ever known.

At least, she believed so.

What had she missed in his documentation? She'd honed her skills of observation and detail to an exacting degree. Through practice, sampling, and sketching every specimen available to her, she'd created a catalog of scientific knowledge in her brain. With an excellent memory and concise method of deductive reasoning, the idea that she had failed to reason out the problem with the experiment irked her frustration.

At a loss for the time being, she strode to the window and glanced at the foreboding cloud cover. *Snow.* Everything about the view outside predicted an imminent snowfall. A strong wind bent the tree limbs of the sole remaining chestnut tree spared by the fire years ago, and not a creature could be seen, most likely burrowed beneath the hedgerows or sheltered by the dense Scotch firs that lined the perimeter of property farther from the house. Even the air seemed raw and crisp, no matter she remained inside and viewed the world through glass. These conditions were a precursor to significant precipitation. She would record her observations in her weather journal later this evening when she was too tired to do little more than move a pencil across the page.

Snow complicated even the simplest tasks. Before dinner she would check with the housekeeper, Mrs. Mavis, and ensure they had provisions in case this sudden unsettling cold spell hampered them for a few days. They were too far from town to be caught unaware in bad weather. Food items, candles, firewood, and the necessary supplies for daily living, would all need to be secured. A few of the stable hands would see to the work of bedding down the horses. Eggs would have to be collected, and then there were all her animals to tend.

These tasks would have been accomplished with a smile if she'd mastered her research this afternoon. Instead, she could only review her grandfather's notes and attempt to understand his reasoning. It took her the better half of a year to learn his notation system and decipher many of his complicated trials. But omitted text . . . that created a difficult hurdle, far beyond her until she fully understood the theory behind his work. When questioned, Grandfather waved away her inquiries as if his notebooks were no longer a language he understood.

Returning to the workstation table, she stared down at the open book. She needed the missing pages. Nearly a third of the entries were gone, and the current passage was incomplete. She touched the paper and smoothed a fingertip over the scrawled notes, careful not to smudge the graphite. If only she had someone other than Grandfather to ask for assistance. When she closed her eyes and wished hard enough, she could still hear her parents' voices, though so many years had passed she wondered if it wasn't an imagined attempt to soothe the bottomless ache in her heart.

Her parents perished in a fire nearly twenty years ago. Theodosia was carried to safety from the estate in her grandfather's arms. At five years old she mourned the loss of her parents, but she never anticipated the loneliness that was to follow, despite the loving attention of her grandfather and the extensive kindness of the household staff.

She shook her head and forced her eyes open wide, quick to blink away the threat of tears. She wouldn't conjure memories now. She couldn't. Seeking distraction, she flipped the journal closed and moved away from the table. She had animals to attend to and other important tasks before dinner. Where was Nicolaus, anyway? Only a fool would go out in the unforgiving winter cold.

She needed to check in on Grandfather before it grew much later, but first she would find Mrs. Mavis. If the weather planned to wreak havoc on Leighton House, the least she could do was prepare for the worst.

Chapter Two

Whittingham urged the exhausted team through a final bend of the roadway and onto the gravel drive of Leighton House. The hour was later than he'd like, yet all things considered he was relieved they'd completed the seven-hour trip before darkness claimed the sky. Snow had begun to fall during the last few miles, and with Coggs inside the carriage keeping company with George, the driver, Whittingham had had time to organize his thoughts. Talbot's latest article concerning chemical ratios and compounds suggested a rare isolation of dephlogisticated air. The series of scientific trials sounded inconclusive at best, and Whittingham had a bounty of questions concerning the earl's results.

Yet any scientific discussion would wait until morning. His only want at the moment was to abandon the boot in search of a warm fire and brandy. With luck, Talbot would be available and hospitable at this hour.

He pulled the reins and settled the grays as the carriage rolled to a stop before an elongated walkway of limestone stairs. Two footmen were quick to greet him, and George reclaimed the driver seat to accompany the men to the rear of the estate, where the horses would find shelter and a well-earned meal. Whittingham managed the endless path to the estate's door with only a few black oaths. Thankfully, Coggs had the decency to keep his trap closed.

They were shown through the entrance by an additional footman. The grand foyer gleamed with polished black tile and sleek white marble. Several wall sconces and table lanterns lit the area with warm golden candlelight and the immediate effect was soothing, just what he desired. The cold weather, restricted movement, and extensive travel had all combined to tighten his muscles. He leaned too much on his fennel-wood walking stick and resented the necessity, but fatigue reigned master at the moment.

"Good evening, gentlemen." The butler stepped forward as a servant moved in to accept their overcoats. "I am butler Alberts, at your service. May I inquire about the purpose of your visit?"

The efficient butler crimped a stiff welcome and Whittingham offered his calling card. "Please pardon the late hour. Our travel was complicated by the weather. Lord Leighton is expecting me." He shifted his position, desperate for respite aside a roaring fire in hope of relieving the throbbing ache in his leg. Now indoors, the thaw had begun and although not literal in meaning, he almost wished the bloody muscles would stay frozen. At least for the time being.

"I will inform the household of your arrival." The butler turned and motioned toward the left. "If you will come this way."

He didn't say more and Whittingham followed, Coggs a few steps behind. He knew the concerns his valet negotiated. The tiles were slick, Whittingham's muscles stiff and clumsy, and his gait even more uneven than usual. But with a narrowed glance over his shoulder he reminded Coggs not to voice these observations until they were privately installed in guest chambers. As added insurance, he offered his man-of-all-things a blunt directive. "You may wait in the hall."

The butler led Whittingham to a welcoming drawing room decorated in varying shades of charcoal and butter yellow. Windows stretched to the vaulted plasterwork ceiling despite they offered no view, the thick velvet drapes drawn closed to conserve warmth. Bookcases lined the walls, their repetition broken only by a satinwood writing desk and matching sideboard where a tea service graced a silver tray. Was there no brandy to be had? His eyes settled on the firebox, and though his leg protested each step, he didn't stop until he leaned his walking stick against the arm of a Hepplewhite shield-back chair near the hearth. Then he settled on the cushions. He immediately calmed, drew a long, cleansing breath, and waited for Lord Leighton's appearance.

"Milady, a visitor has arrived."

Theodosia sat beside her grandfather with a book across her lap, and though he dozed on and off through her soft-spoken readings, she had no doubt he listened to every word. She looked to the doorframe upon hearing Alberts's voice, careful not to shift too quickly on the settee. "A visitor? At this hour?" She carefully placed the book on the footstool near the tinderbox, and rose. "It seems foolhardy to travel with the threat of poor weather. Is everything all right?" She glanced to the window and back again. A few light snowflakes danced against the dark pane. "Who is it?" She sent a prayer heavenward Lord Kirkman didn't choose this evening to further his suit. She'd made it abundantly clear the last time he'd proposed that she didn't welcome his attention.

"The gentleman presented his card and stated he was invited to Leighton House."

Theodosia answered without raising her voice, though the butler's reply was laughable. "Invited? There must be some kind of mistake." She accepted the white card and viewed the squared lettering printed across the center. *Lord Matthew Strathmore, Earl of Whittingham*. She sucked in a short breath. Whittingham? *Whittingham*. That persistent and annoying gentleman who beleaguered their household with queries, requests, and commentaries about the articles she'd submitted on Grandfather's behalf. Whittingham. She'd intercepted three letters from him last month, burned in the firebox like all the others. How dare he take it upon himself to travel to Leighton House? How very rude and imposing. Why, if Grandfather knew—

"Excellent." Theodore Leighton, Earl of Talbot, appeared beside her, alert and spry, as if he hadn't spent the better part of the evening half asleep beneath a thick quilt on the settee. "I hoped my letter of invitation reached the earl without delay, and I see that it has."

"Your letter?" Struggling for understanding, Theodosia turned toward her grandfather, concern in her voice. "Are you confused?" She gentled her tone and swallowed a lump of emotion.

"Not at all, dear." Grandfather grinned widely. "I received an inquiry from Lord Whittingham a fortnight ago and answered the earl straight after."

A fortnight ago? Theodosia scanned her memory, neatly categorized and nearly infallible. Two weeks ago she'd taken to bed in the afternoon with a troubling cough. If she hadn't such a profound knowledge of herbalism and its uses, she might have been stricken for days. In that, the staff assured her Grandfather was well cared for, but Alberts must have brought him the post before she could sift through the letters and remove any that might be better left unanswered. All in the span of one afternoon.

"Theodosia?" Her grandfather looked at her in question. *Whittingham.*

"You invited him here?" She forced cheerfulness into her voice despite her whispered question, which caused her pulse to beat triple time.

"Indeed, I did." Her grandfather warmed to the subject. "The earl had a bevy of questions, all of a scientific nature. So what better company for you and me? He didn't spare enough ink to explain the details, but I believe his feathers are ruffled over some article printed in the *Philosophical Transactions of the Royal Society.* It must be an older article, as I haven't submitted anything in ages, yet I wouldn't miss the chance for an intellectual debate of the best kind. Nor would you, my dear. I know that to be true."

Theodosia swallowed past the truth. She could never confess she submitted articles to London's leading academia journals using the vague signature, Theo Leighton. Wasn't it the journal's fault for not pursuing whether or not the article was written by her grandfather, the Earl of Talbot, a respected former contributor? The wax seal and imprint may have caused a bit of false presentation, but otherwise she believed herself in the scope of fair play. *At least until Whittingham's letters began to arrive.* What was it in her article that caused question? And how soon would it be before Grandfather understood the truth of the situation? Would he be angry or admire her spunk?

"It's too late for visitors, Alberts," Theodosia directed sternly. "Please show Lord Whittingham to guest chambers and inform him Grandfather will meet with him on the morrow."

"Good heavens, Theodosia, the hour is not even half six.

We wouldn't wish to appear unhospitable. The earl has traveled from London, a full day's journey."

Unwilling to upset her grandfather yet determined to gain time to gather her thoughts, she offered a compromise. "And thereby he's likely exhausted. I'll greet the earl in the drawing room and have a generous tray sent up to the guest rooms for anyone who has accompanied him in his travels. I agree a lackluster impression is undesirable, but we are not at the ready to receive guests."

"That's true." Grandfather glanced down at his wrinkled waistcoat and tugged at the hem as if he could somehow straighten the fabric. "I need to be at my sharpest to match wits with one of London's leading scholars."

Theodosia caught Alberts's subtle concerned frown at Grandfather's reply, but she made no indication otherwise.

"Then we're agreed." She looped her arm through her grandfather's elbow. "Alberts, be so kind as to inform Lord Whittingham I will greet him shortly."

"Of course, milady."

She smiled with a breath of relief as they moved toward the door. "Now let's get you settled upstairs and I'll have Mrs. Mavis bring up a fresh pot of tea. Come morning we'll see what Lord Whittingham's visit is all about."

Ten minutes later Theodosia returned downstairs. Grandfather was tucked into his bedchambers for the evening and she had a visitor to confront. She paused with her foot on the last tread of the staircase. No, she had a visitor to *greet*. She straightened her shoulders and shook off a lingering feeling of ill ease. Why did she assume Lord Whittingham sought to dispute the facts in her article? He might very well be here to applaud her elucidations. His letters expressed a series of questions, but that was not to say they would be confrontational. Either way, she couldn't keep the earl waiting any longer and she forced herself into motion, aimed at the east drawing room.

The Earl of Whittingham paced the perimeter of the room a third time, relieved his normal gait was nearly restored. The muscles of his injured leg were warmed due to the overlong wait for someone, *anyone*, to appear. Considering his fatigue from the day's travel, he would have appreciated a prompt welcome. Naturally, he'd arrived after conventional visiting hours and Talbot might be about other business, but the ormolu clock on the mantel indicated he'd waited over fifty minutes, and while the hour grew late, his patience grew thin.

No sooner had he formed this mental complaint than a hollow footfall in the hallway revealed someone approached. He hadn't heard a sound since the butler informed him Lady Leighton would be in momentarily, though neither lady nor gentleman had ever materialized.

At last the door cracked open and an elongated shadow appeared on the pale wool carpet. A slim silhouette was quick to follow.

"Good evening, Lord Whittingham."

She seemed nervous. Her left brow twitched the slightest bit. It was the first thing he perceived until the brilliant silver-gray color of her eyes captured his attention. For a fleeting moment firelight danced and gleamed in her irises, rare and startling, before she moved farther into the room. He stood several strides away, a comfortable distance, though he suddenly experienced a moment of uncertainty.

Odd, that.

He was a master of observation, able to intuit and remember most details others hardly noticed. In that manner, he noted the pinch of Lady Leighton's upper lip, as if she wanted to say something but kept the words locked tight.

She was a young, slight woman, delicate in stature with not an extra ounce to spare. Her ebony hair, thick and wavy, was coiled at the neck and tucked over one shoulder of her prim rose-colored gown. Her features were fine and reminiscent of an expensive china figurine, exquisitely made yet incredibly fragile. She was not at all what he'd expected, though he noted belatedly he'd had no expectations of meeting a female, never mind the granddaughter of the Earl of Talbot.

"Lady Leighton." He strode past his walking stick, abandoned by the fireside chair, and hoped his limp wasn't nearly as pronounced as he imagined it in the moment. "Please pardon my late arrival and accept my gratitude for the timely invitation."

"My grandfather invited you."

Her words sounded more a rebuff than friendly greeting, and as she advanced he realized she watched him as closely as he did her, their eyes unwavering and intensely matched.

"Have you eaten?"

Her tone remained terse, and the air in the room crackled with tension. Had he disturbed her with his arrival? Drawn her away from something important? Or was this her usual manner? Not that it mattered a whit. His purpose was to question Talbot about the inconsistencies of his latest article, not make idle chatter with his slip of a granddaughter.

She blinked in wait of his answer, and again a flicker from the fireplace flames caused her eyes to glint like polished silver. Indeed, the color of her eyes was rare. Less than one percent of the known population possessed gray eyes. Of course, scientists agreed hereditary factors combined with frequency dependency and scattering of light caused the phenomenon. He'd read more than a few articles on the subject but had yet to meet anyone with such exotic gray coloring.

"Lord Whittingham?" She cleared her throat politely. "Are you hungry?"

She must think me a weak-minded dolt for staring so intently at her eyes while I remained silent.

"I'd feel better after a hot meal, but under the circumstances and inconvenience of my late arrival, will make do with a tray in my bedchambers if your staff would be so kind."

A large tabby slunk into the room, and after a deliberate stare in his direction, settled in a cozy spot between the bellows and hearth broom. Its tail looped through the handle of a copper teakettle that rested on a brass trivet by the fender. Apparently, the animal found comfort here in the drawing room. A condition he wished was contagious.

"Of course. I will instruct Mrs. Mavis to have a tray sent up directly. Alberts will show you abovestairs. Thank you, Lord Whittingham."

Was that it then? She would dismiss him more promptly than she'd greeted him? What an odd young woman she was. Not a matter to consider though, as he would have limited interaction with Lady Leighton. For that he was thankful.

Theodosia assessed the gentleman earl with a speculative eye. It would benefit her to glean any information concerning her adversary, if circumstances proved it necessary to reveal the truth of her deeds.

Even across the room he appeared taller than most. His broad shoulders and wide chest filled his fine tailored coat without a finger's width of room to spare. His hair was a dark brown, repeated in his large, piercing eyes. Their color brought to mind the rich mahogany keepsake box where she kept her most treasured possessions locked away upstairs in her bedchamber. She watched as his notice moved to the fireside chair and back, where a walking stick waited, its scrolled ivory knob agleam from the flames. He appeared somewhat restless, his eyes meeting hers, although it could be nothing more than exhaustion after his long travels.

She hadn't expected a young man. Somehow her mind had drawn the image of an elder scholar, a gentleman whose nose had grown longer and hair grayer from time spent within the pages of a book.

Whittingham appeared nothing of the kind. Yet if she ascertained anything from their initial introduction, it was a sense of unyielding strength. Strength of mind and body. Would he have strength of character too? And exactly what did he want with his visit here to Leighton House? Had he come to compliment Grandfather's article—*my article, actually*—or challenge the information set forth?

Only time would tell.

Chapter Three

As was her habit, Theodosia rose before sunrise, her mind busy with ideas, curiosities, and a to-do list twice the length of her arm. These morning hours were the ones she cherished most. A time when she tended her plants and animals uninterrupted and reveled in the peaceful beauty of quietude before the world awoke and intruded.

She stopped by the kitchen and pocketed a fresh biscuit from a warm basket near the hearth, as well as a few small food items. The cook and household staff were accustomed to her early morning visits, as focused as she on their tasks for the day. She then continued through the rear of the house into a long corridor that connected the outer buildings to the manor, the limestone walls cold and shadowy, though several lanterns and wall sconces lit her way.

When her childhood home had burned and Grandfather hired men for the rebuilding, he'd designed their new estate with a scientist's desires in mind. Aside from the manor house with its necessary rooms for social functions and second-floor bedchambers, there was now a laboratory for performing experiments, set apart from the main living quarters. There were also a conservatory and orangery with a multitude of large glass panes atop the roof and along the walls, which allowed for maximum sunlight wherein the citrus trees, rare orchids, horticultural seedlings, and rescued animals made their home. Strategically located grates with red-hot embers generated warmth and allowed the interior plants to thrive despite the varying temperatures outside.

Farther from the house and still connected by the long, enclosed corridor was a compact room used mostly for testing theories and conducting trials that required water or buoyancy. Theodosia saved such discovery for the gentler months.

The house and outlying buildings were all bigger than she and Grandfather needed, the staff larger and upkeep more difficult, and yet Theodosia knew no other existence. With the help of several trusted servants, she'd grown through an unusual yet happy childhood into adulthood, despite the abrupt absence of her parents.

Now she let herself into the conservatory and firmly closed the door behind her, anxious to shut out the brisk air in the hallway. From the inside looking out, snow covered most every glass panel and climbed up the side windows as if it wished to return to the skies. Several inches had fallen overnight, and with sporadic squalls whipping the dusty flakes into tight whirlwinds in flight on the wind, she wasn't surprised snowdrifts blocked most of the light. Luckily, with the heat generated through reflection and insulated by the glass panes, paired with her careful attention, the dormant plants housed within kept well through the colder months.

Using the candle she'd carried through the hall, she lit several lanterns and watched as golden lamplight flooded the room before she turned her attention to the animals in her care. Whenever needed, she nursed injured creatures to improved health until able to return to the wild. Her efforts included a young owl with a damaged wing, several rodents and rabbits who had escaped predators, and once, several months ago, an injured fawn. Yet nothing so exciting had found her since the summer months, and she selfishly kept a few remaining animals as companions, often conversation partners, assured their fate would be better decided in the spring.

"Hungry, aren't you?" She lifted the wire lid of a shallow glass bowl where she kept a Great Crested Newt, and extended her hand, palm up. "*Triturus cristatus.*" The three-legged newt scuttled quickly to her warmth, fitting neatly across the diameter. "Here you go, Isaac."

She retrieved a few crumbles of last night's leftover beef from the pocket of her apron and watched as the alert little fellow consumed a meal that would last him through the end of the week. "You're quite a pretty boy with your chocolate coat, aren't you?" She ran her fingertip down the amphibian's back before it scurried onto a rock and farther into the brush inside the bowl.

"Brown seems to be the fashionable shade these days, doesn't it?" She spoke to no one in particular, though in the glass box across the aisle, a garden snake, dark green with a bright yellow collar, poked his head up as if interested in conversation. "Not that I've given much thought to Lord Whittingham's coloring." She moved aside the mesh lid and smiled down at the three-foot-long reptile. "Did you miss me, William?"

As if the snake understood, he unwound himself from the broken tree limb inside his roomy box and slithered upwards. "Now I know you're not hungry; you've done nothing but eat the last few days, and that's a good thing. With all this fresh snow there's no catch to be had. You'll have to make do, just like Isaac." She gently stroked the snake's head as he reached the top of the container, and allowed him to encircle her sleeve in much the same fashion he'd waited around the limb.

"Let's go check the lemon trees. One of them has yet to recover from the pruning cuts I made weeks ago."

William explored the leafy foliage while she watered the saplings and checked their progress. Pleased the snow hadn't covered the ceiling panels in that area of the orangery, she collected William, deposited him in his box, and completed her morning tasks. It wasn't until ten thirty that she'd changed her clothes and entered the breakfast room to find her grandfather already at the table.

"Hello." She pressed a gentle kiss to his papery cheek. "How are you this morning?" Would he remember they had a visitor? At times his memory failed, but she accepted the lapse as a natural part of the aging process and dared not examine the fact too closely. He was her only living relative and her relationship with him precious indeed.

Some subjects, such as her future, isolated existence in Oxfordshire, and lack of fashionable polish, were rarely discussed and often avoided. Thankfully Grandfather didn't press her and she secretly believed he would be lost without her, most especially as he grew older, their relationship one of mutual devotion.

She had no complaints. She preferred the quiet of the country estate and rejoiced in the ability to practice science, roam the hills to collect botanical samples, and read to her heart's content, all of which would be denied her were she to be raised conventionally. Having disconnected from the accepted vision of feminine preoccupations and adopted the practices of otherwise masculine pursuits, she was afforded freedoms beyond the norm and was loath to consider ever giving them up. London and its plentiful social demands existed as a parallel universe she didn't wish to visit, no matter her grandfather possessed a distinguished title.

True, a touch of remorse accompanied the fact she was the last of Leighton heritage, but were she to marry and produce children, they wouldn't carry the family surname anyway. Perhaps some things were meant to be short-lived. Her parents hadn't stayed with her overlong. Her heart twisted with the honesty in this fact and she forced emotion away, another learned habit.

"I expected a breakfast room full of conversation." She took her seat at the table. "Has the illustrious Earl of Whittingham not graced us with his presence this morning?" Fear of discovery prompted her surly remark, and Grandfather might very well chide her for the unfair jibe.

"I expected the same." Grandfather patted her hand and motioned to a footman at the ready to serve hot tea. "But Mrs. Mavis informed me that the earl requested a tray in his room. I sincerely hope he isn't unwell from the long trip he accomplished in such unforgivable weather."

Theodosia blew a breath of relief. Perfect. The longer she could keep her grandfather from the Earl of Whittingham, the better. Perhaps she could intercept and assure Whittingham there was no need to beleaguer her grandfather with questions, or more the better, address his interest and keep any further interaction with Grandfather at the most superficial.

Yet even as she formed the illogical and somewhat convoluted course of scientific intention, she was aware of the variables and the unlikely odds of meeting with success.

"Yes, it must be fatigue. In kind to your concern last evening, the earl must wish to make the finest impression and therefore has decided to wait until later to discuss whatever prompted his visit."

"That could be true."

Anxious to abandon the subject, she reached for the jam pot and passed it toward her grandfather. "Would you like some marmalade for your toast?"

"Marmalade?" Grandfather scowled. "You know I don't like marmalade. I detest it. I never put it on my toast. It's too sweet."

Caught by surprise, she replaced the jam pot on the tablecloth and flicked her eyes to the footman stationed by the door. He didn't so much as blink an eye, though she knew he heard every word of unexpected admonishment.

"Of course. How could I have forgotten?" Emotion rippled through her reply. "It *is* terribly sweet, isn't it?"

Her grandfather watched her with a frown, a conflicted shadow of worry in his eyes. "I don't eat it anymore, Theodosia. That's all I meant. I once enjoyed marmalade, but I dislike it on my bread now."

Grandfather didn't say more and turned his attention to his plate, though Theodosia had little appetite. She took a long sip of tea and released a deep exhale. At a loss for conversation, she forced herself to consider the earl's visit. What would she do about Whittingham? She'd give anything to know his purpose here. And how would she keep him from Grandfather? She placed her hand atop her grandfather's sleeve and patted lightly, more to comfort herself than him.

"I suppose I'm not going anywhere for a while." Matthew looked out the window at the new-fallen snow. More than six inches sat on the sill below his bedchamber window. Outside accumulation drifted in banks wherever the wind cared to move it, while the sky remained bleak and threatening, an indication more precipitation was likely.

"Although you might have woken me at a more acceptable hour." He turned from the window and skewered his valet with a glare.

Immune to criticism, Coggs busied himself with shaving tools and necessary items for the beginning of the day, his demeanor undisturbed. "You were exhausted from traveling, as you never oversleep. A sure sign the impetuous decision to come to Oxfordshire took its toll and then some."

True to a fault, Matthew had driven himself as hard as the team. A seven-hour ride across unfamiliar country roads with intolerable temperatures would test the endurance of any man, never mind one of bookish orientation. "Kind of you to have a tray sent up."

Coggs flashed a sly smile. "The estate staff is a lively bunch. Very welcoming."

"I'm sure you've acclimated without hesitation." Matthew stirred cream into his coffee and finished off the breakfast tray without interruption. "If it's only Lord Talbot and his granddaughter, one has to wonder why they need an estate so grand. For the most part, it appears to be new construction and the house alone is massive. I'm curious as to the outlying buildings." He strode to the window and eyed the elongated wing that jutted to the west. "I don't have a clear view, but I suspect there may be a conservatory on the property. Talbot has spared no expense in surrounding himself with a scientist's every desire."

"Then you have found the best place to be snowbound, haven't you?" Coggs motioned with the razor. "Shall we begin? The sooner you're presentable, the sooner you'll have answers to the impatient questions racing through that astute mind of yours."

"Indeed." He took the chair and allowed Coggs to proceed. When the last of the shaving soap was cleaned from his chin, he answered the one question he knew his valet hesitated to ask. "The pain is subdued. Not at all as insistent as yesterday."

"Very good, milord."

Matthew lifted a brow at his valet's formal reply and otherwise made quick work of dressing.

He found his way belowstairs—*always so many blasted stairs*—and with the help of a passing maid, located the breakfast room. He approached as Lady Leighton exited, her head bent and lips moving in what could only be a conversation with herself.

"Good morning, Lady Leighton."

She startled, as jumpy as a rabbit, her brilliant gray eyes widened in surprise, though she reclaimed her composure a beat later.

"Lord Whittingham, good morning."

She paused, her gaze sweeping over him in what he assumed was an inventory of his appearance. He regretted the use of his walking stick, though to abandon its necessity for vanity's sake was a fool's path to ruin.

"I noticed the weather has worsened." He shifted position, self-conscious in the conversation for no reason he could claim. "I hope my visit isn't an imposition on your hospitality. While I'm anxious to speak with your grandfather, it would appear time is on my side."

"Grandfather is indisposed at the moment."

Peculiar girl. How anxious she sounded to deliver that disappointing news. "I see." He glanced left and right, taking in the silk-covered walls of the hallway and elaborate crystal chandeliers. "Would you be so kind as to direct me to the library or reading room then? I wouldn't like to waste the day when there's a book in want of company."

His words caused her to smile, and for some unknown reason he experienced a sudden tightening in his chest.

What had he eaten for breakfast? Whatever it was, he'd consumed it too quickly.

"Our library is grand. You'll find an endless supply of volumes in every subject imaginable, enough to keep you well absorbed for hours." She stated this matter-of-factly.

"Then I'm sure I'll be able to pass generous time."

She brightened at this remark and he wondered at her curt manner. The only occasion when she'd appeared pleased was when he mentioned keeping otherwise occupied.

"Might you take me there then?" He watched her closely, curious if his request would meet with a refusal, or polite acquiescence.

"I could show you the entire estate, if you'd like."

A mischievous smile played around her mouth. Her lips were the exact color of the rare camellia flower, indigenous to southern Asia. He'd come upon the blossoms in his studies of herbalism, in search of relief for his recurring muscle pain. Some species of camellia flower were hybridized to produce seeds with curing oils and their leaves used for flavorful tea, their color a delightful rosy pink. Unfortunately, their strength hadn't supplied the effect needed, though staring at Lady Leighton's lips overlong could produce a pleasurable sensation.

"Lord Whittingham?" Her slender brows rose high on her pale forehead.

Had he made a fool of himself again?

"Pardon my silence. It's not a lack of attention, but more an interest in science that occupies my thoughts and carries them into theory." He offered her a half smile, unsure of her reaction to his admission.

"I'm often of the same mind." She nodded in agreement. "Now if you'll follow me, we can begin with the main estate and then, if you're still interested, I'll show you the additional buildings my grandfather had built to his design. Leighton House has several rooms that you may find intriguing."

"Thank you. I would like that." He studied her face, her eyes especially. "I feel as though we may have begun on the wrong foot." He cursed his choice of words. No need to bring more attention to his limp than necessary. "It would appear we're snowbound and you've graciously offered your time in exploring the estate, so please call me Matthew. We're past formal titles and far removed from the stuffy confines of Almack's in London, with no need to stand on propriety."

If he hadn't been watching her closely, he would have missed the slight narrowing of her lids, as if she questioned every word from his mouth or thought his motives unkind. He hadn't taken their home by siege. Lord Talbot had extended an invitation.

"Almack's? I'm not familiar, but aside from the weather's inconvenience, I think it best to keep our relationship cordial, yet formal."

She didn't pause for his reply, and in an abrupt pivot that had the fabric of her skirt rushing to keep pace, she started down the corridor to the left.

Chapter Four

Men. An unusual species. Hard to dissect and understand. Often obtuse. Generally overbearing. Admittedly, Theodosia had limited interaction with their kind, but from what she'd read, gathered through conversation, and observed from afar, she'd formed a working hypothesis.

Lord Whittingham, *Matthew*, remained an enigma. While he came with all the polish of London, his general manner and subsequent conversation left her unsettled and unready to form a conclusion. She noticed he walked with a slight limp, more pronounced last night than this morning, though he kept a walking stick in hand while they traveled the hallways.

The conventional rooms were all met with polite acknowledgment, but she knew as a man of science Lord Whittingham would enjoy not just the extensive library, but the additional uncustomary rooms of the house. Their unusual design would also supply a diverse topic of discussion if needed when he and Grandfather finally conversed face-to-face.

She brought him to the apothecary first. She took great pride in the room, the walls whitewashed, and the gleaming floor as reflective as a mirror. Tied in bundles above their heads, dried herbs, fragrant and bountiful, waited patiently to be put to use, their blossoms faded into pastel shades by the subtle yellow sunlight that leaked in through the far windows. The open cabinets boasted jars, bottles, and vials, all with a different substance, while bins overflowed with boxes and tools, bowls and towels, set beside a marble mortar and pestle.

Lord Whittingham wore an appreciative expression as he advanced into the room.

"I had no idea your grandfather practiced botanical medicines." He eyed the powders and glistening balms on the lower tier of the shelf nearest him and leaned in to sniff a jar full of pale green liniment. He withdrew quickly and Theodosia bit the inside of her cheek to refrain from giggling. It served him right for putting his nose where it didn't belong.

"*Crocosmia.*"

He whipped his eyes to hers. "Pardon?"

"An African flowering plant in the iris family. It's sometimes called copper-tips or falling stars. The fragile petals are parallel-veined and formed in vertical chains. Ground to a fine powder, its dried leaves emit a strong odor similar to saffron and used as a cure for dysentery."

"I knew that." Whittingham straightened his shoulders and canted his head the slightest. He took an extra moment to continue. "You've listened closely to your grandfather's research or mayhap found a few tomes on pharmacology worthy of your time?"

His assumption, that she'd gleaned the knowledge through eavesdropping or in search of relief from boredom, chafed and further proved her singular theory concerning the thickness of the male skull. But she wouldn't take the time to educate him beyond his beliefs. Herbalism was her own preoccupation. Grandfather wasn't interested in that particular branch of science.

"Shall we?" She gestured toward the doorway and they continued wordlessly to the next room. With the key from her pocket, she unlocked the latch and moved into the conservatory. She'd visited this morning, so she had no need to check the animals. Instead she briskly moved down the center aisle and farther into the glass-paneled orangery, aware he kept pace without falter.

"This . . ." He scanned the interior with a wide grin. "This is a sight to behold."

He walked to one of the stone columns that supported the glass-paneled walls and touched the window briefly with his fingertips. The cold air outside immediately condensed with his body heat to leave his fingerprints on the glass.

"It's one of my favorite rooms. I spend a great deal of time here." She had no idea what provoked her to share such a personal detail. She hardly sought a friend in the earl.

"I can understand why." He held her gaze before he continued his exploration.

He investigated the room with all the inquisitiveness she'd expect of a scholar, and she enjoyed watching him, although that realization was a bit unexpected. It could only be that, like she, he appreciated the scientific advantage to having such a research area. Mollified, she dismissed it as just another oddity she had no time to examine.

Matthew meandered about the orangery, impressed by the expert construction and attention to detail. It was one thing to read about science and another entirely to live it. Talbot had constructed two rooms—*and who knew how many more?*—devoted to the pursuit of scientific methodology.

No doubt there was an astronomy room, or perhaps a room devoted to weather patterns and meteorology.

The orangery was filled with exotic plants. Their colored foliage and lush pendulous branches created a visage of an exotic location, far away from England, deep in the jungle or untouched woods. The moist air was rich with the pervasive scent of loamy soil and pungent herbs. Sunlight dappled the slate tiles in patches, while the snowfall insulated the glass room as if a kept secret. Every curious example of flower or plant sat in assorted pots on the tables and floor, while within it all, Lady Leighton stood, a tea-rose blush upon her cheeks. Indeed, she looked as if she enjoyed it here and belonged among the other rare varieties.

"Shall we continue to the library?"

"What do you do here, Lady Leighton?" He strode to an apricot-colored bloom, its petals as plush as velvet to the touch. "Do you tend to all these plants, or does your grandfather have staff on hand to manage their care?" His imagination began to place her among the rows of flowers, a watering pot in one hand, a little song ahum on her lips while she worked. He shook away the outrageous image.

"It takes a large number of servants to keep the estate functioning, including the science rooms, but I do enjoy the time spent here."

It was the most she'd granted since they'd met and the most relaxed he'd seen her. "Your grandfather must be pleased and surprised by your interest in academics." His comment brought a change to her demeanor. Had he mis-stepped?

"Are you implying erudite subjects are beyond female comprehension?" She huffed a breath that dared him to smile. "I know every genetic form of life, from genus to phylum and beyond."

"I don't doubt it."

"Perhaps you're among the dull-witted scholars who believe women aren't capable of accomplishing more than delicate embroidery?" She paced a stride and back again, and he found himself captivated with her volatile, if not intriguing, reaction to his otherwise innocuous comment.

"I'm not, and if you knew my sister we wouldn't have this conversation at all." He stifled a chuckle. His sister, Amelia, was a hellion who spent most of her childhood, and a good portion beyond, keeping him on his toes. When she'd married, he'd at last found a modicum of peace.

"And your sister, I'm certain, possesses grace and refined deportment, adept at the pianoforte and never out of step during a dance."

"You haven't met Amelia. Besides, dancing is overrated." Her eyes fell to his leg, the chit too clever by half.

"Women as a whole have been treated unfairly by men, scrutinized and judged at every turn. We're expected to simper and flutter our lashes upon the gentlest word, enraptured by a bit of imported lace or the newest fashion plates, no matter that many women possess more intelligence than their counterparts." Her expression grew serious, a fiery light in her eyes that emphasized the importance of her words.

"I believe the human brain is a masterpiece composed of wonder and intelligence. Where it is housed, whether in an old man's head or a lovely young lady's, has nothing to do with my respect for its function, and I have met exceptions to and confirmations of that belief in every walk of life. You won't suffer such inanity from me. There's nothing at all wrong with being bookish." He tapped his walking stick on the slate tiles for emphasis.

"Bookish."

He watched her lips as she tested the word and accepted

his answer. His own mouth twitched with amusement. Apparently, he'd met with approval.

"We should move on to the library." With another swish of skirts, she proceeded toward the door and he followed, the tip of his walking stick punctuating each step.

They arrived at the entrance, the panels of solid walnut closed tight and not the least bit welcoming. Again, he watched as Lady Leighton selected a key from a silver chatelaine and unlocked the latch.

"Are all the doors kept secured?" It seemed tedious to be forever opening locks when one lived on the premises. "There are no young children here, are there?"

She raised her left shoulder in the slightest shrug, as if it was a habit she knew she needed to break. "It's the way of things here at Leighton House."

She didn't offer more, and he followed her into a large rectangular parlor that might have been labeled a sitting room if not for the most obvious reason: There was nowhere to sit. Leather-bound books lined shelves, floor to ceiling, while periodicals, magazines, and newspapers were piled in neat stacks against the crenellated baseboard and atop each seat cushion. Oval mahogany tables held collections of every kind, clockworks and compasses, magnifying glasses, kaleidoscopes, prisms and crystals, and everywhere he looked he found another opportunity to investigate. His mind rejoiced and his fingers itched to touch, experience, and discover.

He raised his eyes to prim Lady Leighton, who waited patiently near the hearth, and he wondered at his own expression. Dare he say, she appeared amused.

"You didn't mention how intriguing the interior." He nodded and swept another glance at the nearby shelves. "Books are only one aspect of the library's many charms."

Indeed, he included Lady Leighton in that remark but knew better than to mention it.

"One could while away hours in here." She grinned with a now familiar touch of mischief, and her eyes caught the light. "I often do."

He realized then she was really quite alone. At least it seemed that way. He walked to one of the mullioned windows and looked out over the snow-covered acreage to spy the stables and a few modest cottages farther from the house. There was a barn to the left and beyond that, an unexpected structure. As he looked more closely he realized it was nothing more than a frame, seemingly composed of burnt wood. Could it have been a house? Would that explain the extensive construction here at Leighton House? And why wouldn't the workers have dismantled the worthless and dangerous structure, victim to strong winds and otherwise likely to cause peril? He hesitated, but the question was out before he thought further of it. "What is that ruin to the south? It appears nothing more than a burnt-out shell."

He might have mentioned seeing a sea monster on the lawn for the stricken expression on Lady Leighton's face. The rosy bloom he'd only just admired transformed to pale alabaster and any joy in her silver-gray eyes extinguished to ash.

"I'll leave you now, Lord Whittingham." She didn't wait for him to reply. "I'm confident you'll find more than enough reading material to pass the afternoon."

He stepped forward, his arm extended in ridiculous fashion, as if he sought to make amends, though he had no idea what had caused her dismay, and when he finally managed to make use of his tongue, his words were lost to the sound of the closing door.

"Good day, Bookish."

* * *

Theodosia hurried down the corridor, a jumble of emotions aflutter in her chest, as chaotic as a rabble of butterflies. Lord Whittingham, the positively unnerving man, had the annoying habit of causing her to consider things better left alone. They'd shared a walk of hardly thirty minutes, and within that time he'd touched on myriad subjects she preferred to keep tucked away.

Her somewhat isolated existence.

She grabbed hold of the newel post and began the stairs.

A lack of social polish.

An unconventional preference for academics.

Her feet pounded the treads as if she could stamp out Whittingham's far too observant suggestions. She reached her bedchambers and slammed the door.

The loss of her parents.

She collapsed against the panel, out of breath and patience.

How long would the overbearing earl be a houseguest anyway? The question brought her attention to the window, and despite her sullen displeasure, she walked to the rectangular seat and climbed upon the cushions. Unfortunately, the somber skies matched her mood. Ominous clouds, dark as slate, limned the horizon with the threat of more snow. She couldn't remember a time when the winter proved this relentless and harsh. Emotions bubbled to the surface again and she forced them down. She should find Nicolaus and bend his ear long enough to exorcise her conflicted solicitude.

Still tethered to Lord Whittingham's invidious question, her eyes sought the burnt remains of the estate house, and the few memories time dared not erase rose with clarity in her mind. Her father, grandfather's eldest son and only heir, was a brilliant man, tall and strong, as handsome as he was intelligent. He knew how to make her smile with endless laughter as he tossed her high into the air or onto the buoyant safety of a nearby haystack. He'd chase her through the wildflowers until they were both out of breath and then he'd lift her to his back and carry her all the way home, as easily as if she weighed no more than a feather. If it wasn't too close to dinnertime, he'd stop at the pippin tree and hoist her into the branches, his deep voice a comforting song locked in her heart.

Choose us two rubies, Theodosia, sweet as your smile.

How she strove to find the finest apples among the leaves, wishing to please her father if only to return a thimbleful of the love he shared.

Her mother was beautiful, generous, and smart. She devoured books, her love of learning contagious. She'd taught Theodosia to read fluently by the time she was four. But unlike Theodosia, who considered herself ordinary, her mother was graceful and lovely. Her mother's heartfelt words of encouragement were never far from mind.

You may choose any path to happiness, Theodosia. Follow your heart and capture your dream. Intelligence has no limits.

Theodosia didn't wipe away her tears as they fell; the relief a long cry promised to be too precious to ignore. How dare Lord Whittingham intrude on her solitude and bring to the surface all her tightly held emotions and buried insecurities? His questions were likely nothing more than conversational curiosity, though having struck a nerve they evoked an insightful examination of her person. Either circumstance was unwanted and thoroughly uncalled for, no matter everything he perceived was true.

Still, unscrupulous fear gripped her heart. Fear of discovery. Fear of loneliness and unending solitude. And fear that her simple life was being upended, changed and transformed beyond her control. All caused by the intrusion of one man. Now, for more reason than one, the sooner Lord Whittingham left Leighton House, the better.

Chapter Five

Matthew spent more than two hours perusing Talbot's collection of scientific journals and reference books, the majority of his time occupied by Young's "Experiments and Calculations Relative to Physical Optics." Having listened to Young lecture at the Royal Society in London on his wave theory of refracted light, the readings were engaging and relevant, most especially when considering the reflective property of Lady Leighton's eyes.

Still, with a handful of hours to waste before dinner, he wondered how he would while away his time and left the library to roam the halls and pursue his curiosity further, the mark of a true scholar.

He happened upon the kitchen quite accidentally and recognized Coggs's voice above the din, his valet often at the ready to woo a willing female. He gave a slight nod to gesture that Coggs should move into the hall.

When they were alone in the corridor, he hurried his valet to answer. "What are you doing here? Haven't you learned your lesson yet? Don't do anything that will appear disingenuous or be misconstrued. We're houseguests of Lord Talbot and your actions are a reflection of my character."

"You needn't remind me of that."

"Apparently, I do." He tapped his walking stick against

the floor molding so he wouldn't use it on Coggs's shin. "I saw that young maid giggling at your every jest. You enjoy the attention. Don't deny it. I have known you long enough to realize a warning is justified." He paused, but then thought additional cautioning necessary. "I never received another invitation after your debacle at Pembrook's."

"That was an isolated incident."

"That's what you say every time it recurs."

Coggs appeared nonplussed. "Pembrook recovered, didn't he?"

"That's not the point."

"Already angling for a return to Leighton House, aren't you?" Coggs raised his bushy brows. "All these rooms of scientific experimentation must have your mouth watering."

"Strange pairing of descriptors, Coggs, even for you."

The kitchen door opened and two fair-haired maids passed through. One held a tray with a teakettle service, while the other carried a tidy plate of biscuits. They kept their eyes forward, though the shorter of the two darted a glance in Coggs's direction, which earned her a chide for her boldness by the taller maid.

"Hurry along now, Bess. Lady Leighton doesn't like to be disturbed once she begins."

Begins what?

Matthew held his tongue, though the question ignited a wick of curiosity.

"Just don't make any trouble." He forced his eyes to his valet.

"I'm affronted."

Whittingham grinned in mockery. "I'm sensing a disturbing role reversal in our relationship." He poked his walking stick into the toe of Coggs's boot and continued after the maids, though he had no idea where they led. When they turned a far corner, he slowed his gait, the ache in his knee a sharp reminder he hurried without sufficient care. No doubt more snow was imminent. He muttered a curse and took a left, down an airy corridor with portraits hung on either side.

Crimson-and-gold striped silk wallcoverings provided a backdrop for what could only be the house gallery, though the frames on the walls weren't filled with paintings, as one would expect. Instead the display was composed of letters, articles, and handwritten notations. He paused and read through the first on the wall, an article published two years prior on chemical nomenclature.

Odd, how the gallery showcased Lord Talbot's achievements and not the members of his line. Where were the oils of Lady Leighton's parents? A favored hound? The traditional earldom heritage portrait of Talbot and his descendants?

He might have remained longer in the gallery if he hadn't heard what could only be described as an exclamation of joy. Recognizing Lady Leighton's voice, he executed a quick pivot and changed course, careful to avoid the tabby who sauntered across his path.

Theodosia vigorously rolled her pencil between her palms in excitement. It had worked. Her umpteenth attempt to solve the Standard Model equation proved correct. The physics formula described the fundamental particles that comprise the universe, and she enjoyed researching the vast heavens. She spent many evenings staring at the constellations, identifying phenomena, or meteorite hunting. On occasion, she even made wishes. But regardless of her purpose, she looked to the night sky often enough to become intrigued and thereby engaged in study. It was how she became familiar with the work of Lagrange, the mathematician and astronomer who developed the Standard Model equation, which she now worked through with success.

Exhaling a prideful huff of contentment, she placed her pencil atop the paper and made for the door. She needed to find Nicolaus or Grandfather and share the news. The dynamical problems of integral calculus were beyond the comprehension of many people if they hadn't studied theorems at a scholarly level. Grandfather would be pleased at her accomplishment. Lord Whittingham would be impressed. *Not that he would ever know*. This realization put a spring in her step all the more.

Entering the hall, she made a quick left turn and walked straight into a linen cravat. She barely contained a knowing groan. She'd collided with Whittingham, the intrusive houseguest she'd only just conjured and dismissed from her thoughts. Stepping back, she rubbed the tip of her nose. Despite the soft buffer of his neckcloth, his chest was as hard as a stone wall, the effect somewhat dizzying.

She regained her composure thereafter, although her deep, clarifying breath provided the fragrance of an appealing shaving soap, something woodsy with a touch of citrus.

"Lady Leighton, accept my apologies. I didn't hear your approach. You have a light step."

He'd reached out to steady her and his strong grip on her arm added to her disoriented recovery. She couldn't help but look at his hold on her sleeve, then his boots, and last his walking stick. She wouldn't dare render him unsteady, though while she still reeled from their collision, Lord Whittingham appeared unerringly composed. He removed his hand and she swayed forward the slightest.

"It's my fault, milord. In my hurry, I failed to pay attention." At such close proximity she couldn't help but notice the gold flecks in his dark brown eyes. Very becoming if one fancied things like that.

"Again with such formality?" He tutted a sound of disapproval. "As I already mentioned, I'm here for a short visit, whereafter we'll likely never cross paths. I reside in London and you on this grand estate in Oxfordshire. For the ease of conversation, why not forgo titles and use Christian names?"

"I don't think that's necessary." She took a single step backward. "Even more so for the reasons you've stated. Temporarily snowbound or not, we'll soon have no interaction beyond the unexpected situation of your arrival."

"I was invited."

"Yes, you mentioned."

"As you'll have it, Bookish."

He smiled then, as if in wait of her objection, and if only to vex him, she refused to react to his absurd teasing of her fondness of reading.

"I thought you were in the library." A swift change of subject proved an effective diversion. She had no intention of sharing her mathematical victory now.

"I was. For over two hours, actually."

He shifted his stance, though not a telling indication showed on his face and she wondered if he was uncomfortable or if his injury caused him pain. The latter notion bothered her on some inexplicable level.

"And no matter the Talbot library's enticing collection of every scientific tome in print, I couldn't stay there indefinitely. Besides . . ."

He paused, seemingly waiting for her response. This time she acquiesced. "Yes?"

"The door was left unlocked and I thought it better to escape while I had the chance."

This earned him a smirk, though she didn't wish to encourage him to continue the tease.

"Where are you off to in such a hurry? I've found it easy to get lost in these halls."

"Because you don't live here, milord." *And thank God for that.*

He nodded slightly and cast a glance down the corridor as if deciding what to say next.

In that silence she noted his crisp linen shirt beneath the same welcoming cravat that smelled of shaving soap; and too, how his broad shoulders filled his wool coat without a hairsbreadth of extra fabric, straight down to his tapered waist. He must have a fastidious tailor. But then, in London everyone was preoccupied with fashion and style, and this reason, like so many others, proved why she would never fit in among society there.

"An infallible truth." He muttered.

She repeated the phrase though her inner conversation had taken a different turn. Now to deter him from prying any deeper into her soul. "If that's all then—"

"And your grandfather? Is he available for conversation during this endless afternoon? He did initiate my visit, after all."

"I wouldn't know." She hemmed her bottom lip and made a swift decision. "What is it you do in London, milord?" It was always safe to ask someone to speak of their own interests. It often prevented said person from asking too many questions in return.

"I suspect vastly different preoccupations from yours here in Oxfordshire." He leaned one shoulder against the wall and crossed his arms over his chest, as if he had all the time in the world and therefore prepared for unending conversation. His walking stick dangled from the fingers of one hand in a slow sway that could be hypnotic if one stared overlong. "I think the more interesting question is, what do *you* do for amusement?"

She shot her eyes to his. "Amusement?"

"Is there an echo in here?" His mouth formed a half smile that tempted hers to produce the same. "Yes, amusement. Do you solve puzzles, collect buttons, work at watercolors or poetry?"

"I read."

"That can't be all you do, Bookish." He leaned closer, his head canted down to accommodate their height difference. "Even I don't read *all* the time."

He stated the last bit in a secretive, low-toned whisper, and her pulse jumped, caution alive in her blood. Her retort came out too sharp. "I suppose being from the city you require an endless chain of entertainment, discontent to spend a quiet afternoon listening to the birdcalls or watching the stars."

"Not at all. As a matter of argument, stargazing is among my favorite preoccupations. Still, there's much more to life than the care of plants in the orangery."

"I keep a few animals." She straightened her shoulders, more than a little defensive at his censure. "And practice maths."

His brows shot high at her final word. "All I'm suggesting is a widening of interests."

Does he feel sorry for me? Pity me? A rush of memories brought back the endless sympathy she'd received for years after her parents died, and any previous enjoyment of their conversational sparring faded, replaced in a heartbeat by anger.

"Considering I made your acquaintance less than a day

ago and our relationship is to be incredibly short-lived, you've overstepped, Lord Whittingham."

He studied her, and despite that the urge to brush past him seized her to the core, she kept her feet still, unwilling to flee and appear affected.

"Perhaps I have." He pushed upright. His walking stick tapped twice against the tiles in the uncomfortable silence. "If you will excuse me, Lady Leighton. I must dress for dinner."

Chapter Six

"That was refreshing." Matthew stifled a grin as he accepted a towel from Coggs. "I can't remember when I've been so pleasantly intrigued."

"By your shave, milord?"

"No." He scowled in his valet's direction.

"Pardon, milord?" Coggs replaced the shaving soap and brush before he carefully dried the razor. "To what, then, do you refer?"

"Nothing." Matthew allowed a chuckle this time. "Well, not nothing, but nothing I wish to share with you."

"How unkind." Coggs assumed an offended expression. "We might have traded stories. I've collected a titillating earful from the parlor maid downstairs."

Matthew tossed the towel aside and donned his smalls before he sat on the edge of the mattress to pull on his stockings. "Didn't I warn you to keep your nose on your face and out of other people's business?"

"Quit your grips." Coggs came forward with a pair of buff leather breeches in hand. "It was more a matter of me standing in the right place at the right time. And for what it's worth, I thanked her thoroughly."

"The kitchen staff?"

"No, the parlor maid, for her interesting information."

He sent Coggs another glare as he stood and fastened the waistband of his breeches in wait of his black top boots. His valet quickly produced the pair. The heels had been modified to compensate for his limp, and when Matthew wore them, his gait appeared only slightly uneven. But the damnable boots were uncomfortable as hell, and like the carriage ride through the cold, tomorrow his body would pay the price for his decision.

"You needn't waste your breath and repeat the rumors you've collected. Gossip is impolite and considered a pastime for the addle-minded." And didn't he know it. He played at indifference, but he'd heard the assumptions bandied about concerning his impairment and lack of social presence. Gossip was a waste of words and precious time, albeit he'd done nothing to rectify the gratuitous pity when he refrained from dancing or horsemanship, instead choosing a less compromising lifestyle. He blew out a deep breath and forced his good leg into his right boot.

"You know what they say." Coggs continued undeterred.

"Mind your own business?"

"No." A touch of annoyance tinged Coggs's answer. "The kitchen is the heart of the home and the servants' gossip keeps it beating."

"I see. I didn't realize." His valet was a certifiable tell-pie. In contrast, Theodosia was a delightful diversion, and without examining his feelings for deeper meaning, he remained intrigued and more than a little taken with her.

"Suit yourself." Coggs's retort came from behind the formal wool coat suspended on a hook where the valet worked to remove the most miniscule specks of lint. "We'll be long returned to London when Kirkman proposes a third time. With such dedication to your studies, I suspect we'll take wheel as soon as the weather clears and the roadways prove suitable for travel."

"Who's Kirkman? The steward in love with your parlor maid?" Matthew shoved his foot down hard into his left boot and stood with a deep grunt. He paced a length, pleased with the feel and comfort, if only temporary.

"Hardly."

Coggs handed him a white linen shirt, pressed to perfection, and Matthew pulled it over his head.

"Lady Leighton will make a lovely bride."

Had the fabric not been wrapped around his head, he might have comprehended the news quicker. As one would have it, he yanked his shirt down so hard, the seams strained. "What? Lady Leighton's to be married?"

"I wouldn't wish to spread rumors, milord."

"Your swift change of opinion is admirable." Matthew snapped his neckcloth from the wardrobe in the guest chambers and walked to the cheval glass, his patience at war with better sense. Coggs would never last. He never did. Matthew concentrated on the strip of linen, intent on arranging his cravat in an understated but elegant barrel knot while he mentally counted to twenty. He barely reached twelve.

"Of course, one can never be sure of these things, but Lord Kirkman has already proposed to Lady Leighton twice and it's believed by the household staff that three's the charm."

"Is that so?" Matthew kept his expression unchanged, though he would confess to a lick of curiosity. Lady Leighton was rare. Quite striking. Provoking, and downright amusing. This collection of attributes was a far cry from the ton's preferred compliments of *swanlike grace* or *delicate disposition*. And that made all the difference. She was different. Different and interesting in the best way. *A pleasing way.*

Not that it mattered. Though he recognized that for a lie, intelligent scholar that he was.

* * *

Several doors down in an adjacent hallway, Theodosia prepared for dinner with the help of her young maid, Dora. Had she not been preoccupied with the current situation and what might occur once her grandfather and Lord Whittingham finally met, she would have comprehended her maid's suggestions more fully and refused to dress in her fanciest gown. As it was, Dora leapt at the chance to prepare the formal wear and underthings, never before worn, and flurried about the room as talkative as a chatter-box. That may have been why Theodosia so readily became absorbed by her worry and preemptive attack to whatever sparked Lord Whittingham's visit.

Now, faced with the freshly pressed garment and the layers of underclothes needed, she wished she'd listened to Dora more closely. And while she could change her mind as easily as she changed her gown and insist on dining in a simpler, more comfortable design, she didn't dare return belowstairs later than expected, in case Grandfather and Lord Whittingham began a conversation without her.

"I do like the way I've arranged your hair with this lovely embroidered bandeau, milady." Dora brushed her fingertips across Theodosia's temple and tucked an errant wisp behind her ear. "I can't remember the last time you've allowed me to fuss."

"There was no need for it, and it's only because I was distracted that you managed to succeed to such lengths." Theodosia glanced in the oval cheval glass where an un-familiar face looked back. She was most often in a service-able day gown. Something with several deep pockets for all her necessities, whether feeding her adopted animals, managing the house, or conducting experiments. Diamond jewelry such as the glinting earbobs and matching necklace that adorned her this evening were a rarity at best.

"If only Lord Kirkman could see you tonight." Dora stifled a girlish giggle. "One glance and he would become tongue-tied."

"If it prevented another proposal from tumbling out, then I like the idea." Theodosia smiled at her own jest. She stepped back from the glass to see her entire reflection. Far from the daring fashion worn in London, this gown was still flattering. The rectangular bodice and lacy sleeves were becoming, the periwinkle blue a compliment to her eye color, and the high waist and endless layers of semi-transparent silk over silk, created an illusion she was more ephemeral than permanent. This suited Theodosia perfectly. The sooner she could resolve Whittingham's inquiry and dispatch him back to London, the better. "Is it still snowing, Dora?"

"I believe so." Her maid set down a pair of silk slippers with matched silver beadwork and scurried to the window. "Oh yes, I'm afraid the weather has worsened. I can hardly see a thing."

"Well, then." Resigned to the fact she was at the mercy of the weather, Theodosia slipped on her shoes and glanced one last time in the mirror, more than a little surprised at how elegant she appeared. Perhaps, at a moment like this, she wasn't so different after all.

"Would you like gloves, milady, or a fan? Do you need your reticule?" Thoroughly carried away with accessories, Dora stepped forward with an armful of frippery.

"I'm only going downstairs, but thank you." And then at the last minute, Theodosia snatched a hand-painted paper fan from her maid's grasp and rushed from the room.

She nearly flew down the staircase, aware by the longcase

clock in the hall, she was four minutes late for cordials in the sitting room. Would Grandfather be himself tonight? She could only hope. At times his age showed a different side to his personality, but she refused to believe his mental capacity compromised in any manner, despite recent unexpected mood changes. Grandfather was well-known for his work in all branches of science. A sharp, learned mind like his didn't fail, most especially in odd bouts of confusion and forgetfulness.

She approached the sitting room, half out of breath, her closed fan swinging in a frenzy from the ribbon loop at her wrist.

"Milady, might I have a word?"

The housekeeper approached, her face wrinkled with concern.

"What is it, Mrs. Mavis? I need to get inside." She looked toward the sitting room door while her heart pounded a chaotic beat.

"I won't keep you, but I knew you would wish to be informed."

Theodosia nodded. Impatience held her mute.

"His lordship insisted Cook include marmalade on the menu this evening. There's no reason for it, no dish for it to accompany, but his lordship wouldn't hear otherwise and I thought not to upset him, being we have a guest in the house."

"Think nothing of it." She tossed these words over her shoulder and breezed toward the sitting room with a deliberate effort at serene poise as her slippers crossed the threshold.

Chapter Seven

"Grandfather." Lady Leighton entered the room and strode directly for Lord Talbot. She extended her hands encased in elegant white gloves and clasped his tightly as she pressed a kiss to his cheek.

"Theodosia." He said her name with affection, the aged earl apparently smitten with his granddaughter. "You look beautiful."

Theodosia? Theodosia. It fit. An honored namesake of her respected grandfather, no doubt. Where were her parents anyway? Did they not live here in Oxfordshire?

"Thank you." She smiled. "I didn't intend for anyone to wait on my account."

"To see you in such finery is worth any wait. Besides, Lord Whittingham entered not a minute before you." Talbot turned in his direction and Matthew adjusted his grasp on his walking stick in order to complete a proper bow.

"Lady Leighton." He straightened and accepted her hand. "Theodosia." He murmured just loud enough for her ears, "What a fine name, Bookish." She didn't say a word, though she snatched her fingers away before he could press a kiss in greeting.

"We haven't yet begun our conversation, in anticipation of your arrival." Talbot walked to the sideboard and poured a liberal portion of brandy into two crystal glasses. He brought one to Whittingham and then motioned Theodosia toward the settee. "Come and sit with us. Perhaps then the earl will share the reason for his insistent visit."

Matthew fought the desire to remind them he'd been invited, as everyone in this house wished to label him a refined marauder. Best he dispel that impression. "It was your article in the *Philosophical Transactions of the Royal Society* last month that snared my attention. I found your discussion of the law of definite proportions to be accurate and informative, though I have a few questions concerning the whole-number ratios used to formulate compounds. Several of the calculations are curious."

"Grandfather." Theodosia chimed in from her opposite position on the settee. "I'd enjoy a glass of port, if you'd be so kind." She placed her fan on the table as she spoke.

"Of course." Talbot rose and moved to the sideboard.

As soon as Talbot's back was turned, Theodosia eyed Matthew and leaned forward as if to impart a secret she didn't wish her grandfather to hear.

"It's too late to begin a conversation of complicated scientific method. My grandfather is likely tired. Wouldn't you rather talk of more current news?" Her eyes widened with the question, a hopeful plea in their depths.

"Discussion of your grandfather's contribution is the sole reason I made this long trip through harsh weather conditions. The invitation to visit and share theoretical viewpoints is a rare opportunity and I wouldn't squander a moment."

Theodosia did not appear mollified.

"Here you are." Talbot set a glass of port on the inlaid satinwood table beside his granddaughter's fan and reclaimed his seat. "Now what shall we talk about this evening?"

Matthew couldn't be sure, but he thought Theodosia

stifled a gasp. Or mayhap he imagined it. There was no way to know. One thing was certain, she didn't want port. Her glass waited on the table, ignored.

"Lord Talbot—"

"Call me Theodore." Talbot smiled and took a sip of his brandy. "If we're to share conversation and a satisfying meal, we should dispense with formality. Out here in the countryside we're more relaxed than our city relations. Besides, all that decorum grows tedious."

Matthew turned toward Theodosia with the intention of waggling his brows in mocking reference to their earlier squabble over Christian names, but he noticed her eyes never left her grandfather, a slight grimace holding her expression firm as Talbot raised the glass for another swallow.

"It must become confusing with a Theodore and Theodosia in the house."

"Not at all." Theodosia dragged her eyes to his, though with a blink she changed the subject. "What occupies your time in London, Lord Whittingham, aside from taking impromptu trips across the countryside?"

"You must call me Matthew." He donned a congratulatory grin. "At the request of your grandfather, of course. Besides, by your own admission we'll likely never see each other again, so what difference does it make?"

The conversation proceeded no further as a footman appeared to call them into dinner. Claiming his walking stick, he was quick to his feet, yet Theodosia made a point of slipping her arm through her grandfather's elbow to allow him the escort into the dining room. Matthew told himself he shouldn't feel disappointed. And honestly, he couldn't imagine why he would.

They took their places at the long rectangular table, illuminated by chandeliers above, though at least a dozen candles burned in an elaborate silver epergne at the far end of the damask tablecloth. Talbot seated himself at the head, leaving Matthew with a delightful view of Theodosia directly across the china.

For a few minutes no one spoke as linen napkins were unfolded and placed delicately to the lap. A footman provided wine efficiently, while a wisp of a maid bobbed in and out with all sorts of delectable tidbits to begin the meal.

"Cook must have prepared all day for this selection."

Theodosia commented with a smile, though it didn't reach her eyes. What had upset her? They'd hardly exchanged a dozen words.

"Now, tell us about your studies, Whittingham."

Talbot spooned a liberal portion of deviled kidneys onto his plate. From the corner of his eye, Matthew saw Theodosia wrinkle her nose at the dish.

"As chief officer of the Society for the Intellectually Advanced, I spend most of my time in scholarly pursuits. The position requires I remain in London, where I have the esteemed responsibility to investigate accurate reporting of scientific news and discoveries, both past and present. Your recent article was the topic of a heated debate at our last meeting and instigated my first letter. As you may recall, I invited you to speak and share your findings."

"A recent article, you say? I don't recall. Nor do I remember a letter." Talbot's face screwed into an expression of confusion. "What was the topic again?" He put down his fork and offered Matthew his focused attention.

"It was in last month's edition. Your article on—"

"Oh, what have I done?" Theodosia let out a sigh of disappointment as her glass toppled over. Red wine splashed across the ecru tablecloth, a helpless victim of her mishap.

Conversation halted as a footman rushed forward with a hand towel, the soiled fabric quickly covered with a smaller cloth in a darker color. Within minutes a platter of glossed dates and dried apricots covered the stain and effectively tucked it out of sight.

Without missing a beat Theodosia resumed the conversation. Perhaps she sought to pull attention away from her accidental spill.

"For as long as I can remember Grandfather has explored the sciences and shared his knowledge with me. As a child I beleaguered him with questions, but he always took precious time and explained the answers in a clear and patient manner."

"You still beleaguer me with questions," Talbot added as he examined the flatware beside his plate. "But then any great scientific mind is apt to question things." He picked up the fork and paused, before he replaced it on the table. "And you have questions too, don't you, Whittingham?"

Matthew finished chewing a savory bite of salmon. "I do. In relation to your calculations of fixed ratio and mass, I couldn't replicate your result. As a matter of course, I discovered—"

A large serving dish appeared in his peripheral vision.

"Have you tasted the imported ham?"

Theodosia waved the footman closer to the table as she spoke.

"Thank you." Matthew followed the plate with his eyes as it was placed before him. Every time he began a discussion, Theodosia interjected. Could she wish to be the center of attention? That hypothesis didn't bear investigation, as he'd already ascertained she'd prefer they didn't dine together at all.

Still, her fetching gown and sparkling diamonds might support his theory. She looked stunning this evening, her hair pulled back to expose high cheekbones and a pale, slender neck. He lingered too long in appreciation and found her eyes matched to his when at last he pulled his gaze upward.

"It's divine. Exquisite, one could say." Matthew held her stare without waver. "The ham, of course."

She continued, though her cheeks acquired a lovely blush. "We always have ham during Christmas, and with the holiday season approaching, I suspect Cook is testing a new recipe. I smell cloves and ginger." She cut a tiny bite from the slice on her plate and chewed it elegantly.

What is the lady up to?

"Whittingham didn't come to Leighton House to discuss our menu, dear." Talbot nodded vigorously to accompany his words. "Exactly why did you come here anyway? Are you interested in the sciences?"

It was then that the pieces began to fit. He should have suspected it sooner, but he was too caught up in the intriguing petite beauty with ebony hair and silver-gray eyes across the table.

She looked at him then. A clear, intense, knowing stare, and whether she wished it or not, that look communicated everything.

"Let's talk of other things, shall we?" He finished his wine and allowed the footmen to whisk his glass away to be refilled. "I suspect the snow will be finished on the morrow and the roads serviceable in another day or two."

But Theodosia didn't comment, her gaze tight with impatience. She'd turned away from the conversation for a moment, her attention cast to the window as if assessing the weather outside, despite it was dark and her view obstructed.

"Pass the marmalade, please."

Talbot extended his hand to receive a bowl of apricot marmalade. Was that a customary condiment at their table? Whittingham associated the fruit preserve with breakfast, though he supposed some might use it to sweeten a piece of ham.

When Theodosia failed to respond, a footman swiftly retrieved the bowl. She turned, belatedly, and he noticed a sadness in her eyes that wasn't there before.

"I would like to visit this society of yours." Talbot covered the food on his plate with several dollops of preserves. "You stated earlier you once invited me. I don't recall the message. Does the invitation still stand?"

"Grandfather." The word sounded sharp in the otherwise quiet dining room. "Grandfather." She gentled her tone. "I hardly think a trip to London during the coldest months of winter is advisable. I couldn't bear the thought of the long day's travel. My compliments to you, Lord Whittingham, for your valiant excursion to Oxfordshire, but my grandfather is not as hearty as you, nor easily pleased." The last few words were said as she eyed his marmalade-covered plate.

"Nonsense," Talbot rebuffed, his tone indignant. "There's nothing wrong with me. I can travel as well as anyone. I happily accept your invitation." His voice grew more determined as he replied.

Matthew found himself in the awkward position of being trapped in a private discussion. While Theodosia sought to protect her grandfather in his later years, Talbot rebelled against his age. Was the earl aware how often he lost the thread of conversation? How odd some of his actions? Was it a matter of lucid thinking mixed with confusion that had produced the intelligent, articulate piece printed in the Royal Society's medical journal, or had someone assisted? Theodosia mentioned her grandfather had taught her much through the years.

And the letters he'd written inviting Talbot to present his findings? Had Talbot forgotten about the invitation to speak in London or had his granddaughter effectively prevented him from reading those same letters as a way to protect his pride and reputation?

Matthew's mind spun furiously with its usual investigative method: ideas conjured, proven or eliminated with lightning-fast proficiency.

How compromised were Talbot's capabilities? Perhaps someone else altogether had submitted the article. Someone with a depth of knowledge but limited experience.

Someone like Theodosia.

The clever minx.

Chapter Eight

"I disagree." Theodosia flared her eyes at her grandfather. Now was not the time for him to become angry or belligerent. She'd feared his contrary position on marmalade to be the biggest threat, but oh, how she'd underestimated the situation. "I shouldn't like to travel in this weather. Most especially as the holidays approach. Why don't we plan a trip to London after the thaw in the New Year?" She forced a brittle smile. *Please, Grandfather, please don't add humiliation to my long list of heartaches.*

"That may be the wiser decision," Matthew interjected. "The Society would be delighted to host a reception for you at any time. The accumulated snowfall is an unforeseen complication nonetheless. There's no need to rush."

"But there is."

Grandfather's tone became somber, and not for the first time, Theodosia wondered to what extent her grandfather knew that his mental capacities were diminished. Did he fear the same things as she? Did he realize he could no longer hold a conversation without getting lost in the words? Or that he often forgot tasks as simple as the usage of flatware?

"We can revisit the subject another time." She pushed

on. "Let's not spoil the meal with this discussion. Besides, it's not every day Leighton House has the privilege of your company." She struggled and finally forced her last word out. "Matthew."

He looked at her again. It was as if he was staring at her all the time, though in his defense he was seated directly across from her for the purpose of congenial conversation. Still, she wondered if he considered her an oddity. A pariah. A woman raised without the polish of city life, or worse . . . a spinster bluestocking.

He was handsome. Too handsome, some might say. She saw the way the maids twittered when he walked past, and for all his dependency upon his walking stick, his limp an impairment he likely cursed, it caused him to appear stronger, heroic, and that much more interesting. But she wouldn't consider any of this because none of it mattered. As little as forty-eight hours earlier, Lord Matthew Strathmore, Earl of Whittingham, was nothing more than a name on paper. Paper she fed to the flames in the hearth in fear he would somehow materialize.

And yet he had, as if she'd evoked some witch's spell.

His eyes searched her face, in confirmation he knew her thoughts, and she bristled, straightening her shoulders as she sought a fortifying sip of wine. Best to keep him at arm's length. *Or farther*.

"I'm pleased to visit Leighton House, and as I mentioned, the Society will welcome your visit any time of year."

He seemed to understand, and with that came equal portions comfort and embarrassment.

"I'm relieved. With the Christmas season on the approach, there's enough planning without the addition of travel to the schedule." She attempted a smile, in hope they could return their dinner conversation to a lighter topic, though deep inside, her heart thundered. Matthew was a highly respected scholar. He would have no trouble deducing what she worked so hard to keep concealed.

"How do you celebrate? Do your parents—"

"I won't be put off like a child." Grandfather dropped his knife to his plate and stood so quickly the chair toppled over. "I'm for London tomorrow."

Theodosia eyed one of the footmen at the ready to assist as needed in the past.

"Grandfather." She rose as well, her hand extended to capture his, though he pulled away in anger. "I didn't mean to upset you. Why don't we finish dinner and discuss it afterward?" She chose her words so carefully, but all the while knew there would be no calming him now. He'd experienced a fit of outrage only one other time, and two footmen had been needed to resettle him. She sent a silent prayer to heaven it wouldn't come to those terms this evening while Lord Whittingham watched.

"May I help?"

As if he read her mind, his calm tenor met her ear, but she couldn't bear to look at him for fear emotion would cause her to crumble.

"The matter is settled. I will travel to London and speak at the Society and you won't stop me, Belinda." Grandfather's words became an agitated edict. His voice resounded in every empty corner.

It wasn't his childish behavior or petulant demand that pierced her heart, but the use of her mother's name. He'd never done that before, confused her for another, or conjured memories from the past to mingle with current reality.

And all at once, she was nothing more than a body in the room, her soul numb and mind blank. Vaguely aware of two servants who led her grandfather from the room with a promise of his quiet bedchambers and a cup of chocolate, she never glanced at Matthew. Shame, indignity, and utter mortification fought for control within her as she rushed from the room, blinded by tears.

He found her in the library. It was nearly midnight by his glance to the clock in the hall, and highly improper, but while he'd cursed his leg and the vicious complaint of pain from his hellish top boots, he couldn't return to guest chambers, his mind feverish with concerning images of Theodosia. Had he not taken his eyes from her through the meal, he might never have noticed how she paled, how she fought to control the tremble of her lips whenever she drew a deep, calming breath, or the subtle tremor of her fingers as she replaced her spoon to the side of the plate. She endured and rebelled much like he, unwilling to submit to the pain.

Still, the situation was highly unusual, and while he found his interest piqued and empathy eager, he concluded that a strong, independent, intelligent woman like Theodosia would not welcome his company at this time. Although she hadn't anyone, did she? And for all intents and purposes he happened to be their guest, if not a complete stranger. Yet isn't that how one became friends with another, as strangers first?

Still untangling the knots of these contemplations, he entered the library with hope she would be there, and she was.

Framed by the incandescent glow of the flames in the firebox, she stood with her back toward the door, grasping a looming multi-shelved bookcase, though he assumed she didn't seek something to read.

She needed strength and support. Comfort in books and knowledge. And the circumstances weren't all that unlike his life at another time. He knew that search as well.

She remained in her evening clothes. The gauzy layers of silk glimmered with a sheen from the hearth, so much so, she could be an illusion if one believed in such fanciful idiocy. Long ribbons of ebony hair cascaded down her back, nearly to her waist, and he watched her shoulders rise and fall in a broken motion.

Was she crying?

He swallowed audibly, stalled by a moment of hesitation.

"Either come in or leave already."

Her raspy command took him by surprise, but it offered an invitation he would not refuse. Leaning more heavily on his walking stick, he made his way across the room, relieved when he stepped to the carpet, the tap of his stick on the tiles too much a reminder of his own shortcomings. He'd learned all too quickly in London, women desire a knight on a white horse, not a man with a limp and a cane. Not that he'd ever assume to aspire to that role at present.

She didn't turn and he didn't know how to begin. The last thing he wanted was to further her distress.

"Are you well?" It seemed the most mundane beginning and he cringed at his inadequacy.

"I will be." She shifted against the bookcase, but only partially turned.

He noticed the glisten of tears in her eyes, though her cheeks were dry, her lashes too.

"So now you know." Her whisper caused his heart to ache.

He nodded. "Your grandfather is struggling." *Aren't we all?* Matthew took a deep breath.

"Yes. One could say that."

"The mind weakens with age. It's the natural course of things. Everyone gets old."

She jerked her head to the shelves again with a short sniffle. "Not everyone."

He'd hit a nerve. "That's true."

Pervasive silence invaded the room. Still she didn't look at him, her back tight with tension, and he wondered if he should take his leave. Curiosity, another curse of his character, demanded he remain. "Why did you do it?"

"The article?" She gave a delicate shrug. "For too many reasons to name."

"Tell me the two closest to your heart."

He waited, and so many minutes passed he believed she would not answer at all, but then she did.

"To protect my grandfather's legacy and reputation as a scientific scholar." She drew a ragged breath as if she needed extra air to force the remaining words out. "To prove that I could. That I have worth."

He wanted to pull her forward, turn her around, and give her shoulders a shake. Did she believe a journal article would accomplish the latter? Had she so little belief in herself? But he knew better than to delve deeper than the facts. "A published journal article cannot prove your worth."

"Not to you, but mayhap to me."

They stood that way another minute or two and when she didn't say more, he stepped away. He rounded the bookcase, his feet silent on the carpeting as he positioned himself on the other side. With the removal of three heavy leather volumes, he created a hole large enough for him to speak to her face-to-face.

"Bookish." He knew to tread carefully.

She watched him, her eyes glistening with unshed tears.

"A beautiful mind is more valuable than a thousand beautiful faces. Aren't you lucky to possess both?" He wanted to reach forward and stroke his fingertip across her cheek for no other reason than to offer comfort. She was such a little thing. Alone. Grappling with the care of an aging loved one. Where were her parents to assist at this complicated time? Compassion and a strong sense of long lost chivalry rallied inside him.

"What error have you found in my article?"

Discussion of concrete science would hopefully provide calm. Emotion was just another crutch. At times it supported and then at others, adversely hindered. "Despite its publication, some of the calculations require a leap of faith."

"Some things do," she insisted.

"Not maths," he countered. "But we can work through the unclear formulas tomorrow if you'd like."

He watched her shoulders relax and her posture lose some of its earlier rigidity.

"Do you always roam the halls when you're a guest in someone's home? It's near midnight, isn't it?"

It was an attempt at levity and distraction, and he wouldn't miss the mark. "Only when a vexing woman believes herself on the shelf."

"While I appreciate your pun, taken literally, it is true."

"You don't really believe that." He chuckled softly until she continued.

"How did you injure your leg?"

"Aah, the skill of evasive conversation and subject substitution."

"Does it pain you?"

"Yes." He scrutinized her reaction. "Sometimes more than others."

"I find that true of many things in life."

She disappeared from the window created by the withdrawn books, and he moved to the end of the aisle.

She was closer to the fire now, her skirts swishing back and forth as she paced. "You've tried camphor?"

"Yes." He followed, though a dull throb of pain pulsed through his thigh.

"Salt baths? Chamomile?"

"Both, as well." He stopped, unwilling to let his discomfort show on his face any more than she'd likely detected it in his body.

"Lavender has soothing qualities."

"They are fleeting at best and leave me smelling like a dainty lady."

This evoked an unexpected smile, and in that one moment he knew he wanted to kiss her. She was an odd, becoming, interesting young lady and the combination was absolutely intoxicating.

I need to kiss her.

This complex, brilliant, delicate woman before him. She was an intricate puzzle of which he hadn't many pieces.

"What about ginger salve?" She slapped her fist to her palm as if she'd just discovered an eighth planet in the solar system. "Used repeatedly, it could provide the relief you seek."

Only one thing would provide relief at the moment.

"I'll try it. You'll supply me the ingredients, I presume."

"We'll mix it tomorrow." She huffed a short breath. "After you show me the mistake in my calculations."

"Shrewd negotiations for one so young." He took another step, wanting to be nearer. "They weren't necessarily mistakes."

"Regardless, I'd like to take a closer look."

As would I. "Certainly." He reduced the distance between them to less than a stride. "It's the least I can do after insinuating myself into your home."

"You were invited," she offered quickly. "By my grandfather," she amended right after.

"Yes. I was." He stood very still. He wanted to remember everything about the moment, his usual observation of detail at work. In a few days' time he would be returned to London, with its damp, inhospitable weather and slick city cobbles. There lay problems he would consider another day. And when he found himself embittered, he would conjure this unusual and timeless memory. Of kissing a woman who was more a stranger than acquaintance, but more like him than any friend at all.

He closed the distance between them and used a bent finger to tip her chin upward. His thumb drew a soft line against her cheek and she shuddered slightly beneath his touch. "It's true, Theodosia, you have so much potential. That's a compliment of the highest caliber. Were we living in different times, your astute intelligence would be respected and celebrated." The latter part came out as a murmur, but he was certain she heard the words.

The mood in the room shifted. The air all at once held a fraught tension but of which impelling force, he didn't know. Her eyes narrowed the slightest, the only indication she was equally aware.

He doubted she knew much of physical chemistry. Yet talking science would continue to bring her ease. "What do you know about the laws of attraction?" He gently pulled her into his arms. For all her bold intellect, she was nothing more than a startled rabbit in his embrace. Startled, yes. But what did she fear? She reacted before he deliberated the question, and all too soon she broke away to move behind a nearby yew-wood chair.

"Science is a vast universe. I've read dozens of books on a plethora of subjects."

"I don't doubt your learnedness." He took one step to the right. *Though I have an inkling you intend to prove your depth of knowledge.* This was mused to himself.

"Most people blink near 17,000 times a day."

Her unexpected fact offered an excuse for him to connect with her lovely gray eyes. "Interesting, that."

"Did you know a woman's heart weighs less than a man's and beats faster?"

He laid his hand across his chest. "Are you certain? Mine is racing at the moment." He watched with amusement as those same gray eyes flared wide.

"The average person has 100,000 hairs on his or her head."

"You haven't counted, have you? Life here in the countryside must be duller than I assumed, although each strand of yours is more fetching than the other 99,999."

She might have clenched her teeth at his compliment, but she was speaking again an exhale later. "Lobsters have blue blood."

"As do my ancestors." He grinned at the turn of phrase and strode closer.

Theodosia took two steps back. "Koalas, a marsupial native to Australia, sleep twenty-two hours a day."

"Just think of all the invigorating conversation they miss." He moved to the left to offset her slick maneuvering. "Do you always spout random facts when you're unsettled?"

"I don't and I'm not. I'm proving the depth of my intellect." Her chin notched a tad in proud defiance. "Fifty percent of one's body heat is centralized in the scalp."

"I daresay I dispute that." He aborted a chuckle. "At least not in my experience."

Unaware of his insinuation, she dashed away from the chair and around the rug, lost behind a mahogany bookcase before he caught sight of her, though surely she heard the irascibility in his voice.

"Diamonds are the hardest substance known to science."

"Again, speaking from experience, I'm not certain that's true." His mind went to a wicked place.

"I know a great many things." Her voice was filled with challenge. "It's believed the moon is twenty-seven percent the size of the earth."

"Aah." He paused to don a smirk. *Proof indeed that size matters.* "You've memorized a collection of interesting discussion points, but you needn't attempt to convince me. I'm satisfactorily impressed. In fact, I never doubted your claim."

"Do you expect me to act a widgeon? To flutter my lashes and giggle incoherently whenever you spout a bit of flattery? I told you earlier, I'm not like the ladies you escort about London." A flash of her gown revealed she'd wandered farther into the bookcase rows. "I've a brain in my head just as capable as any male's, unlike starfish, who don't have brains at all."

This time he did chuckle. "Considering some of the men I've met in London, that's not an exclusive quality." He stalled near the third bookcase and viewed the shelves suspiciously. Wherever she'd wandered to, at least the doors were completely out of range. "I would think a woman of your ilk . . ."

"Of my ilk?"

Her voice drifted to him as he rounded a row where he abandoned his walking stick for the warning it provided of his approach. "Yes, of your ilk. Your presence. I would presume you're full of confidence and bearing. You're smart and beautiful. I daresay that's not a common occurrence in London."

A long stretch of silence followed. Had he said too much or was she simply digesting his compliments?

"You believe that to be true?" Her tone said everything her question did not. She appeared at the end of the aisle.

"I wouldn't say it otherwise." He stepped toward her and his jaw tightened as a wicked spiral of pain gripped his leg.

"Are you all right?"

Bloody hell, she'd noticed what he worked so hard to mask. Limping was hardly the rage, neither fashionable nor vaguely interesting if the injury hadn't occurred on a battlefield. His impairment was sadly unappealing and he would accept no one's pity.

"As right as rain." Pain sang through his leg, but he refused to so much as blink.

She exhaled deeply as if contemplating whether or not to believe him, and then she surprised him yet again by scurrying away to reappear a blink later with his walking stick in hand.

"Does it hold you back or offer support?"

"Both, although it's mostly an annoyance." He was reluctant to accept it but did so in the end. He'd no idea how long they might chatter here in the library, and he wouldn't relinquish time due to his injury, even if that meant accepting a crutch. And too, there was the matter of that kiss.

Chapter Nine

Theodosia handed Matthew his walking stick, but in truth it was she who had become unsteady. What was happening? Every emotion rushed to the forefront and the impact was somewhat dizzying. When he'd pulled her into his warm embrace, her heart divided. One half yearned to draw closer while the other panicked and caused her to flee. It wouldn't do to form any attachments to the earl. Girlish fancies and long-lost dreams were foolish investments.

Still, before her stood an imposing man, tall and handsome, with a devilish smile and beguiling gaze beneath too-long lashes, who seemed to say everything she needed to hear and somehow make her world much better by doing so. He was smart and strong and far too charming, a veritable intellectual riddle, science combined with tender emotion. But she couldn't allow herself to care, no matter that when he looked into her eyes a curious warmth unfurled in her chest.

"Thank you, Theodosia."

He spoke softly, intentionally, as if he savored her name on his tongue, as gentle as a caress.

"You're welcome," she answered, crisp and efficient, striving to deny the pulse of desire and curiosity alive in her blood.

He stood with his shoulders against the bookcase, and no matter they remained a pace apart, she sensed his body heat, smelled his shaving soap, and the enchanting allure of experiencing his kiss begged her forward.

She didn't move when he lowered his mouth to hers. On an intuitive level, once he'd entered the library and they began their coy banter, she knew somehow she would find her way into his arms, and now the moment was here. His mouth nearly touched hers when logic took hold.

What was she doing? She hardly knew Lord Whittingham. He'd arrived on their doorstep not even two days ago, and now she stood in the house library pressed against his chest. Didn't she have adequate heartache without compounding the problem? Wasn't each day difficult enough? Anyone with the most common sense would recognize this as a bad idea. She'd never see him again once the snow melted and he made his way back to London, a place she'd vowed she wouldn't travel to again. Somewhere with too many agonizing memories to ever confront.

She wriggled free and took two huge steps away, but he caught her by the wrist. With a flick of his hand, his walking stick crossed her lower back to cage her in as he insistently slid her back into his arms. He wasn't satisfied until she was closer than before.

"Mayhap this annoying walking stick has one good use after all." He studied her so closely, she couldn't break the spell of his heated stare while confusion and hesitation faded away.

"Matthew." A thrilling spiral of desire coursed through her and she all of a sudden was impatient, her lungs tight, each inhale too fast and at the same time, too slow.

"Breathe, Theodosia. Just breathe."

His walking stick clattered to the floor and he brought his hands up and cupped her face to drag her mouth to his.

The first touch of his lips sent a shock of awareness to her core, as sharp and piercing as a lightning strike. This. What was *this*? Was this attraction? Lust? A yearning so strong, her heart broke and mind blanked, their function irrelevant. A physical reaction so fierce she knew her knees would betray her in another moment.

And they did.

Supported by the bookcase at his back, he hauled her closer, his hands locked tight, their kiss unbroken. All logical thought ceased. For this one moment there was nothing else. She surrendered to his kiss and melted like a snowflake in the sunlight, anxious to absorb every nuance of the experience.

He smelled divine, a woodsy mixture of citrus and spice that caused her a dizzying sensation though she fought against it. His hold was strong, one hand placed at the side of her neck where his fingers stroked her skin, the other splayed across her back to keep her close while his mouth tasted and explored, his kiss ever more hungry and insistent.

His tongue slid across her lips and she gasped, then withdrew far enough to meet his eyes. Had he done that deliberately? The intensity in his gaze caused heat to flood through her body. Apparently so.

She understood the natural course of things and had read countless volumes on physiology and anatomy, but when she pleaded with her brain to review everything she knew about mating, the useless organ produced nothing but a tingling awareness somewhere deep in her midsection.

"Stop thinking, Bookish." He moved closer to her mouth, his words slightly muffled as he began their kiss again.

She curled her fingers into his coat, the soft wool as tempting as his silky request and she succumbed, a wild pounding in her veins as she opened her mouth the slightest. His tongue stroked over her lips, between and inside before she could object, although only a simpleton would bring to a stop such a cataclysmic riot of emotion when it proved so heavenly.

Something bloomed in her chest. Dare she label it joy? She loosened her hold and smoothed her palms across his chest to his arms, the solid biceps beneath his sleeves too wide for her grasp, but she hung on anyway, their flex and movement a fascinating phenomenon. How hard he was all over. How perfectly made.

Bloody hard. I am too bloody hard.

Matthew shifted his position the slightest for fear Theodosia would detect how unmercifully aroused he'd become with just one kiss. Something, something intangible and precious, drew him to her with undeniable force. He wanted to protect her, fix all the ills and resolve all her problems, but the reaction was laughable. He hardly knew her beyond a day's interaction.

When she opened her mouth and he delved between her honey-sweet lips, her naïve exploration and bold daring was an unforeseen punch to the gut. How he would recover afterward he did not know, but he refused to allow the evidence of his ardor to frighten her now.

Her hand clung to his upper arm and the other stroked against his cheek, her fingertips testing the fresh whiskers there. The innocent exploration caused the problem in his breeches to increase accordingly. Still he couldn't break away just yet. He nudged her jaw with his thumb and angled her chin back to deepen their pleasure. She wiggled against him in a moment of restlessness. He couldn't be the first man she'd ever kissed, could he? What of that Kirkman fellow?

The thought of another man kissing Theodosia in the

same manner brought a spike of anger so sharp it cleaved his pleasure in two. He withdrew with blood pounding loud in his ears, and forced a laugh. His voice sounded husky for the effort. Why the hell was he thinking during their kiss anyway?

It took a quiet minute to regather focus, though she didn't readily remove herself from her position against his coat.

"That was rather . . ." She spoke in a soft voice, her eyes cast down as if she searched for the right word.

"Wonderful," he supplied, the word said low and dark, though she shook her head the slightest.

"Unexpected." She glanced upward, her lips turned in a secretive smile.

"Indeed," he murmured back.

They didn't say anything for another few breaths.

Then he leaned in and broke the silence as he whispered against her ear, "You taste as good as you look, and that's absolutely delectable."

Perhaps the vibration caused an uncomfortable reaction because she pulled from his hold and stroked her hands over her arms, as if she sought to soothe away a sudden chill.

"Thank you." She studied him, her eyes glassy in the fractured light. She seemed to want a change of subject. Her shoulders eased. "Why are we whispering? It's past midnight and no one else is here."

He stared at her as a slow smile crept across his face before he whispered back, "Foremost rule of the library, I believe."

She returned his grin. "I should go upstairs."

Her voice sounded normal now, as if she'd dismissed their moment and was ready to leave it in the past, but he knew he'd never forget this interlude for all its pleasure and amusement.

He straightened against the bookcase and leaned down to retrieve his walking stick. "Yes. You should."

"Good night, Matthew."

He didn't like the sound of those words this evening, but they were inevitable, weren't they? "Until tomorrow then, Theodosia. I'll show you my calculations, if you'll show me yours."

The humor wasn't lost on her and he received another quick smile.

"Until then."

She left straight after, and once she was out of sight he sagged against the bookcase, despite his leg felt much better and he needed no support.

Unapologetic sunlight flooded Theodosia's bedchamber the next morning and she pried her eyes open despite she hadn't slept well. When she first climbed between the sheets, her heart racing from her interlude downstairs in the library, she took time to relive Matthew's words, the pressure of his mouth upon hers, and examine the multitude of emotions that coursed through her. After which, she still couldn't find rest with so many unanswered questions prodding her brain. The little sleep she did manage was interrupted by vivid dreams.

And so, when Dora entered with a breakfast tray and news that Grandfather was well but requested to stay in his rooms for the morning, Theodosia didn't wonder about it overlong. Instead, distracted by the shimmery feeling alive within her, she ate her coddled eggs and toast, finished her tea, and deliberated the day ahead, anticipating the time she'd spend with Lord Whittingham. *Matthew.* She dressed in one of her better day gowns, a mint-green block-printed cotton with white sawtooth trim. Of course, there were several pockets in the skirt, as her schedule included a stop in the orangery to care for the animals.

Now, seated on the vanity stool while her maid twisted the lengths of her hair into a braided coil, she considered the two earls down the hall.

"Grandfather is well then, Dora?"

"Yes, milady. Fit as a fiddle. Mrs. Mavis had Cook prepare his favorite breakfast and he was pleasant to the footman who delivered his tray." Dora held the braids in place and began to add pearl pins. "His lordship mentioned wanting to organize a few things."

"Yes, he's as fastidious as I am when it comes to arranging his belongings." She glanced around her bedchamber, where every item was neatly in its rightful place. "And Lord Whittingham? Has he gone downstairs to breakfast?"

"I believe he requested a tray as well." Dora attempted to stifle her laughter, though she wasn't successful.

"What is it?" Theodosia cast a glance over her shoulder, causing several pins to drop to the floor.

"It's nothing more than a bit of girlish tomfoolery, but three different maids asked to deliver the tray. I doubt we've ever had a guest who earned so much attention."

Theodosia couldn't believe the nonsense going on below-stairs. Matthew was handsome and charming, and true, the house rarely saw visitors, but to vie for the opportunity to deliver a tray of food . . . she smirked at how ridiculous it sounded. Her mind didn't operate that way. Or mayhap she had never been exposed to society's expectations to create the flirtatious habit. It was just another reason on a long list why she'd never fit into London society. The somber reality didn't warrant any more thought, though she secretly wished a footman had taken Matthew's breakfast tray up.

"Well?" She twisted on the stool and waited for her maid to continue.

"I hope I haven't gotten anyone in trouble, milady." Dora's cheerfulness fell away. "It was only a bit of amusement in the kitchen."

"Not at all." Theodosia patted her braid and stood. "My hair looks wonderful. I have a busy day ahead." She hesitated, almost embarrassed to ask the next question, though as lady of the house she needed to be kept abreast of all goings-on. "So *who* delivered the tray?"

Spoken aloud, the question sounded more foolish than when kept in her brain.

Dora's smile returned. "Mrs. Mavis scolded the girls and sent one of the footmen upstairs instead."

"Very good." She felt a sense of relief that was uncharacteristic and absolutely absurd, but she didn't say more and hurried down the hallway. She paused before Grandfather's room, unsure whether to knock. Sometimes the smallest disruption caused the largest problem, like not having marmalade on the table for every meal *or* having marmalade on the table for every meal.

And too, they would be together at lunch and if he didn't come out of his rooms then, she would definitely visit and speak to him. Perhaps a little distance was necessary today.

Confident in her decision, she hurried on in the usual manner and stopped by the kitchen to gather what she needed. She headed toward the gallery, the walk through the extended corridor an ideal chance for her to arrange her schedule before she reached the workrooms. Until she saw Matthew. He stood before the farthest frame on the wall, his attention focused on the glass. She hesitated in disturbing him and didn't mind having a few minutes to take him in.

The kiss they'd shared last night came back in a hurry, the tingling sensation and giddy, bubbly feeling that spread throughout her body with every beat of her heart. She quickly squashed these emotions, unwilling to allow them control. She needed to concentrate on her calculations. The last thing she wished was to appear a bird wit. For some reason, now more than earlier, she wanted to show her abilities in the best possible light.

"What did you say to me last evening? Either come in or leave already?"

He remembered? *He remembered.* A faint smile teased her lips. He turned then and the sunlight from the far windows limned his face in a golden glow. No wonder the maids were squabbling. He cut a dashing form. Dark hair, broad shoulders, tall and strong with enough charm for three men. His wardrobe proved impeccable and tailored masterfully. Her gaze fell to his left leg and she shot her eyes up again in a clumsy gesture she wished she could erase.

"Better. Bearable. I've overdone it with my travel and exertion the last day or two, so I'd still appreciate the salve you mentioned."

She looked away and shook her head slightly, upset with the awkward situation she'd created. "Of course. Would you like to do that first? I thought we would compare maths before we went to the apothecary. Sometimes I need to change my clothes after mixing potions." Her voice trailed off as he approached and she started toward him to cut the distance by half.

"What kind of elixirs? Magical mist? Warlock spells? Love potions?" he questioned with brows raised, and she laughed before she thought better of it.

"Nothing of the kind, although your suggestions sound intriguing."

They met in the center of the gallery, and for a moment they both stood there looking at each other. What she wouldn't give to read his mind.

"The sun has decided to visit Oxfordshire at last." He indicated a nearby window with the tip of his walking stick. "The roads should be clear in the next day or two."

"Of course. You'll want to return to London." An odd twist squeezed her chest tight and she wondered if breakfast disagreed with her. Perhaps it was only trapped air or an unladylike hiccup. Not that she wanted to experience either malady in his company. "Let's not waste any time then."

She reached in her pocket for the chatelaine of keys and they proceeded down the corridor.

Chapter Ten

Matthew followed Theodosia into a small sitting room at the end of the hall. The interior was sparsely furnished with two mahogany armchairs and a rectangular table with fine woodwork inlay. A large pedestal sideboard held books, quills, and paper items instead of the usual crystal liquor decanters, and between the velvet-draped windows sat a writing desk as cluttered as its cousin on the opposite wall.

Wall sconces provided ample light, though the first thing Theodosia did after she unlocked the door was to draw the curtains wide and allow sunshine to chase away the chill.

"You lock the doors . . . for your grandfather's benefit." Matthew waited for her to sit before he assumed the other chair beside the table.

"His safety, mostly." She busied herself with the arrangement of a sheet of foolscap. After she pulled the inkwell closer, she turned to him and continued. "At times, he's the man I've known all my life. Brilliant in his work and warmhearted in every other way. He raised me, you know. My parents perished in a house fire when I was five years old."

"I'm very sorry for your loss." The words sounded

hollow, thoughtless, and in that moment, he began to truly understand the unfair composition of Theodosia's life. How much happiness had she known? Had the majority of her life been spent here, tucked in a house with her grandfather and otherwise disconnected from society?

He didn't wish to bring a pallor to the day. He would likely depart tomorrow; if not, the day after. If he could make their shared time entertaining, she would have a few amusing memories after he'd gone. It wasn't much, but it was easily achieved. And he welcomed the obligation.

"We don't need to dwell on it. I don't." She picked up a pen and dipped the nib into the ink pot. "We can't predict our future nor change our past."

His mind raced, anxious to transform the threat of melancholy into something lighthearted. "Well said, Bookish." He picked up his pen, at the ready to review the formula in question. "Not that I would change one second of last evening in the library."

He was rewarded with a sweeping crimson blush along her cheekbones and a twitch of her petal-soft lips.

"That was rude."

"I'm not accustomed to being categorized as such." He couldn't help but tease and intentionally misunderstand. "Whatsoever is rude about a reference to Dalton's *New System of Chemical Philosophy*? It was an enthralling read from cover to cover."

She laughed softly and her eyes regained their sparkle. "Your explanation is not sound or substantiated by valid evidence. You discovered *me* in the library and therefore had no time to read as we—" Caught in a conversational trap, her blush reappeared, as did her smile.

"If you're going to be all *scientific* now, I suppose we should work on the calculations in question." He began to scratch numbers on the paper. "Do you have the work you referenced and your notes?"

"I do." Seemingly anxious for the diversion, she hurriedly flipped pages in a notebook atop the table. "Here are my equations for the chemical ratios and compounds." She indicated a series of numbers. "This is where I thought we should begin."

They worked diligently on reproducing the result for over an hour, but Matthew couldn't verify her calculations no matter which equation or leap of faith he employed.

She appeared utterly deflated.

"The rules of math are challenging and unforgiving." He placed his pen down on the blotter and leaned back in his chair.

"Are you going to notify the *Philosophical Transactions of the Royal Society* journal and reveal I've made a mistake? Will you expose me for the imposter that I am?" Her face worked through a series of uncomfortable emotions.

"No. Of course not." He almost chuckled. "Whoever approves the articles printed in the monthly journal should be held accountable for shabby research, not you."

"Thank you." She barely whispered the words. "I'd rather not have been humiliated."

Something painful flared in her eyes before she looked away.

"I propose we leave off for a bit and take a walk to the orangery. I liked it there very much and my leg could use the exercise."

"Oh." She quickly tidied up the desk. "I didn't realize."

"How could you?" He chuckled. He stood and reclaimed his walking stick, quick to head toward the door so she wouldn't see his grin. She really was a delightful secret hidden away here in Oxfordshire.

They moved toward the conservatory, the mood light and conversation easy.

"What has provoked your interest in botanical studies?" He followed her inside. With the sun shining brightly, the glass panels along the ceiling and walls warmed the room considerably and again he was impressed at the extensive attention to detail.

Theodosia approached a glass bowl and lifted the wire lid. They didn't explore this area when he'd first visited two days ago. *Two days?* That's all? Most likely it was due to the length of time they spent in each other's company, but it was as if their relationship was more comfortable than those he'd had in London for months, maybe years.

Of course, in the city, everything from fashion to friendship was held to a judicious standard. Theodosia would have had a maid trailing her throughout the day, and he'd have been obligated to leave her company after twenty minutes, his visit acceptable only during calling hours. Restrictions like that made acquaintances less familiar.

And then there was their kiss. It would have been much more difficult to achieve.

He blinked away his mental musings and refocused his attention, but as he did so his brows shot high in surprise. "Are you wearing a . . . snake?"

"A garden variety, and a completely harmless one at that." She smiled at the creature and stroked a finger down its scaly back.

He cleared his throat and shifted his position, all at once at odds. Bloody hell, there was something strangely *erotic* about seeing Theodosia in her mint-green day gown with a snake twined around her arm. He had no explanation for it, but he recognized a physical problem, a growing one, in fact. He forced his eyes to a row of seedlings and attempted to change the subject while angling his body to disguise his state of semi-arousal. "What are you nurturing here?"

"I'll explain in a minute." She walked closer and the snake climbed higher, its head against her lace-trimmed bodice. "Snakes are fascinating creatures. This one is a common variety, but the boa constrictor, a large snake indigenous to Central and South America, can grow to more than fifteen feet long."

"Indeed." He watched the sleek reptile continue its travels toward Theodosia's shoulder.

"Surprising, isn't it?" She flashed a brief smile. "The constrictor strangles its prey before ingestion and is the only species capable of asexual reproduction."

"That hardly sounds like fun at all."

She giggled, her unexpected reaction a pleasant surprise.

"Would you like to feed William?" She canted her head to the left to indicate the reptile near her shoulder. "He doesn't bite."

"William?" He darted a look to the snake and back again.

"Yes. William. William Snakespeare. I name all my animals, even though they'll return to nature as soon as they heal. I've treated owlets, baby badgers, and a few hedgehogs too. If I happen upon an injured creature or animal in trouble, I can't help but to offer aid. I suppose I sound stranger than you'd thought me already?"

"No." He looked at her then and his mind spun in another direction. She wasn't strange at all. *Remarkable* was the word on the tip of his tongue. The ladies he knew in London would scream their heads off at the sight of a mouse, never mind walk about casually with a reptile wrapped around their arm. Theodosia's desire to help injured animals was admirable.

A more disturbing suggestion interrupted his contemplations. Did she view *him* as a lame creature who needed her attention? Was that why she'd offered to make him salve? Or was it simply the fact he was a houseguest? *A lame houseguest*. It did provide opportunity for her to practice her apothecarial skills. These thoughts bombarded his brain and collided with common sense. By the time he muddled his way through the tangle, Theodosia had fed Snakespeare and returned him to his temporary home.

"Most ladies would swoon at the mention of a snake, never mind the thought of wearing one as an accessory." He came to stand beside her as she moved to another display.

"I don't swoon." She laughed again and the sound was infectious. "I can't fathom anything meaningful enough to cause a faint." She lifted the lid of the bowl on a low wooden table. "Come here." She waved in his direction. "You may as well meet everyone. This is Isaac Newt. He has only three legs." She pointed to a brown lizard the color of strong coffee. "The most important member of my menagerie has free run of the house."

"Dare I guess who that might be?" He released a long-held exhale. "Sir Thomas Mole? Sir Francis Drake? I find I'm not half as clever as you, Bookish." And then, against better sense, he asked a question that burned a hole in his brain. "Are these your only companions? Have you no other acquaintances?"

He'd prodded too deeply and all amusement faded. She blinked several times at his questions, her slender brows dipping over her lovely gray eyes. Valiant as a soldier though, she regained balance, quick to answer.

"The milder months bring social events to Oxfordshire. Grandfather and I often have outings and the villagers are ever kind to us when we visit."

He wouldn't point out the bleak and problematic reality in that statement. Theodosia was a beautiful, vibrant— *bloody hell, too intelligent*—woman to waste away in the countryside. What kind of existence was this? Didn't she realize how fulfilling her life could be away from here?

He would suffocate from boredom, his mind and studies malnourished from the lack of stimuli. No wonder she compartmentalized her day into scheduled work sessions and befriended outcast animals. By god, she gave them names as if they were her friends.

"Come to London." The words were out before he could stop them. Never mind the impropriety of the suggestion, he had a tight knot of problems awaiting him when he returned, but the words burst out as if they had a life of their own, more command than request.

"What?" She laughed, and it was the happiest he'd seen her all day.

Relief coursed through him. Why was that? Why? *It doesn't matter why*. She clearly liked the idea.

"I'm not going to London." She brushed her fingers over the downy leaves of a potted meadowsweet plant. "I thought that was decided when my grandfather tried to accept your invitation. London is the last place I'll ever visit."

He examined her face, searching for the slightest betraying emotion, but found none. "Just a thought."

He moved away from the aisle and further toward the lemon trees. He'd miscalculated more than the math problem earlier. What was he thinking?

I wasn't.

There lay the problem. He needed to return home, recalibrate his purpose, and forget about this unexpected anomaly.

His heel caught the edge of the slated path and his leg jarred enough to arouse a dull throb of pain. "Let's proceed to the apothecary. I'm interested in the concoctions you create there." At least he could provide unmatched conversation. Of that, he had no competition or doubt.

* * *

Theodosia followed after Matthew this time as he kept a brisk pace down the corridor. Her mind raced with equaled fervor. Why had he invited her to London? Considering the scene Grandfather had caused at dinner, Matthew had to know she remained in a delicate predicament. She couldn't leave her grandfather in Oxfordshire, nor could she take him along. The weather, lengthy travel, and his current state of mind precluded that decision. But it was of no consequence anyway. London held nothing for her except painful memories, and she wouldn't volunteer to revisit the past.

They arrived at the apothecary door, and with a click of the lock silently moved inside. She lit several lanterns and stirred the coals in the grate. Flames sprung to life in the box, eager to add light and warmth to the room.

"You've evaded my questions too many times to count, so I'll ask again. How does a woman like you become interested in botanical science?" He came up beside her at the worktable where she crushed aromatics with a pestle.

"A woman like me?" She darted her eyes in his direction before she returned her attention to the task.

"Young. Pretty. How old are you anyway?"

"Four and twenty." She tapped the pestle gently against the marble. "And you?"

"I've five more years."

"Botany was one branch of science I could share with Grandfather where he didn't already know everything." She added shaved beeswax to the ginger paste in a bowl and stirred it thoroughly. "I'm not creating anything special. Any herbalist might have made you this same ginger mixture." She glanced over her shoulder as she reached to a high shelf to retrieve a bottle of white liquid. Her fingers slipped and the bottle slid backward.

"Here. Let me help." He came up behind her. "It's the least I can do since you're going to this trouble for me."

He reached above her to fetch the liquid and she twisted, anxious to move out of his way, but he'd come too close and unwittingly trapped her. They stood chin to nose for a moment before he spoke.

"My apologies," he muttered. In his hurry, he brought his arm down and by consequence brushed a bundle of lavender strung from the top of the cabinets. Tiny purple buds, as feathery and light as dandelion fluff, showered over them.

"You're destined to smell like a dainty lady after all," she quipped.

His eyes gained an intensity that caused her pulse to skitter and he took an abrupt step backward.

"Wait." She reached up and brushed several pieces of lavender from his hair, tentative at first. Then she smoothed through the too long strands with a familiar manner no salve or elixir could replicate. For a fleeting moment she savored the contact despite the impropriety.

"Thank you." He swallowed and placed the bottle on the worktable. "Shall I?" He canted his head toward hers.

"No need. I'll give my hair a good shake later on. For now, I'd rather smell like flowers than the salve I'm creating for you."

"Ginger," he remarked. "I wouldn't have considered it."

He watched as she placed the bowl in a pan of water near the fire.

"I experiment often." She glanced over her shoulder at a blue container on the far counter. "That's my newest attempt at face tonic."

"What?" He nabbed the round tub she'd indicated and peeled back the lid. "What's in it? Not what I fear, I hope."

She laughed and he seemed to relax, their congenial

mood restored. There was safety from misplaced emotions in mundane conversation. She retrieved the bowl and continued their discussion.

"Rose oil, bitter almond, and distilled water." She tilted her chin and moved her head from side to side. "I use it every evening before I go to sleep."

"That's a waste of time . . ."

Her smile fell away and he hurried to finish his statement.

". . . when no lotion could ever improve upon your appearance."

At first, she could only return his stare. Her hand grew still. But before he spoke further she rededicated herself to the task and furiously worked the mixture in the bowl. She finished, sealed the container, and handed it in his direction.

"I hope this helps. All you need to do is rub it over the muscles that pain you in a brisk massage as often as you wish. It should alleviate the pain, albeit temporarily." She glanced at his leg and held back a hundred questions. Instead, in her usual manner, words peppered the air in a nervous habit to fill the void. "I can write down the ingredients, if you find it effective and choose to have someone prepare it for you in London."

"Thank you." He tucked the container into his coat pocket and an odd silence settled between them again.

"I should check on my grandfather." She looked at the bracket clock on the wall before returning her attention to him. "It's almost lunchtime, and if he hasn't emerged from his bedchambers, he may need coaxing."

They left the apothecary, and as she locked the door she could feel Matthew's attention so intently she hesitated in turning around. He must think her an odd collection of traits. Intelligence and isolation were often ingredients for madness.

"It must be difficult for you."

He didn't mince words. He was a scholar who knew the value of controlling a conversation. And while they were only acquainted with each other a few days, she could hear the change in tone, the unmistakable note of pity. She couldn't bear it and quickened her steps, rushing away into the gallery.

Chapter Eleven

"You know the way back, don't you?" She knew it was poorly done of her. How she ruined the day. An inordinate and delightful day that should be treasured for its rarity.

Like the kiss.

Like his kiss.

But she couldn't help it.

"Wait."

The word sliced through her and she slowed her steps. A grumble of curses punctuated by the sound of his walking stick on the tiles followed. She should be ashamed of herself, but she couldn't allow him to look at her with an air of scientific study, to dissect her existence as if some curious specimen caught under glass.

She made the most of a difficult situation and didn't complain. Nowhere in the plan did she intend to suffer a catalog of questions pertaining to her grandfather's decline or her unusual existence.

She paused and released a deep breath, the sound loud in the sudden stillness of the corridor. What had happened? Did Matthew no longer follow?

At odds with her cowardice, she doubled back and found him in the gallery, his focus on the same hanging as when their day had begun. A day that had held promise, or so she'd believed.

"I shouldn't have left."

It was somewhat of an apology, and her words grabbed his attention, though he was polite enough not to remark on her disregard. "These walls are filled with intriguing articles and admirable letters of accommodation. It's an uncommon gallery. I anticipated a stroll through your heritage." He watched her when he finished speaking.

"Instead you found Grandfather's most esteemed contributions as a respected intellectual in the field of science for over two decades." She drew closer, though the subject evoked a shadow of sadness. "He's funded research and donated generously to medical foundations of every kind, sponsored education through university for countless students, and established a distinctive reputation as a scholar in several branches." She already breathed hard from unsettled emotion, and when tears blurred her vision she bit the inside of her cheek to keep her composure. "So, I don't want your pity."

"You don't have it. Not my pity, at least." He reached out and removed a stray lavender bud from her hair. "Though you've captured my interest, Bookish."

She swallowed, forcing herself to dismiss emotion, to push it down deep where she wouldn't have to consider all she'd lost until it was nothing more than a disquiet whisper in the background of life.

"I grew tired of the empty walls." Her voice came out as a sullen murmur, but it regained strength as she continued. "Our family's history in oils was lost to the fire all those years ago. I've no picture of my parents, other than the fading memories of my childhood."

"I'm sorry, Theodosia."

There was a wealth of sincere empathy in his words and not a shred of pity this time.

"Thank you."

"You intended to check in on your grandfather and I've deterred you long enough, but I've a brilliant idea to chase away the somber mood we've conjured this morning. The sun is shining." He glanced toward the oblong windows as if to confirm his proposition. "Snow melts as we speak, and I suspect the roadways will be passable by tomorrow. We shouldn't waste a bit more of the weather."

She searched his face for a clue to his thinking.

"I haven't seen much of the property from my guest room window, so you'll need to tell me if the mews are to the left or right once I exit the rear of the house."

"To the left." She narrowed her eyes, suspicious of the sudden merriment alive in his.

"Two hours should prove sufficient." He moved past her. "Dress warmly. Very warmly, in fact. And meet me in the front hall."

She watched him walk away, his uneven gait hardly perceptible, overshadowed by his stature and bearing as a good man.

"I'll need my flannel stomacher and the woolen waist-coat I wore during the carriage ride here, Coggs." Matthew washed the last bit of shaving soap from his chin with a cloth left beside the ewer, his final words coming out muffled as he toweled dry. "And two pairs of stockings."

He busied himself with further necessities as Coggs retrieved the requested articles. If he were to bring a bit of joy into Theodosia's life for the afternoon, he would need to begin the arrangements.

"If it isn't fit weather for travel, why are you insistent on braving the elements?" Coggs screwed his face into an expression that displayed his opinion of the plan. "Walking about on snow and ice is hardly the recommended activity, especially when—"

"I'm not defined by my impairment, Coggs. And that reminds me . . ." Matthew returned to the mattress, where he'd discarded the clothes he'd worn earlier. Rummaging through his coat pocket, he retrieved the container of ginger salve and placed it on the bedside table. "No doubt I'll need that later." This he muttered to himself.

"Isn't it customary for the host to provide entertainment for the invited guests, and not the other way around?" Coggs persisted, though he supplied the articles requested.

"Under normal circumstances, I suppose." Matthew continued to dress, his attention divided.

"Is the lady not normal, then?"

"I never said that." He cast a glance toward Coggs that indicated it was he who stood on thin ice. "She's the bookish sort and somewhat alone. I see no reason not to brighten her day with an outing. Do you?"

A beat of silence followed before his valet answered. "Kirkman."

"Pardon?" Matthew pushed his Hessians aside and reached for his worn leather boots. They weren't fashionable but they were far more comfortable.

"The twice-proposing gent. I assume Kirkman would disagree with your intentions."

"I don't have intentions. Nothing more than an afternoon diversion. How often do you think Talbot entertains?" He wrestled with one boot and then began with the other. "I'd wager our visit is as rare as a rainbow on Christmas Eve." He stamped his foot and stood promptly. "Besides, no one appreciates a codnogger." He added this as a reminder to Coggs's propensity for gossip. For some odd, unnamed reason, Coggs's comment fueled him to pursue his idea with additional determination.

Several layers of wool later, he donned his multi-caped greatcoat and leather gloves, took the back stairs to the kitchen, and exited Leighton House at the rear. A gardener or other servant had shoveled a wide path from the main house to the stables, and bearing left, he followed the cleared walkway toward the mews. The passage was narrow, the cobblestones covered with a slick coat of packed snow and ice, and true to his valet's prediction it made for poor traction. But nonetheless he reached the building, unlatched the gate, and entered. Inside, he found his driver, George, playing cards with two stable hands, and so he enlisted their help in his endeavor.

"I'll need your strongest draft horses." He indicated a pair housed in the same stall, one golden blond and the other chestnut brown. "Show me the sleigh."

A young lad led him to the farthest corner of the stable, where, beneath what appeared to be a cord of wood, sat a grand wooden sleigh, its exterior once a polished Kelly green, but nothing more than a dusty reminder of Christmas past now. He'd assumed the estate would have some type of winter vehicle, although he'd rather hoped it wouldn't be so neglected.

"This may take longer than expected." Matthew rounded the vehicle and inspected the leather straps for deterioration and long, metal runners for rust, but found nothing to deter his plan.

"It's not been used for years, milord." The lad removed several logs as he spoke, tossing the firewood to an opposite corner of the stable and out of the way. "Must have been a dandy when she was new."

"Indeed, though we can do nothing for it now aside from give her a little life." Matthew assisted with the unwanted

wood until every trace of bark had been removed. Together
he and the stable hand buffed the leather cushions and confirmed the safety of the sleigh. "She's a beauty. A forgotten
beauty, asleep for far too long, but a beauty nonetheless."
He ran his hand across the high dashboard, further insurance he or Theodosia wouldn't be hit with a clod of snow
thrown up by the horses' hooves.

"Shall I ride with you?" the stable boy inquired, a hopeful gleam in his eyes.

Matthew knew the extra weight at the rear rumble seat
would lift the runners and allow for a smoother, faster ride,
but he envisioned a different outcome. Despite the lad had
helped without complaint, Matthew hesitated.

"Let's hitch up the team and test her out. Would you like
a spin around the stable yard before I bring the sleigh up
the hill to the main house?"

"Yes, milord." The lad jumped to attention. "Yes, I would."

With the horses secured and the stable doors wide,
Matthew flicked the reins and sent the forgotten sleigh
into the snow-packed yard. She glided smoothly on her
runners, as if she'd waited patiently for someone to remember she existed, to find her and give her a purpose, if only
for one day.

After two full turns around the yard, Matthew reined in
the horses, deposited the young boy at the mews, and sent
the team up the sloping hill to the main house. He maneuvered most any vehicle with ease, his skill with the reins
more than proficient despite he couldn't tolerate a long ride
in the saddle. His upper body had become unusually strong
to compensate for his impairment. His leg betrayed him in
the consistent control and strength needed to ride astride,
so he rarely did, though he missed it, the feeling found atop
a stallion, in command of the world from above.

He paused near the rear of the house, where two footmen

assisted with final necessities, and then with a snap of leather, he drove the team toward the front entrance.

"What do you think his lordship has planned? Why would he request you dress warmly? Will you be venturing far from the house?" Dora finished buttoning Theodosia's fur-trimmed velvet riding habit, her questions as fast as her fingers.

Theodosia was grateful for her maid's assistance, no matter she chattered with curious excitement. It distracted from the multitude of thoughts bombarding her mind. At least Grandfather had eaten a satisfactory lunch and napped comfortably in his chambers. She breathed a little easier.

An outing would be just the tonic needed to exorcise the effects of distress on her mind and body. She didn't mind the cold temperature overmuch and she owed Lord Whittingham the courtesy after her less than becoming behavior this morning.

And too, the recent snowfall offered a scientific wonderland to observe. The breathtaking symmetry of each lacy snowflake was a marvel she found difficult to comprehend, while icicles, long, lean, and piercing, hung from every branch and eave with delicate grace. Rare nacreous clouds in lovely shades of mother-of-pearl and nickel softened the sky, almost made iridescent by their shimmery existence. The world of science was renewed with every snowfall.

Now having donned several petticoats, two pairs of stockings, a chemise, underskirt, skirt, and jacket, she was bundled, warm, and curious. *What did Matthew intend?*

"I was only told to dress well and I have done so." Theodosia checked her pocket for leather gloves and gathered her swan-down muff. Her hooded cape was lined with ermine so she eschewed an additional scarf, already overwhelmed by the weight of her garments.

The sound of horse hooves and halters broke the quiet. Dora darted to the front window unencumbered. Theodosia was slower to follow.

"He's dashing, isn't he?" Her maid whispered, though they stood quite alone.

"He's leaving tomorrow," Theodosia answered, not sure who benefited more from the words.

"That doesn't mean you can't have a wonderful time today." Dora smiled and gestured toward the door. "Now, don't keep the earl waiting after he's gone to such trouble to please you."

That much was true. Theodosia knew the condition of the sleigh and the work it must have taken to prepare their outing, never mind the thick fur blankets she noticed on the bench and the brazier full of hot coals on the floor, poised to warm their feet.

"I suppose there's no harm in taking a short jaunt." She started toward the door, working to draw on her gloves as she moved. "What could possibly happen on an afternoon sleigh ride?"

Chapter Twelve

Theodosia approached the sleigh with caution. She may have rationalized her decision upstairs and confidently deflected her maid's interrogation, but beneath several layers of flannel and wool, her heart beat a furious rhythm.

"What's all this? You've taken on quite a challenge for one afternoon's distraction."

Matthew had come around the other side of the sleigh and she noticed he seemed surefooted on the snow-packed drive despite the lack of a walking stick.

"What good is a sleigh if it never sees snow?" He chuckled, and his deep tenor rippled through her. "Besides, the world is brand-new after a snowfall. I thought we might enjoy the scenery. At least until we decide it's too cold to bear."

She watched him, her mind working now as hard as her pulse. He took her gloved hand in his and helped her into the sleigh. When she was settled on the seat, he climbed in beside her and arranged two fur blankets across their legs. All the while the heated coals in the brazier warmed the soles of her boots.

"Are you ready?"

He cast her a sideways glance, leather reins in hand, and she was struck by his handsome profile and the way fractured sunlight glinted in his eyes. He wore no hat and as he turned, the not-so-subtle wind lifted a fallen lock of hair across his brow. He must be quite popular within society's chosen circle, a man as striking, intelligent, and generous as he.

So why would he take time to arrange such a complicated diversion this afternoon?

"Wait." Her objection came out in a puff of breath as translucent and fleeting as a ghost from the past. She refused to allow him to feel sorry for her. "I'm not lonely."

"Nor am I, but I thought, today, we might be not-lonely together."

He smiled and something sparked inside her, a tremor of excitement that began at her heart and reverberated to her fingertips and toes. She returned his grin and before she could consider it further, he snapped the ribbons and the sleigh lurched forward. Wind stung her cheeks and snuck beneath her hood to nip at her earlobes, the sense of fast flight refreshing and invigorating. She tried to portray a more composed mien, not that Matthew's opinion mattered or she considered herself lacking the city polish he was accustomed to, but once the sleigh took the drive and raced over a series of gentle slopes, her stomach dropped with delight and she couldn't suppress her laughter.

Heavens, it was wonderful to laugh. It seemed too many weeks, months . . . too long she'd gone without the unconditional freedom of pure joy.

She turned and he did as well, their eyes matched in the moment before he averted his attention to the landscape ahead. They coasted along for a good stretch, wordlessly happy in the uncomplicated thrill of the ride. At last they glided into a wide field beyond the main house and gardens, down a small hill to a tall row of holly bushes, where he brought the horses to rein.

As she'd hoped, everywhere she looked, the ordinary was

made beautiful by the weather, pure white and crystalline, an enchanted fairy-tale vision that caused one to pause, awestruck, though she was out of breath from laughter more than anything else.

Matthew wrapped the leather reins around the hook inside the dashboard and clamped the remaining length beneath his boot. The sleigh ride was a fine idea on his part. He relished Theodosia's gleeful reaction throughout the ride.

Glancing at her now, he paused in appreciation. Her cheeks were pinkened to a rosy blush, her pert nose just so, and true delight danced in her gray gaze. In an unexpected rush, he was pulled back to their intimate exchange in the library, the weight of her breasts crushed against him and the flavor of her curious kiss. He found himself mesmerized and distracted in the best way by the intriguing, beautiful woman beside him.

He cleared his throat and broke the uncomfortable silence. "That was refreshing."

"It was." Her breath danced between them before it disappeared. "I can't remember the last time . . ." Her words faded just as quickly.

They sat in silence a few more moments, as he was at a loss to intrude on whatever memories haunted her.

"I haven't been a very good hostess." She shifted on the bench and placed her gloved hand on his forearm. "I should apologize for earlier."

"Think nothing of it." How delicate her touch despite they were both bundled for warmth.

"Well, I do and I'm sorry."

He merely smiled, wishing to change the subject and alleviate her concern. "I get on well enough, able to do most anything, or at least the most important things." He struggled for a way to bypass the stilted niceties that held their conversation hostage.

"Dancing is overrated, or so I've heard."

She returned his words with grave sincerity, and for some reason that small gesture touched his soul. The moment stretched and reformed, and while he watched her intently, a different mood took hold and all previous jocularity evaporated.

"Are you cold?" She'd long before removed her glove from his sleeve, though he wouldn't have minded if she'd clung to him longer. "Shall I take us back?'

"No, not yet, please." She looked about the scenery before she darted her eyes back to his. "Most people find winter weather confining, but I've always preferred nature to a ballroom. I suppose that's where we differ."

"I'm not sure about that." He followed her line of vision to the landscape and spied the snow-dusted ruins of burnt wood and broken beams. "You're fortunate to have this vast scenery at your disposal. I imagine it has supplied you with countless days' adventure."

"And research."

"Yes, of course. Research." He shifted on the bench, angling toward her as he spoke, and his knees inadvertently rubbed against hers beneath the blanket. Her eyes widened with the contact, though she didn't move away. Then he said what he needed to say, despite the words caused an unexpected spike of disappointment in his chest. "I see no reason not to return to London in the morning. The roads should be clear and I've several matters to attend to." His latter statement lacked significant conviction. "I've enjoyed my visit here at Leighton House."

"Truly? You traveled extensively to investigate a dubious journal article, which you quickly proved lacked valid substance and was written by an imposter. Not to mention I've insulted you more than once. I wouldn't label that *hospitality* by definition." She hemmed her lower lip, seemingly abashed at the truth spoken aloud.

Their conversation paused as fresh snowflakes filled the air, much to Theodosia's delight. Her eyes lit with pleasure and she immediately brought her palm upward to catch a few atop her black leather glove. "Under a microscope, scientists have discovered each snowflake is composed of two hundred ice crystals. Yet they're as unique as finger-prints, no two the same."

"Indeed." He couldn't tear his gaze from her profile and how intently she admired nature's gift. "That must have made for chilling work, or perhaps a race against the clock before the specimen disappeared."

She smiled at his teasing and blew the snowflakes back into the air. He watched her lips pucker and relax, and his body recalled that kiss but again. Surely every snowflake that landed upon him melted on contact. He reached for her hands and enveloped them between his.

"I should bring us back. I wouldn't wish for you to become chilled."

Somehow they'd drawn closer, though he'd swear neither of them had moved.

"I'm quite comfortable. Aren't you?"

There was a question he couldn't answer honestly. For the truth would reveal a disputable scientific fact that cold temperature did nothing to relieve a raging erection.

"Theodosia?"

She blinked away a few snowflakes caught in her lashes. "Yes?"

He searched for appropriate words, never before so careful to choose wisely. "I'm glad we've had this opportu-nity to become acquainted." He watched her reaction. His sentiment didn't seem adequate, though he lacked the ability to categorize it in any way more than an unforeseen anomaly.

"I am too, Matthew."

It was his name on her lips or mayhap it was because he hadn't stopped staring at her lips or it was none of those things and all of those things, but he found himself acting more than thinking and so he dipped his head and captured her mouth.

She didn't resist.

Her hands climbed his sleeves and wound tightly around his neck, and despite layers upon layers of thick wool and flannel, he felt her touch on his skin.

It was well below freezing in the open air, but his blood boiled with a riot of desire and emotion and she tasted— she tasted just as he remembered, sweet and curious and delightfully inviting.

Their tongues met with anxious friction, each velvety slide another stroke to his fervor, and he let go of thought, not something he was apt to do often, and allowed himself to get lost in their kiss. How easily that was achieved, the light-headed freedom of feeling instead of thinking.

Her hair smelled like lavender, tucked inside the warm hood to enhance the fragrance. Her fingers pressed into his upper arms as if to hold on tightly, though they sat quite securely in the sleigh. And her mouth, her lush clever mouth, opened beneath his and returned his kiss ardently, chasing when he retreated, succumbing when he pursued.

It took no effort for him to imagine her in bed beside him, all pearly white skin and delicate pink blush, her glossy black hair spilled around her shoulders, her body a gift offered for his exploration. Mayhap it was the forbidden layers that separated them now or a strange curiosity that provoked him to these indulgent erotic images, but they came, one after another, and he allowed them to drench his mind and saturate his soul. Once abed, he was as equal as any man, a passionate, giving lover. It didn't matter that nothing more would come of their association. Theodosia's kiss would not be easily forgotten despite his misplaced lust.

He realized belatedly he should put an end to it and so, reluctantly, withdrew. Their foreheads touched though their mouths parted. Steam filled the space left between them and he concentrated on the hypnotic rhythm of her exhales, committing it to memory.

"Was that to thank me or say good-bye?"

"Neither." He shook his head the slightest. "There's no need to label it."

She looked away and back again.

"You should come to London." Again, it wasn't what he'd planned to say. "The museums and libraries would please you."

Something changed in her eyes. Some emotion he didn't understand. Without an answer, she righted herself on the seat and straightened her hood. She pushed her hands into her muffler and took a deep breath.

"We must go." She tried for cheerfulness, but he recognized the strain. "I've already spent far too much time away from the house, and while Grandfather appeared content when I left, I should look in on him again."

He leaned down and unhooked the reins. Unsure what to say, he chose silence and urged the horses into a gallop as they crossed the field, overtook the hill, and whipped up to the main house.

Theodosia steamed in a tub of scented water, warmed to the core, her mind busy with unanswered questions. Her normal uneventful and predictable world had been upended since the Earl of Whittingham had come to Leighton House on his mission of discovery and revelation. Indeed, those words served well. She had no way to decipher the new and confusing emotions coursing through her, quick to acknowledge they were simultaneously pleasant and distressing.

She leaned her head back against the rim of the tub, thankful Dora had left to allow some much needed quiet and contemplation. Too preoccupied with the day-by-day struggles of coping with Grandfather's lapses in memory, Theodosia had never peered too far into the future. Her parents' untimely deaths caused her not to conjure the past. And while she saved specific memories like keepsakes in a box, she didn't dwell on the course of her life any more than necessary.

But now, with the earl's arrival and her heart somewhat curious, she wondered what lay in store and how her future would evolve. Deep inside, when she was painstakingly honest, she knew Grandfather's health was deteriorating. She'd read endless books and articles on the subject, too afraid to face the inevitable truth. No one lived forever. Hadn't she learned that lesson with her parents? As a child she'd dreamed, but then there was the fire and hope died in the flames, extinguished and buried in ash. Would everyone she loved leave her too soon?

She'd never considered taking a husband. Never debated whether or not children were part of her plan for the future. She'd grown into womanhood with freedoms and habits most men acquired as part of their manhood. Knowledge was her closest friend aside from a few assorted animals. She wasn't fit for tea parties and social calls, ballroom dancing or flirtation.

And yet, the earl's arrival had stirred something inside her that she once doubted existed.

Desire.

What of it? This wasn't intellectual curiosity. Desire was

strong. Reckless and disobedient. It permeated every part of her and begged to be explored. With a huff of disgust or mayhap resignation, she climbed from the tub and toweled dry. At least there was comfort in knowing Matthew Strathmore, Earl of Whittingham, was a temporary distraction and would be gone from her life soon enough. Gone, like everyone she dared to care about before.

Dinner was an unusual affair. Grandfather held logical, enjoyable conversation and never once mentioned marmalade. At times he recalled theories with admirable accuracy and spoke of detailed experiments he'd conducted years ago. She had no way to explain his sudden lucidity other than a rare happenstance and the fickle nature of aging, but she treasured the occurrence, innately satisfied that Matthew witnessed her grandfather as he once was, perspicacious and learned.

After dinner they'd retired to the library, where the gentlemen took brandy and she sipped a glass of port, and when the conversation turned to recent scientific exploration, she envisioned what life might have been like if she were a different person and circumstances weren't what they were.

Oh, she would never return to London. Of that she was certain, but having spent most of her years isolated in the countryside, her nose buried in a book, a research book no less, defined her person and she could not change to become one of society's countless ladies who flitted from event to event without a more serious thought than which shoe clips matched her evening gown.

Furthermore, she didn't know how to dance and everyone, *everyone*, in London danced. Quadrilles and reels, waltzes and cotillions. Dancing was practically signed legislation. She secreted a smile at the thought. No matter if one particular gentleman considered it overrated.

When the longcase clock chimed eleven, she startled from her reverie, surprised by the late hour. The men might have noted the same.

"Our discussion is highly agreeable and I can speak endlessly on current topics, but I should retire now. I'll need to get an early start tomorrow morning in case the roadways are slower than anticipated." He shook Grandfather's hand. "Thank you again for your kind invitation."

"You're welcome. I hope our paths cross in the future, Whittingham. Our view of science advancement is much aligned."

"I owe your lovely granddaughter a debt of gratitude as well." Matthew bowed in her direction before he retrieved his walking stick from the corner and advanced. "She gave her time freely when I'm certain she had other more interesting pursuits."

When he reached where she stood, he inclined his head and spoke softly. "Although our invigorating sleigh ride will not be easily forgotten and was well worth the frigid trip to Oxfordshire. Take care of yourself, Lady Leighton, and your ever-so-clever menagerie of animals. No more ghostwriting antics or false authorship. The next opposer may not be so easily charmed by your alluring gray gaze and remarkable intelligence."

Taken aback by his personal aside, she floundered for a response equally compelling. This would likely be the last time they spoke. He searched her face as if he waited for something, but her mind blanked, his absence already felt though they'd spent little more than two days in each other's company.

"Safe travels, Lord Whittingham. Thank you for"—she

paused, the next words chosen carefully, for she couldn't mention their kisses or any other of the rare, beguiling moments they'd shared—"your friendship. Don't forget to use the salve." She groaned inwardly at her clumsy last statement.

One half of his mouth climbed in a grin and then he merely nodded his head. And as she watched him leave, broad-shouldered and tall, his uneven gait more charming than anything else, she wondered why Fate had caused their paths to cross and what his future held, and more importantly, her own.

He couldn't sleep. Despite he needed to be rested before beginning the seven-hour return trip to London in barely improved weather, he couldn't manage to shut off his mind or stop the incessant questions that begged for answers. Theodosia was a puzzle he couldn't solve. An intelligent woman with an unusual past, but a conundrum just the same. He rose from bed, dressed again in passable attire, and left the guest chambers in search of relief for his restlessness. He decided upon the library and so took the stairs quietly as he made his way downstairs.

He paused at the newel post and glanced down the hall into the entryway area. A light gleamed, the faintest shimmer of candlelight. He moved with caution, unsure what creature might cross his path, that spontaneous tabby always at him with a suspicious eye.

He arrived at the door where light shown underneath and with the tip of his finger eased it wider so he might peer inside without notice. Theodosia sat near the fire, her feet curled under her skirts where she'd drawn them upon the seat cushion. How lovely she appeared, outlined in firelight, like a masterful painting in a gallery of art. The only way to answer the questions that refused to allow his sleep was to ask them. He'd possessed an inquisitive mind all his life. Curiosity was a curse and a charm all the same.

She turned, the weight of his stare likely the cause, and she smiled slightly. He needed no other invitation.

Chapter Thirteen

"I couldn't sleep," he offered in way of explanation.

"I couldn't either," she answered with a shake of her head that fanned ebony hair over her slim shoulders, each length momentarily glossed in a blue-black gleam from the chandelier overhead.

He took the matched chair opposite her near the hearth, in the same room where he'd first made her acquaintance.

"Would you like some port?" She held up her glass, half full with the rich burgundy wine.

"Thank you, yes." He moved to the cabinet alongside the far wall and poured himself a glass before he reclaimed his chair.

It was highly unseemly to drink wine with an unchaperoned lady while in a state of semi-undress, though he rather admired her disdain for decorum. London would be shocked by their combined lack of grace and zealous social familiarity, but he enjoyed that fact. There was little about London's swells and elites that met his approval anyway. How often they judged an individual on appearance and not their worth of character or intelligence.

He hadn't donned his coat or cravat when he'd left his rooms, though his shirt remained closed at the neck. She wore a silky white wrapper that smoothed silently against her skin whenever she lifted her glass to take a sip. The air grew heavy in their silence, so he sought innocuous conversation. In the end she'd proven a most gracious hostess.

"This has been a liberating visit, Bookish. Even if my initial intention became skewed, I've enjoyed my stay. I'm glad we became . . ." He stalled in search of the right word.

"Friends?" she supplied.

"Perhaps. I suppose I was thinking more in line with confidants." He cleared his throat. "Your secret is safe with me. As long as you won't repeat the offense, I won't tell a soul you instigated an article in that stuffy Royal Society journal. Nor that you forged your grandfather's name."

She looked a bit unsettled by his statement, but he couldn't understand why when all he offered were reassurances. "*Confidants* implies we both have something to hide, and I don't know very much about you."

"I suppose that's true. And as you've often reminded me, we'll most likely never see each other again, so I suggest we end this evening with a few traded secrets."

"Secrets?"

Her expression sobered. Clearly, he'd touched a nerve.

"Nothing you don't wish to share, of course." He took a healthy sip of his port and watched her do the same. Red wine would never transform him into a liberal speaker, but he had a feeling her tolerance would be affected in an altogether different manner.

"I can't imagine I have anything worth knowing." She set her glass down on a side table with care. "I live a practical and simplistic life here in Oxfordshire and I wouldn't have it otherwise."

"Really?" He too replaced his drink. "Forging research

and claiming it as your own seems the stuff of espionage for the Crown."

She laughed, although he wondered if it was amusement or tension that evoked the reaction. The sound overrode the chime of the bracket clock striking midnight.

"I propose three questions each." He canted his head in her direction and grinned.

"Two and no more," she countered, a shrewd look in her eye.

"Done." He sat up straighter in the chair as he collected his thoughts.

"Ask away then." She shook her head in the negative, as if doubtful he'd accomplish a query of worth. "You're bound to be disappointed."

"I'll be the judge of that." He tapped his pointer finger against his chin and skewered her with a stare. "What is the fondest memory of your life thus far?" He really did wish to know more about her, and up to this point she'd been anything but forthcoming. By asking this in particular, he expected her to expound upon a mathematical theory or remind him of one of her accomplishments in her botanical science experiments. Instead her face took on a series of conflicted emotions.

"That's truly two questions within one. My fondest memories are also my saddest, and both include my parents."

Silence followed in which he cursed himself for the fool that he was, wishing to bring levity to their discussion and in turn causing the opposite.

"How did you hurt your leg?"

Apparently, he was more affected by remorse than she.

"Aah, you've selected a very good secret to question." He took a long swallow from his glass. "Over a decade ago I was involved in an incident that risked the life of my closest friend. We were young and reckless, too cocky to believe we could ever get hurt, but we both learned a lesson we shall never forget. In the midst of our adventure, we angered the wrong person and he blindly fired a pistol at us. My friend, the Duke of Scarsdale, managed to escape unharmed, but the bullet caught me in the side of my knee." He leaned down and indicated the spot where he'd been shot. "I deserved it, I suppose, for poking into business that wasn't my concern. Though I'd never anticipated a deadly outcome. That night was hell, but recovery was worse. Sequestered at my family's countryside estate, I thought I'd go mad from boredom."

"You're lucky to have escaped with your life."

"How true."

"No wonder you despise Oxfordshire and the country simplicity it represents. You must have been anxious to return to the busy calendar you've embraced, while a rural setting reminds you of the pain and recovery you suffered. Your offer to come to London gains clarity now."

"I was serious in my invitation." He drained his glass and dismissed the maudlin memories never far from recall.

"I believe you."

She looked so deeply into his eyes, he dared not look away. Her gaze, silver gray and absolutely entrancing, held him powerless. He forced himself to conversation. "The city can't be all that bad a place for the upper ten thousand to call it home."

"London will never be a place *I* call home."

The finality of that statement held the room in silence for several minutes. He watched her finish her wine, and while he knew he shouldn't ask it, their previous exchange provided the ideal conduit. Besides, he still had a remaining question in their bargain.

"Why?" It was a small word, only three letters, but he knew it challenged her to reveal something life changing and meaningful.

She didn't start readily and toyed with her glass, turning the stem between her fingertips while the fire popped and cracked with impatience. He kept quiet and wondered if she knew how lovely she appeared or how her intelligence was an admirable and wonderful gift. How being void of all societal expectation and pretentious insincerity was the very beauty that made her the cherished exception to the rule. Her silvery-gray eyes were hardly a comparison to the innate and wondrous traits she possessed. In science such an anomaly of rare perfection was labeled a miracle, for lack of a sufficient term, and he could see no reason not to categorize Theodosia as one.

When she finally spoke, he startled, unaware he'd become lost in admiration.

"I was fourteen at the time. Grandfather had raised me for eight years already, and my education was extremely thorough. Aside from a clever governess and several tutors, I learned an abundance by observing my grandfather at work. He was always reading, writing, or researching." She paused in the retelling, a reminiscent smile on her face. "But he got it into his head upon my fourteenth birthday that I needed to attend finishing school. Despite a vast knowledge of scientific theory, he knew little of finer feminine pursuits, and while he might have invited additional tutors to instruct me in subjects of dance and etiquette, there wouldn't be the necessary social interaction to hone and test those same skills."

She looked toward her empty glass and he retrieved the wine to refill it. Nothing but the hiss of the flaming logs in the box could be heard in the interim.

"I'll never forget that day. Grandfather acted as though he couldn't wait to be rid of me, but I know he hated to see me go as much as I regretted leaving. Nevertheless, I'd agreed to start the semester and wished to make him proud. Neither one of us could have anticipated the tragedy that claimed my parents or the years afterward. Raising a five-year-old couldn't have been an easy task, no matter he hired staff to assist, and I was forever in his shadow despite an excellent governess who saw to my every need. Grandfather was always kind and generous with his time, though in retrospect I'm sure he had dozens of other pursuits he'd have preferred. With that in mind, I refused to disappoint him, since my attending finishing school was a small request by comparison."

Matthew nodded, though he wouldn't interrupt.

"Mrs. Barton's Academy for Girls was reputed to be distinguished among the ton, grandiose and welcoming. Grandfather had it on good recommendation it was the finest academy for young women. I'm sure it cost a small fortune. Unfortunately, neither he nor I considered the other students in attendance, nor whether I would be accepted."

She blinked several times and took a sip of wine, her eyes downcast as she continued with more emotion in her voice.

"It took less than two weeks for me to become a target of humiliation and embarrassment. It was easy to see I was different from the polished, delicate ladies who'd also enrolled to *finish* off their otherwise appropriate education. I stood out for a number of reasons. I was too smart. My quick answers and extensive knowledge showed my advanced learning, but also revealed how little the other girls had studied. At first, I didn't realize it unwittingly cast a shadow on my classmates. It upset them that I completed my assignments before the due date and included detailed additional research. The instructor was quick to hold my work up with praise and comparison, but this unfortunately created animosity among the students. In a survival tactic with which I was unfamiliar, they banded together in conspiracy, eager with petty complaint and mean-spirited compensation.

"At first there were small, foolish pranks. A spider in my soup or missing stockings later found tied to a chandelier in the assembly room. Holes cut into my best dresses or pockets filled with mud from the garden. Given the opportunity, the other girls of the academy joined in the hurtful antics rather than champion me. A few withdrew and remained silent, too worried they'd draw notice and become the next victim. But with either course, I hadn't a single friend, and anyone who dared to speak to me and express their remorse at the situation did so in a hushed whisper."

She exhaled thoroughly and he longed to take her into his arms and offer comfort. Still he remained in his seat and allowed her to continue, damning himself for asking the question in the first place.

"I did my best to remain invisible. I tried to quell my abilities, but it was too little, too late. The instructors knew I withheld my knowledge, and while exhibiting too much intelligence is never becoming in a lady of the ton, they too had grown accustomed to using my work as an example to motivate the others. Besides, the guttersnipes who perpetuated the rumors and created the embarrassing mishaps were in control and enjoyed wielding their power. They isolated me and I became a pariah of sorts. No one was going to rescue me. I couldn't write to Grandfather and cause him worry. Instead my letters home became a listing of accomplishments that had nothing to do with my relationships with the other girls. I counted my days and planned to at least finish one semester before I returned to Leighton House for Christmas. Then I'd express my desire to remain home."

"Theodosia." He said her name softly, his heart aching for the hurtful acts she'd endured. "Why didn't you seek help from the instructors or leave immediately?"

"And allow those spiteful girls to know they drove me from my purpose?" She shook her head vehemently, her hair shimmering around her white robe. "Anyway, that all became unnecessary. I already knew I was lacking in social grace. I could hardly replicate the demure deportment of the other girls. Still, to be repeatedly shamed and taunted, no matter how strong you believe yourself to be, hurts, and you begin to believe that the perception of others is in fact, true. That the face you see in the mirror is ordinary and plain and the dance steps you attempt are awkward and clumsy . . . made all the more hurtful by the twittering censure of eleven other girls watching. You believe that hair the color of soot is hardly attractive when compared to the gleaming gold or burnished bronze of a cultured English beauty, and the tone of your voice is far from melodic insomuch as it can be heard over the snickers and animal noises made whenever you speak. You stop looking for your chemise and stockings and instead, hide them under your mattress so you have something clean to wear come morning. You learn to always examine your soup bowl before eating, to keep your peripheral vision sharp, and never answer the instructor's questions, even if no one else knows the correct solution and the information is burning a hole through your tongue. Instead you become adept at hiding your *abnormal proclivities*.

"You teach yourself not to cry in your sleep, no matter the nightmare or daydream for that matter, and that different is *wrong*, even though before you attended finishing school you never perceived yourself in that manner."

"Bookish, stop. Please." He stood up and paced a hard line on the carpet before her chair. "I want to find Mrs. Barton and throttle her for allowing those vipers to torment you. You should have informed the instructors. Surely they would have come to your aid."

"Any punishment the girls received would come back to me twofold." She breathed deeply, her expression less pained now. "I simply counted the days, because numbers made sense and guaranteed predictability, and when the holidays arrived I returned home and never went back."

Her voice acquired a note of sadness he experienced deep inside his chest.

"It doesn't matter how many years have passed. I'll always remember their names, and their faces twisted in critical assessment of my shortcomings. The haughty disdain London's debutantes accomplished with high marks. All because I didn't fit into their vision of *genteel lady*. I despise London and everything it represents, whether that's a finishing school, the opera, or the people who attend it. I'm perfectly happy here in Oxfordshire, where I daresay I never look in the mirror in my own bedchamber and dislike what I see by comparison, because there is no comparison. I will never be made to feel that way again."

Her final words were a statement of empowerment, and he couldn't be prouder of her resilience.

"So, now I know." He leaned a shoulder against the mantel, relieved she'd achieved the retelling without an abundance of tears. He crossed his arms over his chest and looked into her eyes just to be sure. He couldn't bear it if he caused her to cry.

"So, now you know."

"But aren't you still allowing those foolish, hateful girls to win if they keep you from visiting London?" He might be playing with fire, but he didn't want to consider never seeing Theodosia again, and the odds of him returning to Oxfordshire were slim at best.

"I don't know." She stood and approached him, her face clear of all earlier sadness. "I don't think about it. Until you arrived, London was the farthest thing from my mind. I'm worried over my grandfather's health. For nearly two decades he's taken care of me, and now it's my turn. He's declining. His mind is weakening. What if one day he doesn't realize who I am? Or where he is? I can't lose him that way. I know no one lives forever. And people leave before their time. I learned that lesson when I was five years old. But I can't lose Grandfather. Not like this."

Now her eyes welled and tears coursed down her cheeks. She didn't cry for the hurt she'd endured but for the fear of what lay ahead for Lord Talbot. He pulled her forward, tightly held her in his embrace, and allowed her to cry for all the wrongs that composed her life up to this point, all the injustices and worries that were out of one's control, and her all-too-real fears for the future. Collectively, she had a great many to list. Her parents' death. The tormenting episodes at finishing school. And now, her grandfather's health. He wrapped his arms around her tighter. She seemed so slight to have endured so much. His heart ached for the circumstances, and yet he was powerless to resolve any of the hurts that caused her misery.

He wanted to kiss her again. To comfort and console, to allow her to lose herself, if only for a moment, but he wasn't so selfish to do so. What Theodosia needed most was a friend, and he could be that man. This evening, they'd shared more than secrets. They'd formed a precious bond. One he would always treasure, no matter where life led.

Chapter Fourteen

Matthew didn't look back at Leighton House as George drove their carriage away. Having decided to leave at first light, he eschewed breakfast for a morning tray in his chambers. An unsettled feeling, one he couldn't categorize, gnawed at him from the inside out, and he thought it best to start toward London, unsure if his uneasiness was a condition of regret or premonition. They left the gravel drive with the velvet curtain drawn, shutting Oxfordshire out as quickly as one banishes an unpleasant memory, though within the interior Coggs was his usual vociferous self.

"Don't despair, milord." Coggs settled into the corner in preparation for the lengthy trip. "No one could have predicted the dismal outcome of this unexpected jaunt."

Matthew shifted on the padded bench, his expression indifferent, or so he believed. Did Coggs perceive some unnamed emotion? His valet was a shrewd man of many opinions, most obtained through a filter of household gossip. With loyalty, the servant had never shown Matthew a wrong turn and instead garnered facts to share in hope of providing assistance. But at other times, his retelling was drivelous tripe that Matthew preferred to label *brain clutter*. Thus, the conundrum, one never knew which Coggs would offer at any given moment.

"Is that what you believe?" He should cut his tongue out for instigating further conversation. "I'm satisfied with my visit."

"All's well then. Your leg no longer pains you?"

"Not at the moment, although a headache threatens," he muttered, and remembered the salve as he touched his coat where he'd pocketed the small container. *Clever minx.* Ginger salve. He would think of her whenever he used it. It certainly brought his aching knee relief before bed last night. As well as the memory of their interlude in the library. He had no ready reason for his behavior since first meeting Theodosia, up until the last lingering thought of her as he left the property. She was an unusual woman. A very pretty puzzle at that. But she was hardly his concern, and the unexpected protectiveness and desire to bring happiness to her lonely existence could only be chalked up to an innate male predilection to protect those in need.

For a few minutes there was nothing but the sound of the horses and carriage wheels as they rumbled over a stone or dipped into a rut, but as Matthew suspected, Coggs didn't stay quiet for long.

"Lady Leighton is quite an unconventional female."

"You think so?" He hoped Coggs would hear the censure in his voice.

"Genteel ladies enjoy embroidery, watercolors, and the art of flirtation."

"Not all of them."

"Perhaps, although I haven't met a one in London who prefers hybrid plants and injured animals to socialites and tea parties."

"Then perhaps you need to leave London more often."

Coggs appeared nonplussed. "I'm only considering the obvious."

God help me. "And that would be?" *That there is something about Theodosia so rare, more uncommon than her exquisite gray gaze and inquisitive mind. London would stifle her, crush her spirit and cause her to feel all those unique and wonderful qualities were somehow wrong. Just like those horribly vapid girls at finishing school.*

"Lady Chester is of an opposite nature entirely, and with your impending nuptials—"

"Nothing has been agreed upon, Coggs." He huffed an annoyed breath.

"You've narrowed your social calls to one lady. I only assumed."

"Assumption. A flaw of the idle-minded and addlepated." He speared his valet with a meaningful stare as he enunciated each word.

"It seemed the natural course of things and expected conclusion to your pursuit of the lady," Coggs persisted. "Besides, you'll be lonely in your later years."

"Never mind my old-aged self." A scoff escaped before Whittingham could stop it. "You need to keep your nose on your face and out of other people's business, most of all mine."

"It's not uncommon to be intrigued by the unusual," his valet continued. "I thought it curious how Lady Leighton captured your attention at great length."

Of course, Coggs would overstep. Hadn't he given his valet every reason to believe he could? Over the years their relationship was more friendship than one of employment. His valet had witnessed struggles of every kind, and their relationship long ago lost its formality. Matthew's damned impairment and unpredictable pain crippled in more than one manner, causing him to depend on others, sometimes for the simplest, most humbling tasks. At its worst, the pain was like a hook under his flesh, debilitating and relentless. He'd learned how to prevent such attacks through compromise in activity, but he'd also experienced episodes that left him temporarily immobile, and Coggs had seen him at such times.

He bit back a curse, angry at his own failings. It wasn't his valet's fault. By nature of their relationship, Matthew's injury provided a sense of security in the servant's position that enabled unsolicited advice and unequivocal opinion.

Still, he wouldn't lose his balance or his temper in this conversation.

"Lady Leighton is none of your concern, nor mine, for that matter. We've barely left the estate drive and I've no desire to spend the long journey poking holes in your poorly assembled theories." He leveled a glare at Coggs that conveyed the valet should seal his mouth permanently.

"I only meant to express that women have certain expectations. You can't—"

The carriage came to an abrupt halt and both men swayed with the unanticipated movement. Matthew rapped on the roof and with immediacy George climbed down from the box to stand at the door not a beat later.

"It won't be but a few moments' delay, milord. A tree has fallen and blocked part of the roadway, leaving a narrow portion just wide enough for one-way passage. There's an approaching gentleman on horseback and I'll allow him to move by, before I maneuver the carriage further."

"Excellent decision, George. Thank you."

True to his driver's report, the thunder of horse hooves could be heard in the distance, although they slowed to nothing more than a trot the closer they came. Curious about the situation, Matthew nabbed his walking stick and exited the carriage. It would be good to stretch his legs and even better to escape Coggs and his convoluted thinking.

Not twenty strides from where he stood, the trunk of a decayed hornbeam tree lay over the left portion of the roadway, and beyond that a single rider came into view. The gentleman slowed his horse considerably, though he didn't wait for the animal to stop, and slid from the saddle in a graceful leap that landed him solidly on his feet. Matthew bit back a curse at the stranger's agility, blaming his foul mood on his valet.

George appeared behind him while conversation ensued.

"Whittingham." Matthew extended his hand to the stranger in greeting and they shook heartily. It wasn't customary to initiate an introduction in the middle of a thoroughfare, but if the roadway needed to be cleared, it would take more than one man to remove the fallen tree.

"Good of you to stop." The gentleman seemed younger by comparison, although it was hard to tell beneath his winter attire. Unlike Matthew, he wore a beaver cap and cashmere scarf. The flaps of his black greatcoat caught the wind. "Kirkman here." He gave a sharp whistle and his stallion, a beast of an animal, snorted in answer before it settled. "Are you departing Leighton House?" Kirkman offered a friendly grin. "I'm on my way there now."

Matthew could only assume the devil was having a holiday. What other reason could there be for this coincidence? "Yes, we left this morning, though we haven't progressed very far."

"The weather has been unforgiving." Kirkman walked toward the fallen tree and Matthew was forced to follow. George scurried ahead to assume the responsibility of the work, although Matthew labeled this courtesy as deficiency instead of entitlement. He wanted to look toward the horizon, admire the snow-covered trees and icy glaze formed by the temporal serenity of daybreak, but he forced himself to watch, no matter he curled the fingers of his right hand into a fist at his inability to do more.

Kirkman lifted the tree trunk with George's assistance and the two men deposited it out of the road. This should have put all things to right, considering it would return him to London that much sooner, but it conjured several other emotions instead. A man shouldn't have to worry about uneven ground or losing his balance by simply lifting a log. Let Kirkman assume the driver completed the task out of respect, but how Matthew would have liked to take it on instead.

Kirkman gave a nod before he swung effortlessly into the saddle, and with a flick of the reins galloped past. The draft created by his passage sunk deep into Matthew's bones. He spit curses all the way back to the carriage, where Coggs hung out of the square window, his nose on the scent of details like a Newgate mastiff. Matthew squelched the desire to place his palm to his valet's face and push him back into the interior.

"What was that about? Who's the dasher?"

The questions began before Matthew had climbed into the interior.

"Kirkman."

"Kirkman?" A fair degree of surprise reverberated in Coggs's response.

"Now let that be the end of it."

Theodosia wouldn't allow herself to watch Matthew leave. She purposely avoided the front windows despite she awoke before sunrise. She took a tray in her room to ensure she didn't cross paths with him in the front hall or breakfast room. She remained in bed and stared up at the canopy, a lovely lace design filled with ladybirds and florals, all in hope she could distract from the inevitable.

She knew she wasn't a stunning beauty, nor was she unbecoming. She was ordinary, and that suited her. What did it matter anyway? She'd rather stay abed with her cat and not face the quietude of her existence. How foolish to feel lonely. She long ago accepted her lot in life and rarely bemoaned her existence.

When at last she dressed, she looked about for Nicolaus and his understanding companionship, but she didn't find him and so resumed her normal routine. Yet this particular morning her emotions were scattered and she struggled to rearrange them in their usual confined order.

Before the Earl of Whittingham invaded my privacy.

Before he kissed me senseless.

Before he made himself known and I confessed every secret of my heart.

She was embarrassed to think a few days' time could create such an impact or conjure so many emotions, but she was too intelligent to ignore what stared her straight in the face. She'd enjoyed his company and now he was gone, leaving an unsettling solitude that no longer felt comfortable.

In a habit that consumed a large part of her world, people left too often, their stories hardly told.

Determined to visit the conservatory and get lost in her plants and animals, she walked with hurried strides, unlocked the door, and shut herself into her personal sanctuary. She fed Isaac, silently stroked William down his long scaly back, and pruned an ornamental fritillary plant that didn't need to be pruned. In spite of her efforts, the tears came anyway.

Resigned to sadness, she walked to the farthest corner of the conservatory and looked out at the rear acreage. She could see the burnt remains of her childhood home and clenched her eyes painfully tight in hope she could hear her mother's voice or father's laughter, but nothing came.

Instead, the first sob caught her by surprise, but there were several after. Lost in utter despair, she consented to allow this one instance of weakness and get it out of her system before she returned to check on Grandfather. Through Dora she'd learned he slept soundly, and it was early yet. She needn't rush her mourning. Wallowing seemed appropriate.

Eventually her tears slowed and her pulse evened. She pressed her forehead against the window. Broken exhales of heated breath fogged the glass where she stood, stealing the outside world from her blurred vision.

She didn't realize what she saw at first. It took a moment of composure and clearheaded thinking, but when she recognized exactly what lay bare before her, her breath caught. On the glass where condensation gathered, Matthew's fingerprints were revealed. She recalled how he'd examined the structure, impressed with the floor-to-ceiling panes and the ability to keep plants viable throughout the winter. Through that inspection he'd braced himself, his nose almost pressed to the glass so he could peer out to the acreage, much as she did now.

She stared at his fingerprints a good long minute. Then she wiped them away, not wishing to prolong her misery further. There was no logic in misplaced emotion. She couldn't afford to allow her heart to be swayed.

She dried her eyes, locked the door, and made her way back to the main house. Moving quietly through the gallery, she'd almost accomplished the hall when she startled, shocked to find Grandfather there. His hair was disheveled and he still wore his nightshirt, though he'd layered a loose, belted banyan atop it. He was barefooted and perfectly still, as if he didn't recognize his surroundings and stood, helplessly, in wait of rescue.

Her heart twisted with the truth of the scene and she rushed toward him, anxious to return him upstairs to dress properly. "Grandfather, are you well?"

It was a pitiful question to ask when one already knew the answer.

"There you are, dear." He sighed loudly. "I thought you left with your gentleman. I saw his carriage take to the drive this morning."

She swallowed a lump of emotion. "I wouldn't leave without telling you. I would never leave." She placed her hand within his, warm and secure, as he had done for so many years of her life. How frail he seemed in this moment. "He's not my gentleman. Lord Whittingham came from London for a visit. Nothing more. He has read of your brilliant research."

"My research?" The very idea seemed to surprise him.

"You're a learned man. Science owes a great debt to your dedication."

"Is that true?"

Conversation coaxed him forward, their words in sync with their steps.

"Of course, it's true." She leaned closer to his arm and smiled. "All of London knows the fine work you've done and how accomplished you are."

"Yes, yes. I understand." Though his brow wrinkled with the struggle to do just that. "When will we begin?"

"Begin?" She continued toward the entry hall, anxious to return her grandfather abovestairs before a footman or other servant intersected their path. The household staff were aware of the situation, but it was quite another thing to be faced with the unbearable explanation on a daily basis.

"Our trip to London." Grandfather shook his head vigorously. "Your gentleman invited me."

"Yes." She forced the word off her tongue as her mind spun for a suitable reply. "We can't travel in this weather. We'll discuss a trip to London come springtime."

They arrived at the front stairs and Alberts stepped forward. An expression of understanding creased his forehead, but he didn't say a word. The knocker dropped and echoed in the silence.

"Go ahead, Alberts." Theodosia nodded. "Answer the door and I'll see to Grandfather." She began the stairs and breathed a sigh of relief when her grandfather followed without complaint. Yet they'd only made it halfway when her notice was pulled below.

"Lady Theodosia." Lord Kirkman stood in the foyer where Alberts accepted his coat and hat. Once he'd separated from the garments, Kirkman moved to the first step, his arm extended in a gesture of assistance.

"It's fine." She forced a smile to her lips in a strained effort. "Will you wait for me in the yellow drawing room? I won't be long." She turned away at the top landing so he wouldn't see her bite her lip. "Come along, Grandfather. I'm sure you'd like to change your clothes before we meet with Lord Kirkman."

"Yes, yes, I need to dress." Holding tightly to her hand, he allowed her to usher him down the corridor to his bedchambers. Mrs. Mavis was there, as were two footmen.

"Please summon Collins to assist."

Collins was the under-butler, and for reasons no one could decipher, Grandfather accepted his companionship without question while others, including Theodosia, failed to persuade or cajole him into cooperation.

Chapter Fifteen

Ten minutes later Theodosia returned downstairs. She'd had a fitful night's sleep and myriad misplaced emotions, and all at once was exhausted, no matter it was only midmorning. Still, Henry Hanes, Lord Kirkman, a baron by land tenure and a congenial neighbor, didn't deserve her anger. He was a childhood friend and comrade for nearly her entire life. More importantly, he knew of her struggles now that Grandfather's health failed. She took a deep breath and entered the drawing room with a forced smile.

"You look upset. Have you been crying?" Kirkman approached from where he'd waited near the window.

She sighed. A pitfall of knowing someone for years is found in not being able to mask expressions as easily. "It's been a trying few days."

"I wish I'd known, although I came as soon as the roads were passable." His voice dropped with concern. When he reached for her hand, she turned away.

"Of course. Thank you." She settled in a chair near the Hepplewhite occasional table, knowing he would be forced to sit on the other side, where the only chair in close proximity was located. "You shouldn't feel responsibility. We get on all right here."

"And thus, the tears." He murmured this, though she knew he considered her in his care, and much the same for her grandfather. "I don't know why you won't marry me, Theodosia." He blew out a breath of frustration that she experienced twice as deeply.

"Because we don't love each other." She might have laughed. She was exhausted and overwrought. The last thing she needed was to debate another of his marriage proposals. It seemed all the expected conversation abandoned them, his frustration palpable.

Kirkman stood and paced a few strides before he turned back. "Marriage becomes friendship eventually, and we've already two decades of that. I know you better than anyone else. You deserve more than this life, locked away in your home with little more than an interest in the sciences to keep you company. I can offer you more."

"But we both deserve more than a loveless marriage, Henry." She gentled the words, though she believed in them strongly. Let that be the end of the conversation.

"Do you find me so unappealing then?"

This time she laughed, though the sound was composed of wry cynicism. "Now, you're being ridiculous." Kirkman was a tall, strong, engaging man who would have no trouble finding a wife if he pursued the subject in earnest. Whatever kept him from doing just that she didn't know, despite she'd questioned him in past conversation.

"Your grandfather isn't going to live forever."

His soft-spoken words intruded on her mental contemplations and she sobered, the truth in that statement all too real.

"What will you do?" he asked. "Live in this enormous house alone, with a few stray animals and an aging staff?"

"You needn't be cruel." How was it her existence was questioned twice in less than twenty-four hours?

"And you needn't be stubborn." He paced before the hearth.

Their conversation was reduced to the syncopated tick of the mantel clock.

"See, we squabble just like husband and wife." He darted a glance in her direction.

"More like brother and sister." She dismissed her own words with a shake of the head. "You deserve so much more than compromise, and marrying me for whatever reason you've decided would be just that. You have a long, wonderful life ahead of you. Wouldn't you rather spend your days with a woman who's captured your heart?"

"I've never known you to be a romantic."

"I suspect there's much more you don't know about me, but that's not the point. One doesn't have to be considered sentimental to yearn for equal love and respect." Would she never get him to understand?

"I didn't come here to argue." He sat down again. "I'm trying to help you see the reality of the situation."

"Perhaps you shouldn't have left so little time to find a wife. That was poorly done of you." Without intent, her words acquired a sharp tone.

"I assumed I would eventually change your mind." His brows rose as he spoke, apparently surprised at the realization that he'd failed to achieve that goal.

"That was equally foolish."

"I didn't anticipate your grandfather's decline. Or the snow, for that matter." He looked toward the window as he listed his excuses.

"So, my heart was to be won in a few months. I've known you almost my entire life. You're like a brother to me. I do care about you, just not in the way that I should were we to be wed."

The room fell to silence again.

"You persist, when it all becomes friendship in the end anyway." He leaned forward, his eyes imploring her.

"As you're fond of reminding me."

"Because it's true. Besides, I worry you will seclude yourself in Oxfordshire forever and ultimately be completely alone after your grandfather . . ." His voice trailed off.

She knew the unspoken words. "Don't act as if you're proposing for my sake, and don't you dare pity me." She struggled to keep her temper even, exhaustion and frustration causing her to have short patience.

"I worry for you. There's a difference." He exhaled thoroughly, his focus still intense.

"And what would you gain? A wife who doesn't love or desire you." She couldn't be more blunt.

"You wound me." He stood and walked to face the fire. "We would get on."

"You need a dose of honesty, Henry." She rose and moved beside him. "You deserve more."

"You'll use my own words to deflect me." He almost chuckled. "I'll not add to your list of worries, Theodosia." He paced away before he changed the subject in an attempt to clear the air. "How can I help with your grandfather's condition? I wrote to Dr. Fletcher in London on your behalf. Do you remember our conversation from last we were together? This is the physician who studies the elderly and their tendency for forgetfulness. At the least he should answer my inquiry as a courtesy. I'm still waiting for a reply, but I'm optimistic."

"That makes one of us then." Speaking of Grandfather's decline was hardly one of her favorite topics, but she'd gladly dismiss their earlier talk of marriage. "You'll come to me with any message you receive, won't you?"

"Of course." He moved to stand directly in front of her. "And then I'll escort you and Lord Talbot to London, where

I will deliver you to Dr. Fletcher's office. He's the most respected physician in England with a special interest in the aged. I'm confident he will be able to enlighten us about your grandfather's advanced lapse of clear thinking."

"Thank you." She looked into the face of a friend. A man she'd played with as a child and respected as an adult. Life shared with him wouldn't be awful. They'd always gotten on together without upset. Was she making a mistake by not accepting his proposal? For a brief instant she considered the situation in a new light, until a voice in the back of her head reminded her she felt nothing more for him than a fond kinship. Nothing at all like the heated press of—"I'd much prefer if Dr. Fletcher would visit us here in Oxfordshire. I'd compensate him handsomely for his expenses."

Henry laughed a hearty chuckle. "You *are* more stubborn than I realized."

He reached for her hand and placed it between his own. She stared at their hands, aware she experienced no feeling beyond contact and a sense of friendship.

"Dr. Fletcher is a busy man. Not only does he see patients, but he pursues his studies and spends a great deal of time educating others. He's a member of several organizations and serves on the board of the Society for the Intellectually Advanced. I doubt a full day's travel to the countryside would fit into his schedule. We'll have to go to him. That is, if the doctor has the time to answer my query and allow an appointment. His services must be in high demand."

"I would think so." She liked to believe Grandfather's condition, whatever it was, wasn't uncommon and, perhaps, would be curable or reversible once they understood the dimensions of his sporadic lapses. And too, mention of the Society caught Theodosia's attention. It was the same group the Earl of Whittingham had discussed. Didn't he say he was newly appointed as chief officer? In the haze of the last two days and the tumult of conflicted emotion, she couldn't be sure.

"I suppose we'll have to take it one step at a time then." She slipped her hand free from Henry's grasp and invited him to stay for luncheon. "Grandfather will be happy to see you."

"Thank you. It will be a splendid afternoon."

He smiled and she returned his grin, though she couldn't help but notice his attention failed to stir her in the same manner as the Earl of Whittingham's.

Whittingham strode into White's in need of distraction. He wasn't one to frequent the gentleman's club often, preferring purposeful academic pursuits, but this evening an insatiable restlessness drove him from his exclusive address at the Albany, straight to St. James's Square. His bachelor apartment was situated in Piccadilly, amidst the wealthy and well-connected, most fashionable gentlemen, but tonight he sought diversion no polite conversation could satisfy. He refused to consider the contrary emotions that took residence in his heart since leaving Leighton House.

"Whittingham."

A familiar voice cut through the ambient male cacophony and he scanned the crowd until he spotted Jonathan Cromford, Earl of Lindsey, across the main floor.

"Lindsey." He nodded his head in greeting and followed after his friend, who led them deeper into the club, through the hall, up the center stairs, and ultimately into the card room. A few tables were occupied by men too engrossed with their play to give them more than a passing glance at their entrance.

"This is an unexpected, yet pleasant surprise." Lindsey signaled a waiting footman and indicated their desire for brandy. "Have you mistaken the club for a lending library, or are you fulfilling the terms of a poorly made wager?"

"Has it really been that long?" Whittingham knew well it had been months since he'd shown his face at the club. He avoided many of society's functions, not one for the ballrooms, as he was in no search of a wife. Not that he considered himself husband material. Nor much of a dancer. He glanced down at his left leg, the muscles at ease, without grievance due to the ginger salve he'd applied earlier.

"Whatever the reason, it's good to see you." Lindsey accepted his brandy and took a long swallow.

Whittingham set his glass aside, more interested in conversation than libation. "How are you? Have you found a resolution to the difficult problem you mentioned last time we spoke?" He had no idea what Lindsey's specific situation was, as Lindsey refused to reveal anything more than a scant complaint of life's cruel fate, but having known the man for several years, Whittingham wished to see his friend content.

"Unfortunately, life continues to kick me in the stones." Lindsey took another swallow of brandy.

"It's hard to believe anything could be wrong. You appear as polished as ever." It was true. Lindsey was the veritable ideal of every marrying mama's wish for their daughter. Handsome, titled, part rogue, part gentleman, the earl was a dashing composition of all the most desirable traits all the while maintaining a reputation of aristocratic aplomb. If he spent too much time at the club, it could only be in avoidance of the trail of swooning females left in his wake everywhere else.

"Appearances are deceiving." Lindsey crooked a half smile and skimmed his fingertip across the rim of his glass.

"Perhaps." *Most definitely.* Matthew's mind conjured a vivid image of Theodosia, her cheeks pinkened from their sleigh ride, her flower-petal lips curled in a smile of delight. Yet her intuitive thoughts and acute intelligence were the most attractive of all her charming qualities. His mind skittered forward by degree. "By the by, are you familiar with Lord Kirkman?"

Lindsey's attention sharpened, his eyes intense as he replaced his glass on a side table. "I am."

A moment passed in silence, much to Whittingham's annoyance. "Care to elaborate?"

"Not at the moment. Why do you ask?"

Lindsey's refusal to share information concerning Kirkman was irritating, if not downright rude. "How do you know him? He resides in Oxfordshire, and I met the man there as I took my leave."

"So, you're acquainted then?"

"Not in the least." Whittingham huffed a breath of impatience.

"Kirkman owns a country estate and tenure of land in Oxfordshire, left to him with the barony, although he frequents London often."

"Interesting, that." Whittingham picked up his brandy at last.

"I can't imagine why this interests you, although Kirkman and I have our own problems to settle."

This snagged Whittingham's interest further. "In what way?"

"I've already spoken out of turn."

Whittingham mulled this over for half a second. "Your reputation as a veritable expert on everything London wishes to keep hidden prompts me to press for information, though I could ask Coggs. He should work for the Crown the way he manages to discover the most interesting tidbits of well-hidden fact."

"I'm sure you could, although his effort wouldn't reveal

a word. Of that I'm certain." Lindsey's expression grew pensive. "Kirkman and I are involved in an affair better left quiet. It's complicated and personal."

"Are you in trouble?" He leaned in, his voice lowered for privacy's sake. "Can I assist?"

"No, on both counts." Lindsey's smile appeared strained. "And there's no reason for concern. Things always work out in the end, don't they? Either that, or one dies in the process."

"That's a rather grim outlook from a man who usually carries the world in his pocket." Lindsey was a man who appeared at ease with even the most difficult situation, but as Whittingham watched him adjust his cravat and finish the remaining brandy in his glass, he took his friend's comments most seriously. "Never mind then. I wouldn't want to compound whatever circumstances have added difficulty in your life."

"I appreciate that, Whittingham." Lindsey exhaled deeply before he stood. "Good to see you. I best make my way home."

And without another word the Earl of Lindsey strode from the room, leaving Whittingham with more disagreeable contemplations than before he'd entered the club.

Chapter Sixteen

"I still don't know how you convinced me to do this." Theodosia hissed the words for Kirkman's ears only, though they sounded loud in the otherwise silent hallway of London's most exclusive hotel.

Mivart's was situated at the corner of Brook and Davies Streets in the heart of Mayfair, and aside from its reputation for extravagant furnishings and the most comfortable stay, it boasted a celebrated French chef with a dedicated staff renowned for their culinary talents. Composed of several conventional terraced houses, the hotel boasted four floors and more guest rooms than Theodosia cared to consider.

"You need to stay somewhere while we visit Dr. Fletcher." Kirkman dared a grin despite he purposely evaded an answer.

"That's not what I meant and you know it." She looked over her shoulder, reassured to see that her grandfather followed closely. Her maid and Collins, the house under-butler, approached with him and additional footmen were in tow with their luggage.

"Exactly." Kirkman added a low chuckle. "Besides, with luck on our side Dr. Fletcher will be available to see your grandfather tomorrow, make recommendations, and you'll be rid of the city by the end of the week. I know you have an undisclosed aversion to London, but perhaps I can tempt you to a social function or two while we're here."

"Are you mad?" She tried for an angry whisper and failed terribly when her words came out too strong. "I didn't come here to dance a quadrille or sip ratafia. The only reason I agreed to visit this infernal city is to help my grandfather. And never you mind why I dislike the city. Let it suffice that I'm here to help my grandfather, not enjoy the sights." She didn't add how much effort it took on her part to return; London was full of bleak and miserable memories she'd rather keep buried.

"Reluctant as you may be, we're here now, and you're correct. Our only focus is Lord Talbot and the hope Dr. Fletcher will have a recommendation."

"I'm sorry, Henry." She shook her head, disappointed in her ungrateful behavior. They'd ridden all day in Kirkman's carriage, his patience likely as short as her own, and yet he remained helpful now when he might have left them at the hotel's stairs and gone about his business. "I'm worried and my emotions are unpredictable at the moment."

"I understand."

She knew that he did. "You needn't inconvenience yourself any longer. We'll be fine here at the hotel. I'm sure you have acquaintances to see or other appointments that need your attention."

They reached the end of a long corridor on the second floor and a servant showed Theodosia and her maid into a large chamber with three doors, each leading to another room, all of which were decadently furnished. One room was for dressing, another for sitting and taking tea, and the last for bathing. Grandfather's rooms were beside her own, as requested, and Collins would also stay there in the role of valet to ensure nothing untoward occurred.

She sidestepped two maids as they rushed by, and returned to where Henry waited in the hall.

"Thank you again." She drew a deep breath. "I don't know how this will end, but I appreciate your help."

"Let's keep a hopeful outlook." He stepped back, ready to take his leave. "I'll return tomorrow morning. We should be at Dr. Fletcher's office by nine o'clock. Sleep well and try not to worry."

She nodded and watched him depart, all the while wondering if she would be able to take his well-meant advice.

Later, after they'd settled in their rooms and Theodosia calmed her spirit somewhat, for she despised the thought of visiting London and yet found herself in the middle of the bustling city, she accompanied her grandfather down two flights of polished mahogany stairs to the dining room on the main floor. Theodosia cared not a whit for Mivart's extravagant menu or fanciful chef, though every maid and footman managed to insert the information into conversation. Unfortunately, Grandfather's curiosity had been ignited by temptation to the delicacies offered in the dining room, and she feared if she said no it would start a chain reaction of disagreeable behavior, most especially when he seemed completely himself, sharply focused and congenial.

They approached the dining room, discernible not just for the hum of diffusive conversation and clink of silverware, but the enticing aroma of succulent dishes. A satisfying hot meal would be inviting and could possibly contribute further to Grandfather's calm demeanor.

Much to her dismay, she soon discovered the restaurant was unreasonably crowded and the tables closely situated, most likely in an effort to accommodate a maximum number of hungry diners.

Truly, what had she expected? According to the pert maid who'd flittered in and out of her room to check the fire and replace the linens, Mivart's chef drew the best of London's society. This, like so many other reasons, proved she'd never be comfortable in London among the ostentatious, popular set. Her eyes scanned the room to take in a multitude of refined ladies dressed in the latest fashions, their expressions as perfectly in place as their wardrobes, their air of pretentious superiority matched equally by their affectation of excellence. All of a sudden, she wanted nothing more than a bowl of Cook's mutton stew enjoyed near the kitchen hearth at Leighton House.

"Right this way."

The host's greeting startled her into movement and she held tightly to Grandfather's elbow as they entered the room and were led to a corner table. At least the location offered a modicum of privacy, angled partially out of view of the other guests. Theodosia sent a silent prayer heavenward that the evening would progress with relative ease.

A server brought wine and soon after they ordered from the menu. Theodosia chose roast partridge and brown onion soup. Her grandfather carefully perused the list of selections before deciding on the savory braised pork with asparagus tips. The server briskly walked away with their orders and Theodosia dared another view of the room. The crush of guests in low light and high spirits all seemed a world beyond her, and she'd rather keep it that way. Kirkman mentioned an important appointment he needed to attend and therefore was not available for dinner. It was better to keep their appearance here brief. She had no desire other than to see to her concerns and return abovestairs.

"I'm pleased we met with good weather for our travels," Theodosia began. "A hot meal will ensure a good night's sleep after such a long day."

"Indeed." Grandfather took a hearty sip of wine. "I can't remember the last time I visited London. It was good of Lord Whittingham to extend the invitation to lecture at his Society."

Theodosia froze, her hand on the stem of the crystal wine goblet. "But we have other plans during *this* visit." She watched closely, measuring his facial expressions for any sign her deepest fear would materialize. She managed as well as possible at home, but she had no idea what she would do were Grandfather to become indignant and agitated while they were in a public place. A long-buried fear of utter humiliation wormed its way out from the grave.

How foolish to believe they could mingle with society so easily. What was she thinking? Her heart began a race, each compression squeezing her lungs tighter, urging her pulse faster. She needed to calm or dinner would spin entirely out of control.

"What plans?" Her grandfather pulled his shoulders straighter and she recognized his rigid posture with a heavy beat of dread.

A server arrived with their food and interrupted conversation long enough for her to manage a restorative breath. She would tell Grandfather anything he needed to hear as long as they escaped the room without incident.

"Let's enjoy our food before it gets cold." She forced a smile in his direction. "We didn't travel all day to be rewarded with less than the best. Your meal looks delicious."

Luckily her encouragement worked and for the moment, conversation was forgotten.

* * *

Matthew escorted Lady Amy Chester into the welcoming foyer of Mivart's Hotel, her maid left to wait in his carriage. He would have rather dined at home or at Lady Chester's familial estate as a guest, but that was not to be. His family was acquainted with the Chesters in an amiable friendship for many years, and this comfortable camaraderie made him the automatic escort choice whenever Lady Amy wished to venture out. Somehow the arrangement had become more frequent of late. Matthew didn't mind as long as he wasn't forced into difficult situations where he needed to choose between escorting Lady Amy and attending to his academic responsibilities.

This evening, Amy's brother unexpectedly canceled dinner plans. He'd in turn messaged Matthew to ask for a favor, and that's how tonight's event turned about, though it might have occurred on another evening by Matthew's own instigation. He had begun to consider his future, and at present narrowed his social calls to one lady in particular. The already established routine of escorting Lady Amy proved convenient and automatic. He'd come to know what to expect and the particulars of the endeavor. While he wouldn't label their relationship boring, it bordered on predictability. In science, predictability was a necessary constant for success.

Belatedly he realized the contrast of this reality with the surprise and delight he'd experienced at Leighton House weeks prior. This acknowledgment brought with it a mis-placed pang of regret.

Still, somewhere along the meandering history of the Whittinghams and Chesters, the two families had concluded in their collective mind that Amy and Matthew made a handsome pair and of late, it followed that he entertained the thought himself. Despite they shared little in common and the lady was fascinated with societal happenings, while

Matthew often spent hours sequestered within the pages of a book, he knew he needed to make some effort in the area of courtship. With that, an easier path to follow didn't exist.

He would *eventually* marry and produce the obligatory heir. Though he had no reason to rush the issue. He'd learned a lesson *or several* from last year's debacle when he sought to hurry his sister into marriage. Amelia managed her own destiny better than he, and in that moment of clarity he vowed to allow the natural course of things in his own life and not force what wasn't meant to be.

In that vein of thinking, almost as if to test a theory, he'd embarked on a courtship with Lady Amy, though he hadn't committed his heart, or any other part of his anatomy for that matter.

If his parents or valet eagerly drew conclusions that a decision had been made, they were all bound to be disappointed. Matthew simply hadn't gotten around to dissuading their assumption, much like he left correspondence overlong or neglected to get his hair trimmed. And it was possible he would never have need to elucidate them. Of late he didn't possess strong feelings in either direction. A strange ambivalence possessed his soul and he'd yet to displace it.

If nothing else, one benefit of Amy's friendship was found in the removal of the awkward risk of rejection, or worse, embarrassment. Amy knew the man that he was and didn't find him lacking. At least if she did, she hadn't voiced that opinion, and the lady was fairly uninhibited about allowing her thoughts to be known. In return they shared a comfortability, where conversation was easy and expectations reasonable.

As for tonight, he enjoyed a rich meal as much as the next gentleman, and making an appearance now and again within the social set was never a poor choice. When he tallied these supporting facts and considered the outcome, it was a quick decision to escort the lady to Mivart's once her brother's message was received.

"I'm anxious to sample the chef's elaborate offerings. Yesterday afternoon at tea, Lady Dorning mentioned she never experienced a finer meal." Amy sent an appreciative smile in his direction. "Thank you for agreeing to this evening."

"It's my pleasure." He offered her a slight nod. She'd already expressed her gratitude before they'd left her parents' home, and as the conversation lapsed into the repetitive, he assessed the room in his normal practice of noting every detail.

Much as he'd expected, the interior was a feast for the senses. Several ornate crystal chandeliers lent a golden glow to the walls decorated in aubergine-and-cream water silk, though festive evergreen garland had been added about the rectangular windows in anticipation of the holiday season. The decorative linens were white patterned on white, but one could hardly see the tabletops for the multitude of sumptuous platters and overfilled dishes. He quickly recognized the pungent aroma of *bouillie* soup with salt pork and cabbage, and his eyes landed on a plate at a nearby table of filleted sole in a sea of butter and lemon slices as fragrant as those in Theodosia's conservatory. He quirked a bemused smile at the remembrance.

It was overly warm in the hotel lobby and he muttered a subtle complaint under his breath. The allure of an intriguing article concerning Dalton's law of multiple proportions awaited on his bedside table, the perfect end to a pleasant evening. He hoped the kitchen was as well staffed as the plentiful servers who bustled about.

Upon returning to London, he'd paid a call to Lady Amy as was his custom twice a week. The twenty-minute visit allowed by the rules of courtship were most often spent in the drawing room under the watchful eye of her maid, or at times, her mother, Lady Chester. Conversation was dually dissected into Amy speaking and he listening, and he often escaped into his own thoughts if she expounded on societal gossip. During those incidences, he wondered if Coggs would make a better suitor for the young lady. Matthew didn't care for the latest *on dit* or popular salacious scandal. History and the lure of the past had always intrigued him more than the speculative predictions of the future.

And naturally, he deemed the freedom of intelligent debate as most precious. Without cause, Theodosia materialized in his mind's eye and he found another small smile. The carefree visit they'd shared at Leighton House was uncommon and beyond the rules of etiquette, but how he'd enjoyed it all the same. That was a good memory made.

"This way, please." A server led them to a table near the corner of the room and he could readily see Amy's disappointment. She'd have preferred the center of the room where she had the ability to observe as much as possible, but given the crowded interior and lack of available tables, she settled without complaint.

London's ladies were forever interested in what other ladies were wearing, how their hair was arranged, or with whom they spent their leisure time. It was true that society offered the fairer sex limited opportunities beyond such subjects, but not every woman suffered restrictive thinking.

Theodosia.

With purpose, he pulled his attention back across the table. Amy hadn't noticed his silence, her gaze strained to take in every nuance of her surroundings.

The crux of the matter lay in the fact he hadn't noticed how specifically enthralled Amy seemed in their being seen at the restaurant, or any social affair actually, because he wasn't intrigued to do so, his normal perspicacious nature and undeniable curiosity absent in each instance. How odd, that.

"There's Lady Hennings." Amy sent a knowing glance to the opposite side of the room. "She dines here regularly, according to Lady Dernsby."

Matthew adjusted his walking stick aside the chair and scanned the lengthy menu. Several offerings sounded tempting. There was neat's tongue, chicken in creamy white fricassee, and braised beef with ginger sauce. *Ginger.* He rubbed his left thigh beneath the table, the muscles much more agreeable. Theodosia's ginger salve had proven a salvation. He shook his head at the poorly made pun and focused again on the entrée selections. The roast pork with brown onion soup sounded too tempting to deny. Decision made, he replaced his menu on the table.

The server returned to fill their wineglasses and deliver a covered basket of warm bread. The man noted their dinner choices and left with a curt nod. Across the table, Amy swiveled her head from side to side in an act of information recognizance. She would have plenty of observations to share at tea tomorrow afternoon.

"You'll make yourself dizzy if you keep looking about like that." He picked up the bread basket and offered it forward.

"Half the enjoyment of being here is seeing who also attends this evening." She reached for a slice and placed it on her plate.

"If the other half of your pleasure lies in the extensive menu and renowned culinary talents of the chef, I'm dutifully insulted." He borrowed an expression of mock outrage from Coggs.

"Perhaps tonight cannot be divided in halves." She

skirted the issue, a teasing gleam in her eye as she resumed her vigilant surveillance.

Knowing better than to attempt conversation at the moment, he too turned his attention to surveying the crowded restaurant. If a fire or other incident required the occupants to leave hurriedly, there were no extra exits aside from the same doors they'd entered. He located the four corners, assured of the same. It seemed there were tables wedged into every available space. A distinctive note of laughter, light-hearted and melodic, carried over the din and he stalled, canting his head to the side in question. With curiosity piqued, he eyed each table more pointedly, quite surprised when he noticed Lord Talbot and Lady Leighton in the dusky corner to the far right. Uncanny. Could that be? He almost stood to ascertain what he saw clearly, before he belatedly stopped himself.

Still, the niggling question of why they were here so soon after Theodosia vehemently refused his invitation to come to London kept his mind busy. The server returned with the first course but he ignored it, unable to let the matter go.

"Your soup is growing cold," Amy chastised him. "What's caught your attention? Who do you see? Is it someone I know?" She craned her neck in an attempt to look over his shoulder.

"Not at all. Far be it for me to ruin this culinary experience with my procrastination." He took up his spoon and began to eat, though his attention remained divided, and no matter he told himself to mind his own business, an admonishment he frequently mentioned to Coggs, Matthew found his eyes drawn to the right corner of the restaurant more often than proper.

By the second spoonful, he'd decided he should approach their table at the end of the meal. Perhaps Lord

Talbot had decided to visit the Society for the Intellectually
Advanced after all. He stole another look while Amy adjusted
her napkin on her lap, and was gifted with Theodosia's profile when she turned.

She wore a lovely tea gown of cerulean blue and he
wondered if her eyes took on a darker shade because of it.
She did have magnificent gray eyes. And her smile. He
doubted there was another who—

"You seem unusually quiet this evening. Is something
wrong? I hope my brother didn't harangue you into this
escort."

Amy's inquiry brought his attention to their table.

"Not at all." He made it a point to pursue conversation.
"My meal is delicious. How is yours?"

"Equally good." She placed her silver on the tablecloth.
"I should save room for dessert. Lady Jerlin said there's
imported sipping chocolate available and a blancmange so
light you hardly know you're eating it."

"It seems a peculiar quality to desire a food you cannot
taste." He forced himself to stay focused on Amy. It could
only be curiosity and the question of Theodosia's sudden
appearance in London that had him at odds. But he didn't
have time to consider the matter further because an exhale
later, the worst happened.

Chapter Seventeen

"I don't want to see a physician." Talbot tapped the table linens with his pointer finger to emphasize this declaration. "I've come to London to visit Lord Whittingham at his Society. He invited me."

"But Grandfather, we discussed this before we left Oxfordshire." Theodosia looked toward the closest tables, her pulse launching into a panicked beat, her mind at the ready to react if necessary.

"There's nothing wrong with me or my memory."

"I didn't say that, although it will be good to hear the physician's knowledgeable opinion." Compassion squeezed her throat as she uttered the words. "Why don't we see the physician first and then when we're finished, we can inquire if Lord Whittingham is accepting visitors? That way, we'll both be pleased with our travel here."

This seemed to mollify her grandfather, and perhaps the sudden stillness of their corner table deceived her into believing his displeasure had passed. No other reason could explain the heart-lurching startle when her grandfather slammed his fist hard enough to rattle the china on the damask tablecloth.

"Where is the marmalade? I specifically ordered marmalade with dinner."

He hadn't, and Theodosia knew it, yet she needed to calm her grandfather before everyone in the dining room witnessed her humiliation. "Excuse me." A passing server snapped to attention. "Could you please send a message upstairs to room twenty-seven that Collins is needed at once?"

She'd hardly finished her sentence, the server on the move, when Grandfather stood, his face reddened with anger.

"You didn't ask him for marmalade. I want marmalade."

The room quieted and then, as if mistaking the outburst for nothing more than an anomaly, conversation swelled to refill its absence.

Theodosia rose from her seat, prepared to coax her grandfather from the room no matter they had hardly finished their plates. "We should go upstairs now if you're finished."

"I'm not finished. I can't eat until I have marmalade with my meal."

A tall gentleman, the same host who had welcomed them as they'd entered the restaurant, appeared beside their table, seemingly concerned about the unfolding disturbance.

"How may I assist?" He spoke politely, though his expression portrayed alarm.

"My grandfather would like some marmalade to accompany his dinner." How foolish she sounded, but her heart thundered in her chest from a sickening mixture of dread and embarrassment. Hopefully, Collins would come downstairs immediately and mollify her grandfather. Until then, she had little idea what else to do.

"I'm sorry?"

Would he make her repeat the ridiculous request? She hemmed her bottom lip to bite back a scream of frustration. Why had she believed, hoped, envisioned, they might take a meal at the restaurant without cause for upset? If ever she doubted her grandfather's failing mind, this episode would forever remind her it was heartbreakingly true. "Marmalade. Is there marmalade available to accompany the meal?"

Seeking to remedy the situation, the server continued in a low, congenial voice. "We don't serve marmalade. Would you care to see a menu for a different selection?"

Grandfather was not to be waylaid, his reply increasingly insistent. "I don't want something else."

This time the room quieted and every eye turned in their direction. One could hear voices in the kitchen, the dining floor had fallen so silent.

"Excellent suggestion and a capital condiment. Indeed, I would like marmalade as well."

A different voice rang across the room. A deep tenor that rippled through her. When she turned she saw the Earl of Whittingham standing at his table's edge no more than ten strides away.

"What are you doing?" The woman who accompanied him shielded her face as she hissed the words in a sharp, plummy voice, though her question was plainly discernible in the otherwise silent restaurant.

"I would like a bowl of marmalade with my dinner." Matthew stared at Theodosia so intently, her heart turned over twice. "One would think an establishment of high reputation would cater to the most vogue preferences of the culinary elite."

"We have blackberry preserves and mint jelly." Torn between the two tables and their unusual request, the server attempted reparation, though clearly he remained confused. "I will speak to the chef immediately."

By now the crowd had begun to whisper behind their napkins and speculate with intrusive conversation. Dora appeared with Collins in tow, and despite the server had hurried away in search of fulfilling their peculiar demand,

Grandfather was led from the table with little argument and the promise his food would be delivered abovestairs.

Theodosia paused. She looked across the room to where Matthew had recovered his seat and pursued what appeared to be a heated discussion. She might have stood there all evening in fascination of what he'd done and how he'd attempted to draw attention to himself and away from her misery, but she was too smart to glorify what was likely done out of pity.

Matthew knew before he stepped into his carriage there would be hell to pay. Contained and limited by the surrounding crowd, Amy had held back at the dinner table, their scant discussion strained. She'd eschewed dessert and regarded passing friends with a brittle smile until at last they took their leave.

Now the tension within the interior was thicker than the sauce on the unfinished plate of food he'd ordered for dinner.

"Why would you do such a thing?" Her tone expressed everything her words did not. "You humiliated me before a room full of guests."

"Lord Talbot was troubled and I sought to help." He refused to engage in an argument. He would never forget the look of stark fear on Theodosia's face as she'd met his eyes across the dining room floor. "Some might consider my effort compassionate."

"Compassionate?" Amy tutted her tongue in dismissal. "You sought to help a strange old man who created a ludicrous and unnecessary scene in a public restaurant, which interrupted the dining of dozens of people. But instead of ignoring the mad fool, you drew attention to our table."

"My intent was noble, Amy." He folded his arms across his chest, whether to separate himself from her or relieve the tightened muscles there, he didn't know. "The earl appeared overset."

"So, you know him?"

"I do. He's a respected scientist who struggles now in his later years," he replied with growing irritation, the words too callous for the empathy he felt.

"In what way? Do you mean financial hardship?" Amy's intolerance sharpened with each additional question.

"No." He hesitated, aware some of Amy's friends were spectacular tongue-wags. The last thing he wished was to incite gossip. "Sometimes as an individual ages, clarity of thought becomes more difficult." He brought his explanation down to the scantest terms, unsure how Amy would react.

"So, he's gone mad?"

He was taken aback by Amy's insensitive reaction. "No. I didn't say that." His patience frayed to a thread. How was Theodosia managing now? He'd turned away from the scene to assess Amy's reaction and then sought out Talbot's corner table, but they were already gone, the restaurant returned to its normal business.

"You didn't have to." Amy huffed her displeasure. "Still you chose to help that stranger and in turn embarrass me. You showed very little regard for my presence."

"That was never my intention." He waited, impatient with her lack of understanding.

"But you behaved ridiculously. Why would you risk my reputation? My name will be on the tip of everyone's tongue come morning and not for the right reasons. I so wish you hadn't felt the urge to defend that man. My brother should have escorted me. I'll be ridiculed for keeping company with you."

"You're overreacting." He knew the upper ten thousand were cutthroat with their assumptions, but that matter didn't cause him as much concern as Amy's callous disregard of Lord Talbot's situation. She worried more about gossip and perception than the earl's despairing crisis.

"I'm still shocked you stood up in front of everyone and made a spectacle of yourself. You behaved as if *you'd* gone mad."

"No one is mad." Controlling his anger was difficult. He was outraged by now. He wrapped his fingers around the top of his walking stick and formed a fist to defuse his temper. "Lord Talbot was confused and Lady Leighton helpless to change the situation. I merely attempted a diversion. No one will think poorly of you, Amy. If the scene is portrayed in the right light, some might consider my actions honorable."

"You wished to assist the lady?" She choked the question out with that same incredulous tone.

"I did." He checked the window, relieved to see they were nearly returned to the Chesters' home and their conversation would end.

"At my expense?"

"I didn't give thought to any particular repercussions. I had no motive and acted as I saw appropriate, but as we're being honest, what expense would that be? You wished to visit Mivart's restaurant, where you ate a fine meal. You saw your friends and they saw you. You'll have plenty to discuss tomorrow afternoon at tea, or not. Your acquaintances perpetuate the gossip mill. Ask them kindly to refrain if you believe my actions cast you in a poor light." He clenched his teeth. She dare not spread an unkind word in relation to Talbot and Theodosia.

"I'm taken aback by your reaction to all this." She

shifted on the carriage bench. "Usually, you're the epitome of kindness."

"Exactly." He didn't waste words explaining how ironic her complaint.

"I'll need time to think about this. I pray this mortifying scene isn't the topic of the papers come morning. Either way, there's no need to call upon me tomorrow, nor the next day after. I'll send word when I've reconsidered our sharing company."

"I understand." He exhaled, a surprising sense of liberation flooding his veins. Mentally his time was already claimed. He needed to see Theodosia, inquire about Lord Talbot and discover why they'd shown unexpectedly in London.

Amy gave a bitter laugh. "I'm sure you do."

The carriage jerked to a stop and George was quick to extend the steps. Matthew escorted her to the door in silence, though there was nothing left to say anyway. Then he hurried back to the carriage.

"Mivart's, George. And waste not a moment."

He'd barely closed the door when his driver snapped the reins and the horses leapt forward.

Theodosia dried her tears and washed her face a second time in the bowl of water left next to the ewer on the dressing table. Grandfather was asleep in the room next door under Collins's vigilant watch. The hour was close to midnight and Dora had retired as well. Only Theodosia's mind hummed with too many unanswered questions to find rest.

She worried for her grandfather's health. She wondered about her future. And most of all, she attempted to decipher why Matthew would risk public embarrassment in the middle of a room filled with London betters. How pitiful she must have appeared. He could only feel sorry for her. No other answer made sense. At the time, she'd tried not to make eye contact with any of the ladies in the restaurant who sat, aghast, at the developing scene, but she'd noticed Matthew's companion's appalled expression. Her reaction reminded Theodosia of emotions she'd thought long ago mastered.

In the morning, Kirkman would arrive and they would travel to Dr. Fletcher's office. With hope the physician would speak with Grandfather and make recommendations to forestall what now seemed inevitable. *A deterioration of the mind.*

Tears stung her eyes for the umpteenth time this evening. She held the towel against her face and willed them to stop.

A distinct knock sounded on her door and she dropped the towel to the ewer in surprise.

She couldn't answer. Not only was she dressed in nothing but her nightclothes, but it wasn't safe or wise.

The knock sounded again.

"Theodosia. Are you there? It's Whittingham."

Her heart thundered in her chest as she moved to unlatch the door. She had to open it or his infernal knocking would wake Dora, or worse, Grandfather. At least that's what she told herself.

Tightening the sash at her waist, she cracked the door a two-fingers' width and peered into the shadowy light of the hallway corridor.

"Are you all right?"

Matthew was there, handsomely dressed in his formal attire from earlier. He must have taken the lady who accompanied him to her home, and then returned directly to the hotel. But why? She opened the door a bit wider, careful to keep her body concealed. "Yes. I am now."

"You've been crying."

He leaned closer and she fought the urge to withdraw, shut the door, and resist the desire to confess all her fears.

"I'm fine. Truly." How he could discern so much in the lamplight was a tribute to his intelligence and empathy.

"Will you step into the corridor for a word?"

"Whatever for?" She moved farther behind the door panel. She noticed he didn't have his walking stick. "I'm dressed in my night rail."

"You're wearing a wrapper, aren't you?"

His husky whisper caused her skin to tingle with awareness. He seemed to discard conventionality whenever it pleased him, first with his use of her Christian name and now with his improper request. It was one thing to abandon decorum when off in the countryside, but not here in London.

"Yes, I am, but I can't come out into the hall now. It's the middle of the night."

"No one is about *because* it's the middle of the night." He looked left and right before he met her eyes. "Besides, what could ever happen here in the hotel corridor?"

"I once thought the same of the hotel dining room."

"True and fair." His mouth formed a wry grimace. "But now I'll be by your side. You needn't worry. I only mean to hold you a moment."

"Here?" Why did he have to say that last sentence? The temptation of his strong arms around her, offering comfort and support, proved her undoing. She angled into the opening and waited.

"Yes. Here."

He didn't move, but she did.

She closed her eyes and allowed his embrace. Just for a minute, she told herself. Sixty seconds of comfort and strength. She breathed in deeply and was rewarded with the spicy scent of his shaving soap. His cravat brushed her forehead, her ear placed over his heart, and even through his thick wool coat she could hear the steady beat within his chest.

He didn't say a word, though each of his exhales whispered through the fine hairs at her temple. Sensual curiosity caused her mind to race as quickly as her pulse. She would remember this moment. She would recall his empathy and compassion when she was returned to Oxfordshire. Just as his kiss at the right moment had chased away her sadness, his comfort would ease her mind.

"Thank you for what you did downstairs in the restaurant." She began to pull away, but his arms caught her tight. Still, an excuse to leave the respite he offered came too easily. "We've an early morning appointment with a respected physician who studies confusion and forgetfulness in the elderly." Her words were muffled against his chest, but she knew he heard her.

"Dr. Fletcher?" He loosened his grip so they could speak face-to-face, their whispered conversation a silent hush in the hallway.

"Yes. How did you know?"

"He's respected as a pioneer in the study of conditions concerning the elderly, and he also belongs to the Society. Let me escort you to his address."

"Thank you again, but it isn't necessary." She forced out the awkward explanation. "Lord Kirkman, a family friend, has come with us for that purpose. He's familiar with the situation and truly wants the best for Grandfather."

"I see."

Did he? Not that it mattered. They weren't traveling the same paths. He'd taken a lady to dinner tonight, hadn't he? They had no claims or obligations to each other, despite their odd form of friendship. Peculiar, how her heart ached a little at that truth. "Besides, I refuse to become an inconvenience. You have your life neatly organized here in London." It was a bold allusion to his dinner date and he was too intelligent not to realize.

"Hardly that." He didn't explain further and they stood in silence a beat too long.

"I should return to my room." She withdrew the slightest. "I wouldn't wish to oversleep come morning."

"No. We couldn't have that." He leaned in and before she could retreat, he lowered his mouth to hers.

The kiss was wrong for so many reasons. She was alone in a hotel hallway with a bachelor in the middle of the night. She was barely dressed, in nothing more than a thin silk wrapper and night rail. Yet she allowed him liberties that would scald the eyes of any passersby as she held tight in the circle of his arms amidst a deep, openmouthed kiss.

She wanted this more than her next breath. And that made it right for the most important reason.

"Breathe, Theodosia." His commanding growl brushed against her lips as he resumed the kiss.

Why should she bother breathing when every caress sought to take her breath away?

This kiss, *his kiss*, was an unanswered quest. A hypothesis to follow. Something for later thought when clear thinking returned, for now her mind and body flushed with sensation, as heated and delirious as a fever dream. He deepened the pressure of his mouth upon hers and she quickly abandoned any attempt at logical thought, ready to surrender to feeling instead.

The pressure of his mouth was the ideal elixir to calm her nerves, despite it sent her heartbeat into triple time. She opened to him, the stroke of his tongue against hers like a sweep of fire, igniting sparks of pleasure and heat.

His hands gripped her shoulders. His fingers pressed

against the thin silk as if he wished to touch her skin instead. He drew her closer, hard against his chest, and smoothed his hands upward until he cradled her face, his kiss suddenly slower, less urgent, and that much more tender, though she experienced a restless hunger that had nothing to do with food.

Each deliberate stroke of his tongue was echoed by the caress of his fingers at her cheek. Her breath quickened and mind spun, as if she'd had too much champagne and twirled in circles over and over and over again.

"What's happening?" she asked in a distant voice. "I feel as though I'm falling."

"Kiss me, Bookish," he murmured against her lips, a sensual command as he moved his mouth over hers.

Her silky bedclothes were no barrier to his heated touch. His fingertips skimmed down her neck, over her shoulders, one hand splayed at her back. Her nipples tightened in a strange and enthralling reaction to his nearness. Her whole body seemed sensitized, and a yearning ache like she'd never experienced, throbbed with anxious pleasure in her lower belly.

She wanted to kiss him. She wanted to feel his hands on her skin. Caress his muscular chest and learn the shape of his lean body. To touch him and have him touch her and the thought of all these sudden, new, and reckless desires frightened her beyond words.

She allowed herself another sinful moment of pleasure and then stepped back with a gasp, breaking free from his hold to lean against the door for support, her legs as weak as her willpower.

"You're lovely. So very lovely. Those eyes . . ." His words were a low, appreciative hush in the silence.

His gaze was heavy-lidded as he viewed her, and his hair

was a disheveled mess. Had she done that? Run her fingers through the silky strands? The entire episode seemed more dream than reality.

"I thought the time for flattery was before a stolen kiss."

"Stolen? Mine was freely given." He drew a deep breath and restored his jacket to rights.

She swallowed, a little stunned by his honest confession. "I'm sorry if I ruined your evening."

One dark brow climbed high. "This by no means ruins my evening."

"No." She suppressed a shy smile. "Earlier, in the dining room, with your . . ."

"Lady Chester," he supplied, his expression sober. "An acquaintance," he added belatedly.

"Not your sister."

He chuckled softly. "Good god, no. Amelia would have insisted on marmalade too, and somehow the cook would have produced it for fear of crossing her."

This earned him a sincere grin.

Silence enveloped their interlude. So quiet, the crackle of wax and flame in the wall sconce sounded unusually loud.

"It's amusing, isn't it?" Emotion caught her suddenly unaware. How unfair life could be. How sad and sorry her future appeared at this moment. She had to push him away. She couldn't care for him. So many reasons existed to place walls in their path. "To pretend for a while."

"How do you mean?" His answer sounded guarded, as if he perceived the same shift in mood. She could see it in his entrancing brown eyes.

"To pretend Grandfather isn't deteriorating. That my parents aren't dead. Or that I'm destined to be alone with a few compromised animals who need me as much as I need them." She pulled her shoulders straighter and tightened the sash at her waist. "Don't kiss me again. Don't buffer me from the truth of my situation. This is a blink in your existence, nothing more than a page in your history, but for me, it's my life. It's too meaningful. I can't think of my pleasures and wants when I have Grandfather's health to resolve. I'm not that selfish. So please, you shouldn't kiss me again. You shouldn't flirt and tease and call me Bookish. Because when you do, you dare me to believe otherwise and that's far too cruel a trick to play."

"Theodosia." He shook his head while a half smile twitched about his mouth. "You have it all wrong."

She didn't know what to make of that. She'd confessed her greatest fear. That she could somehow lose her head, or worse her heart, and come away broken from the experience. She couldn't lose anyone else. The flimsiest suggestion of that happening evoked fear so strong she refused to consider it.

"You don't have to be alone." His soft murmur tempted her to believe.

"Thank you for checking on me." She turned, her hand on the latch. "I need to sleep. Grandfather and I have a busy day tomorrow."

He nodded and took a step backward. "Good night then."

Amidst doubt and ambivalence, she foolishly wished she'd accepted his offer to accompany them to Dr. Fletcher's office. At least then there existed the guarantee she would see him again. But that same riddle she chased, of wanting what she could not have, was a roadmap for heartbreak. And besides, Grandfather was her most important priority. Any concerns she had beyond that would have to wait.

"Good night."

She closed the door and leaned against it, her eyes pressed together tight.

Chapter Eighteen

Matthew cursed all the way to his carriage. In his rush, he'd left his walking stick in the interior and his leg informed him of the unforgivable error now as he managed the slate steps leading from the hotel. Still, his grumbling had little to do with physical pain.

This evening had proved an unmitigated disaster from start to finish. Since when had his actions become so clumsy, his thoughts so muddled? In the end, what had he accomplished? Not much more than hurt feelings all around.

Parting with Amy was an act long overdue. Whether she deemed him worthy of her attention again didn't calculate into his future. He held no ill feelings. This evening proved they would never suit, and regardless, he'd attempted to force something out of convenience and lack of effort rather than true interest. Her dismissal ultimately improved his life. Not that he would ever wish to hurt another's feelings. Somehow everything became disarrayed once he'd arrived at Oxfordshire.

Hindsight was undoubtedly clear-sighted.

Only last year he'd urged his sister Amelia to marry and follow the expected course of life, but in turn he'd erred in thinking the same applied to his future. One couldn't predict or plan love the same way one proved a scientific theorem. There were no absolutes and the trials were scattered at best.

But then there was Theodosia . . .

He'd scared her with his ardor and insistence, pushed her too hard, too fast, and caused her to feel uncomfortable. She'd retreated this evening. In essence, she lived a rather sheltered existence, absent from society's influence. For him to upset her was truly unforgivable.

He let loose another expletive and climbed inside his waiting carriage. The rap on the roof would be better served to his forehead. Perhaps he could make it up to her and assist in some useful way. He closed his eyes and dropped his head to the cushioned seat, anxious to soothe his displeasure by summoning her image. How she'd looked this evening in the dining room, stalwart and beautiful, at the ready to assist Lord Talbot at any cost. Later, how she appeared in the doorframe, lovely and fragile, her face tear-stained and lips rosy from his kisses.

Or how she fit within his embrace. When she peered up at him, her lashes fluttering in her struggle to comprehend his compliments, her hair unbound around her shoulders like a skein of silk. He itched to caress her skin. Strip her bare and worship her body. He fooled himself into believing she was a passing curiosity easily satisfied with a kiss and kind word.

No.

Theodosia was a raging wildfire in his blood.

Morning came too quickly. Theodosia stretched, yawned, and dressed, though sound sleep had evaded her. Breakfast was taken in the room, and along with Dora's report gained through Collins next door, Grandfather was sharply focused and in high spirits.

Together, she and Grandfather looped arms and descended the two flights of stairs to the hotel foyer amid lively conversation, her maid a few paces behind. She stole a searching glance about the lobby, though she refused to acknowledge she scrutinized every passing gentleman in hope of seeing Matthew. She'd told him not to come, and without fail, he'd respected her wishes. He was honest and fair, and one couldn't fault another for such admirable qualities.

"There you are."

She turned at the sound of Henry's greeting.

"Good morning, Kirkman." Grandfather smiled. "Theodosia wished me to see a physician and I've obliged."

"Yes. We're headed to Dr. Fletcher's office this morning and we should go. My carriage is out front. The address is near Hoxton Square. It will take us an hour's travel with the morning traffic."

"That long?" Theodosia shook her head at the inconvenience, a beat of apprehension awakened. "Why didn't we find somewhere closer to stay overnight?"

Henry grinned, apparently unaware of her worry. "Only the best is acceptable. I wanted both you and Lord Talbot to be as relaxed as possible."

"That was thoughtful, although the long carriage ride may prove his undoing."

They all climbed into Kirkman's carriage and took wheel. Theodosia adjusted her skirts on the seat before she darted her eyes from the window to her grandfather and back again.

"Did you sleep well?" Henry inquired. "Mivart's boasts of having the most comfortable beds in England."

"I'm sure that's true." There was no reason to disappoint Henry's thoughtful efforts. What was done couldn't be undone now.

"I've arranged it all with great care," he continued. "I hope you're pleased with the rooms and service."

Now what was this about? She looked at Grandfather, who stared out the window at the passing coaches.

"Thank you again." She eyed Henry intently. "Is there more?"

"I mean to prove what a considerate match I'd be, not just by my actions in arranging for this trip, but in all respects."

She bit her lower lip to stifle her immediate response.

"He would be a fine husband, dear." Grandfather turned with a sudden interest in the conversation. "We've known Kirkman for more years than I can count. I give you both my blessing."

"No." She gentled her tone. "You misunderstand." She speared Kirkman with a glare meant to render him mute, and passed a glance to Dora, who showed the possession of a valued lady's maid by remaining politely invisible. "Henry spoke out of turn and besides, we didn't come to London to discuss my future plans, but yours, Grandfather."

"Let's hope the physician is agreeable and meets with us in a timely manner," Kirkman added quickly.

"What do you mean? I thought we had the first appointment of the day." She laid her hand upon her grandfather's sleeve, hoping her tone didn't alarm him despite she tried desperately to withhold emotion.

"I wrote to him and explained the situation but never received a confirmation. I'm sure he'll take the time to see Lord Talbot." Kirkman's smile dimmed. "Besides, I wanted to do this for you. To prove how well I can take care of matters if needed. To show you I'm excellent husband material and able to offer more than companionship and security."

"You needn't prove anything." She closed her eyes and summoned patience. Whether Dr. Fletcher would be amenable to their visit was a matter of uncertainty now. A foreboding shadow of ill ease caused her reply to come out sharp. "Why is it you need to marry so quickly? You've told me you must, but you never revealed why."

"I can't." Kirkman shifted his eyes to the landscape outside the window.

"Can't or won't?"

"I'm not at liberty to say." His expression transformed to displeasure. "It's one of the conditions, unfortunately. And worse, it's complicated."

"You want me to accept your proposal and yet you won't even confide in me the reason for this rush to the altar?" She lost some of her anger, too tired to attempt understanding.

"The reason would have no bearing upon your decision, and it's not like I would never tell you. Afterward, I'd be happy to discuss it." Henry nodded, his eyes meeting hers with intensity.

"That sounds like a fool's bargain."

"Not at all." Kirkman scowled. "I told you it's complicated."

"Life certainly is." Grandfather's unexpected interjection brought a hint of jocularity to their conversation, although it thereafter took a polite end.

They traveled several miles in silence, each inhabitant of the lush interior lost in their own pensive considerations. When the carriage at last arrived, Theodosia was desperate for fresh air.

Dr. Fletcher's office was a squat brick building with a single walnut door and two tall rectangular windows. Aside from two smaller gigs, a finely made phaeton was parked outside and Theodosia squinted in the early sun, unable to distinguish the wiry driver on the boot or any insignia to reveal the owner, though the stunning matched grays were unmistakable. Her pulse skipped, anxious and at the same time apprehensive. This was no coincidence, and while her heart warmed with the swift memory of their midnight kiss, she wondered at Matthew's presence here and how their visit might unravel from this point. They didn't even have a legitimate appointment, thanks to Henry's self-serving plan. Would this be just another embarrassment in a growing list?

Not cut from coward's cloth, Theodosia cleared her throat and began walking. Kirkman and Grandfather moved ahead and she followed a few steps behind, careful to lift her hems and not catch a heel on a stone or step into a puddle left by the recent poor weather. Dora trailed, at the ready to offer help if needed. Inside, the offices were simple and sterile looking, with whitewashed walls and plain tiles on the floor. A line of chairs rested near one wall and a stout wooden table sat below one of the rectangular windows.

Without hesitation, Kirkman spoke in a quiet tone to the secretary, who shook his head firmly in the negative. Things did not appear as smoothly arranged as he'd sought her to believe. Distress held her lips tight as Kirkman returned to where they waited in a nearby corner.

"The doctor is unavailable at this time, although his secretary advised we should take a seat and wait. With a bit of luck, Dr. Fletcher will see us before his office hours end." Kirkman's expression seemed to cast more doubt upon the subject than his words.

"You said you'd arranged an appointment." She hardly disguised her frustration, on edge that a lengthy delay would cause Grandfather to become disagreeable.

"I'm sure it will be fine." Kirkman turned to Lord Talbot.

"Would you like to take a seat until Dr. Fletcher can see you?"

"I'd rather not see the physician," Grandfather replied. "I'm feeling fine. Is this why we've come to London?"

Theodosia pressed her lids together tight in a blink that lasted far too long but provided the patience needed. A familiar voice sounded and her eyes shot open.

The Earl of Whittingham exited the far door followed by another, older gentleman.

"Thank you again."

The men shook hands before Matthew turned on the threshold. For a moment her breathing hitched, his fine form showcased by the doorframe as if a work of art. Had he come seeking advice and counsel for his own health? She'd hadn't asked about his leg when they'd spoken last night, and now admonished herself for the oversight.

"Yes, here they are now, Dr. Fletcher." Matthew's eyes caught hers.

The physician was a man of opposites by comparison. White hair formed a circle around a bare pate, his shoulders narrow and build slight. He wore a long, plain coat with deep pockets over his clothes. The two men approached and introductions were made.

"I've taken the liberty of speaking to Dr. Fletcher on your behalf. I hope you—"

"A word, Whittingham," Kirkman interrupted with a cold warning. "You've overstepped."

"Lord Kirkman, please." Theodosia glared in his direction. "No matter how the appointment has come about, let's not forget the reason we're here."

This subdued Kirkman's hostility, at least for the time being, and he moved his attention to Matthew, as if intent to watch the man with upmost perspicacity.

"Why are we here? Why is everyone quarreling?"

Theodosia touched her grandfather's arm, a comforting smile at the ready. "I'd like to speak to Dr. Fletcher. Would you accompany me into his office while the gentlemen wait outside?"

Phrased in such a way, she knew her grandfather would never refuse.

"Of course, dear."

Matthew watched Theodosia and Lord Talbot until the door closed and they were safely tucked inside the physician's office, away from the reception area.

"What is it, Kirkman?" He noted the irritable edge of his question but didn't feel the need to adjust his tone. The ever-proposing Kirkman had graciously accompanied Theodosia and her grandfather to London, and that was well done, but aside from the singular deed, the overreaching, wishful-thinking gentleman grated on Matthew's last nerve.

"What is what exactly?" Kirkman seemed of equal disposition.

"What exactly is your relationship with Lady Leighton?" No need to mince syllables. He didn't care if the question would be interpreted as inappropriate. Besides, he planned to ask Theodosia the same question later. He'd collect and compare his notes as any scientist worth his weight would do. He worked with facts. Why he needed the information was another matter altogether, and at the moment he dismissed it as too taxing for the brain. Instead, he speared Kirkman with a glare meant to hurry him to an answer. When a man deliberated too long, it lent suspicion as to the truth of his answer.

"We're childhood friends and I intend to convince her to marry me."

"I doubt anyone can convince the lady of anything."

"I'm not so sure of that, and as I've stated, I've known her almost two decades."

"Be sure." Matthew indulged in a throaty chuckle meant to invoke unease. "I've known her a fortnight and I couldn't be more certain. Lady Leighton is intelligent and determined." He paused to let that thought sink into Kirkman's brainbox. "A lethal combination."

"Perhaps." Kirkman withdrew his pocket watch and noted the time. "I've an important appointment that can't be missed. I trust the physician will assist, now that a meeting is under way. Shall I leave my carriage at Lady Leighton's disposal, or are you here to usurp me?"

"The latter." Matthew nodded in the affirmative. "Good day, Kirkman."

Nearly an hour had passed before Theodosia exited Dr. Fletcher's office and returned to the waiting vestibule. She saw Matthew near the far window, his back to her, though he glanced over his shoulder and turned at the sound of the door. She stifled a smile. She owed the earl her sincerest gratitude.

"I don't know what you did or how you did it, but I'm sincerely thankful." Her eyes searched his handsome face, noting the gleam in his golden-brown gaze, the wily smile that played about his mouth. A subtle warmth composed of reassurance and affirmation settled in her soul. Somehow Matthew caused her to feel safer, hopeful, just by his presence.

"I merely mentioned to the doctor Lord Talbot would likely be resistant if he perceived his intelligence in question. After a brief conversation and a bit of creative thinking, Dr. Fletcher suggested your grandfather might be agreeable if he thought himself a contributor to a scientific study. The physician's invitation to have your grandfather visit him at home and be treated as a guest while actually under observation was a clever suggestion." At last, Matthew let a smile free. "I assume it went smoothly."

"It did." She exhaled, a sense of relief flooding her from head to toe. "Grandfather accepted Dr. Fletcher's invitation. I'm not sure if he confused your invitation with the physician's, but it doesn't matter. I'm just happy the doctor will have a good length of time to spend with Grandfather. I won't know what to do with myself while I wait, but I couldn't be more appreciative." She darted a look over his shoulder. "Oh, did Lord Kirkman leave?"

"He mentioned something about a private appointment requiring his attention." Matthew nodded toward the window and the uncommon sunshine outside. "Why don't you spend the day with me? I promise you an afternoon guaranteed to chase away troubles."

"I can't just leave." She glanced right and left, assured no one overheard their conversation.

"Did you expect to sit in this stuffy waiting room with your maid all day?" He chuckled. "You do realize Dr. Fletcher will depart at some point and return to his home with your grandfather."

"Still." She dropped her eyes to her hands. "I dislike London and all the crowded attractions the upper orders deem worthy. I'd rather go to the hotel immediately."

"I'll bring you to Mivart's later this evening. Now the entire day awaits." He smiled down at her and waited until she matched his gaze. "I won't take you anywhere you expect to go. I know secrets in this city that any learned scientist would devour with avid interest." He waggled his brows with a charming smile.

Her eyes widened before she could stifle her curiosity.

"Wait." She took his arm though she kept her feet still. "I must send a message to Collins at the hotel. Grandfather's things will need to be forwarded. He does so much better when articles are familiar."

"We'll make the necessary arrangements for Lord Talbot, so you needn't worry." His amusement fell away, his eyes sincere. "Allow me to change your mind about London."

"Only today. Just for a little while." She shook her head, her conditions in place, although she remained aware she might be making a grave mistake.

"By the by, I've been meaning to ask you about Lord Kirkman."

"Yes." She had an inkling she knew his next question.

"What is your relationship with the gentleman?"

"Friendship." She wouldn't offer more.

"Like ours?" He grinned and her heart flipped over in her chest.

For the briefest instance she recalled his kiss, the press of his muscular frame against her and the sensation of his tongue as it coaxed hers into play. She grew warm, once again flustered by the intimate experience. "Not at all."

One dark brow climbed upward.

She shook her head in the negative, anxious to erase the threat of emotion. It was as if her body called to his, her mind all too ready to draw conclusions. She dealt with fact. Facts were safe. Facts were fair and honest and logical. Facts didn't hurt one for unknown reasons or cause unexpected heartache.

He edged closer. "Very good then. Let's get this day under way."

Chapter Nineteen

They climbed into Matthew's stylish carriage, where Theodosia was startled to see Coggs inside. Matthew introduced his valet to Dora with a gleam in his eye and the interaction caused Theodosia a qualm of suspicion, though it was swiftly dismissed as Matthew rapped on the roof and the carriage jerked forward through the slush-covered gutter and out into the wet roadway. The weather had improved, although they still needed to bundle against the cold temperature, and with four occupants inside the carriage, the interior warmed considerably.

"I've instructed my driver to visit Blackfriars first."

His boots shuffled against the floor as if he sought a preferred position. Despite the carriage was large and comfortable, she suspected his long legs, bent at any angle, would become cramped. She didn't dare ask if he'd used the ginger salve she'd prepared for him, unwilling to be disappointed at the answer.

"Blackfriars?" Her mind whirled with the suggestion. What could they possibly seek in such an ominous-sounding place? She knew few locations beyond those written about in popular books, and with no desire to seek amusements in a city she despised, she hadn't an idea where he might take her today. The carriage rattled over a long stretch of cobblestones before he replied.

"Apothecaries Hall, of course. You mentioned an interest in botanical science." He grinned knowingly. "It's the least I can do after you provided me with your exceptional restorative salve."

Impressed by his thoughtfulness, she paused a moment. "You've given this a great deal of thought, haven't you?"

"As all things."

"Even though you had no idea I would agree to this outing?"

He didn't answer.

They traveled in silence a bit farther, though she could sense a level of perception that seemed more acute than any conversation. The air warmed quickly within the carriage and the scent of his shaving soap found her eager to evoke another remembrance of their kisses. She noted the way sunrays streamed through the square window and outlined his profile, the strong set of his jaw and chin, his thick dark brows, and how the light glossed his hair with a becoming amber gleam.

She swallowed, desperately forcing her thoughts elsewhere than the intriguing handsome man across from her. When she huffed a quiet exhale, he turned his attention, almost as if he could read her thoughts. *The scoundrel.* Their eyes met and held for longer than appropriate. She hoped Dora and Coggs weren't as perceptive.

The carriage leaned to the right as they rounded the corner of Black Friars Lane and she forced her attention elsewhere. They parked and exited onto the narrow cobbled street that tilted toward the Thames, no more than a stone's throw away.

"Milady." Matthew clasped his walking stick in one

hand and offered his arm. "My valet and your maid will follow."

He guided them over the threshold of a dark passage where gilt unicorn statues marked the entrance to an elongated courtyard, the façades of several storefronts marked by unusual signs that jutted from each building on blackened wrought-iron brackets. A gust of bitter wind caused a symphony of creaks and groans, the signs asway in unison as if they beckoned her forward.

"What is this place?" She looked at him, anxious to have her curiosity satisfied and at the same time intrigued not to miss a single detail.

"This is the Great Hall, a rare bit of England's history. Over two hundred years ago, a royal charter restricted practicing apothecaries to this single street to barter their concoctions without fear of imprisonment or worse." He gestured to a shop where the signage bore an emblazoned image of a ram's head, its eyes painted blood red. "It's a bit like a wizard's lair, I suppose, and the singular location where botanists were permitted to concoct their unguents and elixirs. You won't find any uppers along this street. If they ever acquired a need of mouse paste to cure stubborn warts or an herbal clyster to relieve constipation, they would certainly dispatch a servant rather than risk exposure of their malady."

"I had no idea."

"Nor did I until Coggs suggested I try a heated snake oil rub for my leg spasms."

"Did it subdue the pain?"

"Not as well as your ginger salve, Bookish."

He motioned for them to enter the nearest doorway and she moved into the dimly lit shop, her eyes wide.

"I'm thankful for Grandfather's foresight in Leighton House's construction." An abundance of odors, some pleasant, others not, inundated her nose while she darted her eyes to the shelves and tables, all laden with bottles, jars, and beige canvas pouches of every size. A handwritten tag explaining the contents was attached to each.

"Aah, how true." He walked to the opposite side of the interior as they perused the items for sale. An elderly man stood in the corner, unbothered by their inquisitive exploration. "You have your own personal hall in which to experiment without anyone the wiser. Though I find the remedy ingredients and their applications more fascinating than the claims of their ability to cure. Sheep's tongue for stuttering in particular."

Theodosia lifted a stout glass jar and read the label aloud. "Take forty to fifty swallows before bed to ensure a peaceful sleep. How odd. I've always believed a glass of warm milk the more relaxing method."

"I suppose it depends if one's hoping for dreams or avoiding nightmares," Matthew answered, a long black pouch in his palm. "Crush feathers into a pulp and mix with white wine."

"Drink while standing in the moonlight." She smiled as she whispered, "That sounds like a witch's spell more than practical science."

Matthew matched her amusement. "Perhaps. This one suggests the user ingest the contents and complete the ritual with the reception of a lover's kiss."

Theodosia felt her face heat. She replaced the jar she held and turned away in hope Matthew wouldn't see her reaction. "I'm not sure that's knowledge."

"Science is a fair degree of mystery mixed with fact, wouldn't you say?"

He'd come up beside her and she hesitated before she turned. "Where's Dora?"

The two servants hadn't entered the shop and she wondered if Coggs's presence was prearranged to keep her maid out of sight. It was a devious yet clever plan, if that indeed was the case.

"I doubt a dragon has found her." He offered his arm. "Come along." He dropped a few coins in the shopkeeper's palm and they took their leave.

Her quick survey located Coggs and Dora across the courtyard in conversation. She couldn't withhold her curiosity. "Did you invite your valet for the sole reason of distracting my maid?"

He chuckled and she suppressed a smile.

"You have a suspicious mind, Theodosia."

She didn't correct him as she should. She begrudgingly acknowledged she enjoyed the sound of her name in his voice. Then she shook her head at the inanity. She wasn't some bird-witted female, charmed by the slightest compliment.

"You don't agree?" he pressed.

"Oh, you misunderstood. I was thinking about something different entirely."

"Reflecting on our midnight kiss in your library?"

Her gasp must have confirmed his hypothesis.

"You needn't be alarmed." He leaned in so close, his mouth brushed the rim of her ear. "My thoughts wander there frequently as well."

At a loss to continue the conversation, she was relieved he didn't say more. Matthew motioned to Coggs and they made their way back to the carriage. He handed her up the steps and spoke to his driver. "George, to our second stop."

Once inside, their discussion resumed.

"Should I be insulted you mentally left our conversation and meandered down a different path?" He waited. "Though I've been accused of the same."

"Are you accustomed to ladies hanging on your every word?" She couldn't help the jibe.

"Not in the least, but I would hope our conversation proved pleasant enough."

"Where are we off to now?" She looked out the window, though she knew little of the city.

"Montagu House."

"The British Museum." A slight smile dared emerge. He had planned a spectacular day. One of the drawbacks of her reluctance to return to London was missing the opportunity to explore extraordinary cultures and curiosities.

"We didn't spend long at Blackfriars because the museum keeps a strict schedule. What day of the week is it anyway, Coggs?"

"It is Tuesday, milord, and near eleven o'clock." Coggs nodded. "The porter will grant you admittance to the reading room for an hour during the second session of the day."

"Coggs knows the schedule by memory. Each day of the week and month of the year are allotted different times in a monthly cycle, and I visit too often for him not to be prepared."

"I've read descriptions of the many collections."

"They're spectacular and must be seen in actuality to be appreciated. Sir Hans Sloane, naturalist and physician, bequeathed a vast collection of books, manuscripts, and drawings to the museum and therefore made the rules. Perhaps he wished for everyone to have an opportunity in the reading room. The viewing of other artifacts and displays isn't as structured and has been since arranged by the body of trustees."

He repositioned his left leg and his boot brushed against her shoe. Aside from her hand upon his elbow as he'd escorted her through Blackfriars and the fleeting brush of his mouth near her ear, they hadn't touched, and she now found it difficult not to want to do so. That realization both thrilled and disturbed her.

"Is something wrong?" His brows lowered with concern. "You look unhappy."

"No, I'm fine." She regained a cheery expression. "We're lucky to view the collections before the museum closes for the holiday."

"Yes." His expression grew pensive. "Christmastime."

He didn't say more, though she sensed he might have wanted to. She wondered how he spent the holidays. Grandfather and she had established a few traditions of their own, and Christmas Eve was a quiet, cozy evening. She couldn't help but wonder if this year would be as calm. Usually, most every evening proved the same, but she was quick to amend that thought. With Grandfather's abilities not as they once were, she had no idea what the future held, never mind the Christmas season.

Would Grandfather be well? Would he remember the past customs they'd shared together and happily resurrected each holiday? Or would she be home alone? Alone with the reality that her only living relative faced a bleak future. One where someday soon he might no longer recognize her. This fear, the worst fear, was too frightful to voice and she smothered it promptly.

She didn't possess many memories of her parents. The fire that claimed their lives had occurred in January, right after the New Year, so she always looked to Christmas to soothe away impending gloom, almost as a precursor to the gray, solemn weeks ahead. In that manner, holiday joy was essential to her surviving the despairing winter months, but now, who knew what it would be like?

They arrived in good time and Matthew couldn't be more pleased. An earlier conversation provided Coggs with his purpose, and after a meaningful glance in the valet's direction, they all set upon the stairs toward the museum's entrance.

"Where would you like to go first?" He gestured toward the elongated marble staircase before them. "Printed books and manuscripts are here on the main floor and also below. The upper-level rooms have works of art, fossils, corals, assorted stuffed and mounted animals, insects, fishes, and lizards, as well as shells, rocks, and herbals."

"Have you memorized the whole of it?"

"Almost." He brought her hand to his arm and moved toward the stairs. "I've never gone to the gallery, too interested in the scientific rather than the artistic. Would you like to explore unknown territory with me?"

She blinked. *Twice.*

She couldn't possibly understand the double entendre. And for a fleeting moment he wondered when everything had shifted. When suddenly Theodosia had become the pursuit of his heart instead of a good deed done or fleeting distraction.

"I'd like to see it all."

He chuckled, and the sound mingled with their boot heels on the stairs. There were few visitors this time of day and he was thankful for that. Coggs and Dora had already disappeared around a corner. Damn, his valet was efficient, if nothing else.

"You'll have to stay much longer in London if you plan to examine every exhibit. There are over 70,000 artifacts. Not that I would object. I gladly volunteer my services as tour guide if it prolongs your visit to the city."

She smiled, though it didn't reach her eyes. London troubled her to the core. She'd confessed her dislike of high society and the harsh reception she'd endured at finishing school, and he appreciated the freedom she relished in Oxfordshire. Still, a part of him, a part that seemed to expand with each passing minute, selfishly wished she would remain here in London where he could see her as often as he desired.

"Then please show me the best the museum has to offer before we breach the unknown together."

There was hope in that statement, hope and truth on a deeper level.

"An excellent plan." He led her to a nearby corner where the trunk of a tree rested on a square platform. "This donation, made in 1760, is an oak stump gnawed by a beaver, a nocturnal semiaquatic rodent."

She flitted her eyes to the artifact and back again, and he admired the glint of wonder and amusement in their lovely gray depths.

"Intriguing."

"I've read they are quite industrious animals, although all that woodwork must grow tedious and a-gnawing."

She coughed at his poorly made pun and he stifled his own groan before pushing on. "Do you like to swim?"

"Nice recovery, milord."

She offered a sideways glance, as if the gnarled stump was so captivating she couldn't tear her attention away, but he saw only coy flirtation.

"I ask because the installation of several sea-bathing machines at Brighton is the most popular attraction for the upcoming season." If she wouldn't stay in London, would she pleasure him with her company elsewhere?

"Come summer I will be nothing more than a faint memory," she murmured in answer.

"Let's continue." Unwilling to allow a solemn mood, he strode to the left. His walking stick tapped against the marble tiles as if keeping time. "Here's the empty shell of the North American tortoise. In the case beside it, you'll find the petrified fossil of a large crocodile head excavated here in England." He paused before he continued. "Had we more time I would explain why I don't believe this fossil belongs to the crocodile family at all. I've studied it on numerous occasions."

"How curious."

He watched her genuine interest alight, the tilt of her pert nose, and lips pursed tight in contemplation. Never far from his thoughts, the urge to kiss her arose with sharp insistence.

"We should . . ." He faltered. "Would you like to go to the gallery? The Elgin Marbles are a rare gift to behold."

She nodded in answer and they proceeded in unison toward the corridor, almost as if she knew, as he did, something more was at stake than an enjoyable visit to the museum.

Theodosia's heart pounded a thunderous beat, whether in anticipation or warning, she didn't know. Her life held too many constraints for her to sort this morning. She enjoyed Matthew's company. A romantic notion that had no right taking residence in her heart yearned for her to know him better. Just the thought of falling into his embrace did all kinds of odd things—unexplainable, emotional things— to her composure.

With Grandfather's mind failing and her dedication to his care and preserving his reputation in good standing, she could never fit in here in London. Not to mention she had no desire to leave Oxfordshire and relocate to a city that had shown her little kindness in the past. But Matthew spoke to her as an equal and valued her intelligence and intrigued her, entranced her, with nothing more than a glance from his golden-brown eyes. And he was unerringly kind and thoughtful, planning this day of distraction when she might have sat in a doctor's office with only worry and distress for company.

"Lady Leighton."

Matthew's gentle bid for her attention broke through her muddied considerations. They matched eyes and her heart seized at the look of honest concern there.

"Milord."

Winter's distant sunlight poured through the high windows positioned near the crown molding. The noises surrounding them—discreet conversations and nearby footfalls—faded away. The moment became timeless, as if divinity entered the room, fragile and precious for its rarity. Their gaze held through several heartbeats, and it was as if words were unnecessary. Perhaps their souls spoke. She couldn't be sure.

He appeared equally affected, until at last he managed words. "The Marbles. Upstairs. The gallery."

She took his elbow and looked at him with a slight smile.

For all the silence between them, her senses brought to bear every subtlety of his nearness. The flexing muscles of his arm beneath warm wool, the glint of light on his long lashes, and his perfectly formed mouth, suited for speaking and other mundane tasks, but truly accomplished at the art of kissing.

A rush of heat tingled under her skin, up her neck to her cheeks, and she prayed he didn't notice.

Chapter Twenty

The gallery was an airy, elongated corridor situated on the east side of the museum with ambitious multipaned windows that stretched toward the sky and allowed for maximum sunlight. Marble figures and plaques lined the walls, while at the center several platforms displayed ancient Greek sculptures. At the far left corner was a small office for the curator's use and on the opposite side an area for artists to sketch and scribble notes.

Matthew heard Theodosia's breath catch, and smiled. He'd accomplished his goal and created a worthwhile memory. He had no substantial reason to explain why it mattered so much, but it did.

At first, they perused the collection in humbled silence. Other visitors, few in number, wandered through with low-toned admiration and discreet conversation. It was as though the Marbles commanded reverence, their existence a rare link to another age.

Theodosia stopped in front of a round platform with a tall figure of a woman dressed in flowing Grecian robes. Theodosia rose to her tiptoes to gain a better view of the sculpture's detail and Matthew couldn't help but notice the way her skirts outlined her perfectly rounded derriere and the graceful arch of her back as she worked to note each masterful stroke by the artist.

They were surrounded by explicit depictions of the male and female form, yet nothing was as alluring as Theodosia in that moment. Sunlight colored her hair with blue-black highlights, her skin rosy from exertion. Every shadow within her posture was perfectly placed to enhance her body, the curve of her breasts as they strained against her bodice, the gentle slope of her neck and delicate shoulders.

He drew a long breath and moved closer, all the more determined to achieve another kiss.

"Breathtaking, isn't she?" He came up beside her and spoke in a low tone.

"I had no idea." She seemed reluctant to displace her attention. "One can read of history and masterful artwork, but until seen . . ." Her voice trailed off as if no words were adequate.

"Many things need to be experienced to understand their impact and pleasure."

She turned to face him more fully. "There are a hundred meanings in that bit of advice."

"Perhaps." He studied her face. Her lovely eyes twinkled in the streaming sunlight.

At odds with his attention, she moved to the adjacent wall, though she found no respite. This particular section of Marbles depicted warriors and centaurs in all their polished nudity. Above and below, bare muscles were sculpted to the most exacting detail.

Unwilling to retreat, she studied the artwork as if her life depended on their memorization, and he did the same at her side, though an undeniable tension built between them, powerful and sensual.

"Have you ever been in love, Theodosia?"

The question must have surprised her. She turned to face

him and blinked thoughtfully, her slender brows forming a vee of concern. "Why do you ask?"

He should have expected a question in answer to his question. After all, she was a deep thinker and self-declared scientist, if not a little defensive on the subject.

"Come here." He caught her hand and towed her forward, relieved she didn't resist. Her boot tips nearly nicked his heels as he hurried her through the entrance of the curator's office, closed the door, and slid his walking stick through the latch before he pulled Theodosia into his arms.

"Now, I'll ask you again. Have you ever been in love?"

"I haven't." She shook her head so slightly, she might not have done so at all. The wall sconces played havoc with the candlelight. "And you?"

"Only once and then many, many times." Did he imagine despair in her eyes? She didn't understand his reply, but he would happily explain, now that he held her tight against his chest.

"I see."

"No, you don't." His mouth hovered over hers, but he didn't claim a kiss. Instead he nuzzled across her cheek and brushed his lips against her ear. "It's you, Bookish. One glance and I was done for. Now the condition is endless because every time I look at you I find I fall in love all over again."

She stiffened in his arms, her spine poker straight. Yet more rigid than her reaction, her reply declared him a liar.

"No. You can't possibly love me."

She wriggled in an attempt to free herself from his hold, but he held firm, determined to explain further. Still she continued to protest.

"You don't even know me."

"It doesn't work that way." He almost smiled. "Love, I mean."

"Yes, it does." She pushed against his arms and he released her. "I wouldn't wish to believe you insincere, and yet we hardly know each other."

"I want to know you. I want to know everything about you."

She looked confused. As if she had no idea how to reply to his heartfelt confession.

"What about the natural order of things?" She took a deep breath. "After being introduced, we would have a courtship."

"Indeed. A compatibility test." The path to the lady's heart lay in scientific analysis. "I agree." He grinned, though whether or not she could see it in the shadowy interior he wasn't aware. "And one more thing." With a gentle tug, he returned her to his arms, and this time she didn't object. "We'll need several repeated trials to confirm the chemical reaction."

Surely this couldn't be happening. Not to her. She couldn't be inside a dimly lit office in the middle of the day in the arms of a man who somehow, piece by piece, claimed her heart. He was intelligent, frightfully so, and strong, honorable, and empathetic. Good lord, if she took the time to compose a list of his attributes, that list would be endless and all the more intimidating. It could only be that her good sense was compromised with worry over Grandfather.

Still, whether reality or fantasy, she wouldn't waste the moment, and when his lips melted over hers, hot and insistent, she didn't give a fig where she stood or how early the hour. Pleasure twisted tight within her, a spontaneous, insistent coil, and she trembled from its intensity.

How had this happened?

How had she allowed this man into her heart when she'd guarded every emotion against his irresistible charms, full knowing heartbreak and disappointment lay ahead?

"Relax," he whispered into her mouth before he brushed his fingertips featherlight across her jaw. "You're permitted to enjoy this."

His raspy command reminded her she was an equal participant, and so she welcomed the onslaught of invigorating sensation as his tongue stroked against hers. She couldn't fight the desire any longer. It was the natural way of things, wasn't it? The physical attraction of female to male?

His touch moved down her neck, drawing a line of fire that seemed to begin and end at the center of her body. He rested his hands gently on her shoulders and deepened their kiss. She curled her fingers into his coat and gripped the fabric as if she needed to steady herself, all the while his mouth worked magic over hers, nipping and licking, stoking her heat. When he moved as if to pull away, she rose on tiptoe to prevent it.

He murmured something indecipherable, low and husky, the sensual sound all the more erotic for its unintelligibility. The air itself seemed intensified and the scent of his shaving soap teased her senses, spicy and male, a reminder of his strength and virility. Lost in acute awareness, she allowed him to trail hot kisses across her cheek to her ear, downward along the arch of her neck where sensation pricked her skin to attention. Again, the throb of desire strummed insistent and strong in her lower belly. He made her want things she didn't understand but wanted nonetheless.

He shifted, and before she knew what he intended, he'd reversed their position, his back to the door as he perched her on the corner of the desk. Without hesitation, he cradled her face with his hands and returned to their kiss. Unsteady, she braced her palms behind her on the desktop, her mind awhirl in kind to her stomach. Every exhilarating tremor of sensation demanded attention.

He slid one fingertip across her clavicle, first left, then right, until he touched the space in the center where her pulse raced. She trembled as he moved his mouth to the same spot and pressed a heated kiss mouth to skin. His hair, silky soft, brushed against her chin and she inhaled, needing to know his masculine scent.

He leaned into her and she moved back to accommodate the change, though it allowed him the advantage, her skirts caught between them and bodice bowed to expose the swell of her breasts.

Fascinated and intrigued, she watched as he left kisses there, tender touches and hot caresses, each more thrilling than the one before, her body all at once impatient and restless. Her breasts grew heavy, the tips painfully sensitive against her chemise so even the softest cotton seemed unbearable now. She ached from the inside out, full of want and need, lost in carnal curiosity. Would he relieve her confusion and ease her pain? She lifted one hand to thread her fingers through his hair, no more than a fleeting stroke before she needed to support herself again.

Everywhere he touched, tiny pulses of heat responded beneath her skin. He traced a line along her bodice and his thumb smoothed away the prickles of her reaction.

"You're so very lovely."

His words were no more than a murmur as he nuzzled her neck with heated kisses. Breathing became a struggle, each exhale strong enough to whisper through the lock of hair at his forehead. She closed her eyes to his exquisite attention, unwilling to stop what was so incredibly good despite logic told her how wrong the choice.

When his mouth passed over the swells of her breasts she nearly lost balance. Unexpected, yet immensely pleasurable, she gripped the edge of the desk and bit into her lower lip, her eyes held tight. He shifted the slightest and his thigh pressed between her legs. Heat singed through countless layers of silk and cotton, and whatever the force that built within her, the insistent desire that caused her to grow wet and anxious, doubled with urgency.

She said something, unsure she formed words, as his mouth returned to hers. Clothing confined her, each breath restricted by her position and suffocating corset, and when his hand skimmed over her breasts, his thumb dragged across her nipple to scorch her from the inside out.

Clothing restricted true discovery. What if he touched her there? Caressed each breast? Teased the tips, now achingly hard with pleasure and pain? Or stroked over each with the burning sweep of his tongue? She wanted to scream with frustration.

Perhaps she'd gone mad. Lost all logic for the price of physical pleasure. She drew a shuddered breath as he placed his hands at her waist, slowly grazing her ribs as if he counted each one and memorized their placement. Meanwhile, she squirmed on the desktop, acutely aware of his thigh pressed against her, the strength of his muscles near her sensitive core.

A lick of cold air met her ankles and calves. With sluggish coherence she realized he'd collected her skirts and pushed them aside. The heat of his palm atop her silk stocking was a lightning strike and she stiffened, drenched in sensation and at the same time left wanting.

"Are you all right, love?" His gravelly questions skittered through her to add to her restlessness.

"Yes." Her voice didn't sound like her own. All she knew was she was falling into an abyss of hopeless emotion as fast as a meteorite quitting the midnight sky, unable to recover, bound to incinerate into nothing but ash.

Perhaps he considered the same.

With a deep exhale, he removed his hand and stepped back. She wanted to cry out for his abandonment. How foolish. How utterly mad.

"I hope I . . ." He stopped speaking as his eyes adjusted to their separation.

"What is it?" She sat up straighter and touched her hair in an absent gesture, all at once concerned he might regret what he'd only just initiated.

She waited, painfully long it seemed, and watched as he swallowed thoughtfully. He tugged on the hem of his coat and then his sleeves, his eyes averted. At last he straightened his cravat and looked at her. When he didn't begin speaking, she thought to ease his discomfort.

"We should return to the gallery. I wouldn't want to miss a thing." It was an odd comment, one that implied she preferred the cold, lifeless Marbles to what had just transpired between them, but she had no experience with romantic conversation and couldn't imagine anything else to say.

Chapter Twenty-One

An interminable span of silence consumed them as they exited the curator's office. With a quick word, Theodosia excused herself to seek the retiring room. Matthew was pleased to see they were of no notice, the gallery near empty aside from an elderly artist who stood with his back turned. As expected, their privacy was short-lived.

Across the way, a gentleman he knew well preceded a small group into the hall. It was a typical afternoon outing. Unfortunately, Amy and her brother, Lord Knolls, were the least likely people he'd enjoy conversing with, never mind the gaggle of friends who accompanied them.

"Whittingham."

"Knolls." He nodded in hope the greeting would suffice, but it appeared the gentleman had other intentions. He stepped away from the group, who cast a passing glance in his direction before moving beyond to the Marbles on display.

"It was good of you to escort my sister about town last evening. You have my appreciation."

They shook hands and Matthew noted that Amy had glanced back toward where he stood, not once, but twice already.

"I was happy to assist." Was Knolls aware how the

evening ended? Matthew would be shocked if Amy hadn't shared her disappointment. The lady wasn't good at holding her tongue, not that there was a call for slander. Her discerning level of character should have assured she not repeat what happened at the restaurant and thereafter, but in retrospect Matthew realized she was absent of that quality. How had he missed that before?

"Amy is a bit put out. She refuses to speak of last evening. I suppose it's one of her feminine ploys to cause me great guilt and plan another outing to Mivart's." Knolls leaned in as if imparting confidential news shared between friends.

"One can never be sure with Lady Chester." Matthew thought better than to correct his misconception. Across the gallery he noticed Theodosia as she entered the hall. Even from afar, he experienced a strong pull to be near her. He hadn't planned on revealing deep emotion when he'd tugged her into the curator's alcove, but one taste of her lips and he was the one jabbering the musings of his heart like a besotted fool.

"If you'll excuse me, Knolls." He strode away without looking back, his walking stick counting a steady beat of patience against the tiles.

"There you are."

Had Theodosia noticed the guests who'd entered the room earlier?

"Here I am."

He offered his arm and led her from the gallery. There stood no reason for Amy to gain more fodder for any exaggerations being spread. While she hadn't told her brother the whole of it, Matthew doubted she would refrain from engaging in speculation with her closest friends.

"I have a better idea." He hurried his step. "One which will keep you smiling for all the remaining days of winter."

"Truly, that's a challenge, I assure you." She murmured this softly, though he heard the sadness in her words.

"I see Coggs and your maid." He gestured with his chin, reluctant to stop talking. "Let's get the third afternoon adventure under way." He continued toward the doors, intersecting his valet's path as they collectively moved through the exit. Once the carriage pulled around, he gave George their direction and then they all climbed inside.

"Where are we off to now?"

"I promised you a London adventure, and I always keep my word."

"But do you always mean what you say?"

"Of course." He winked in her direction. "Especially while standing in curators' alcoves."

Her eyes darted away and back again. It would appear she needed further convincing.

The carriage slowed within a throng of traffic, though George maneuvered through fairly quickly, and less than ten minutes later the driver pulled the team to a stop in front of Astley's Royal Amphitheatre of the Arts.

"Very good. We've arrived."

"So quickly?" Theodosia moved aside the velvet curtain and peeked out the glass window.

"London is a city of illusion and mystery." He grinned. "We viewed the most valuable art and sculpture at the British Museum, while just down the road Westminster Bridge hides an enthralling secret equally rich in culture." He tossed a pouch of coins at his valet. "Coggs, obtain our tickets and be so kind as to purchase Miss Dora a glass of lemonade, or two. We'll follow promptly."

"Of course, milord." Coggs exited and assisted Dora down the steps, though she fairly scurried.

"I think my maid is smitten with your valet," Theodosia mused as soon as the carriage door closed.

"He does have a way." Matthew eased back against the bench and stretched his legs. He wanted a few minutes of privacy, and he could think of no other way to obtain them than by sending his valet on a fool's mission. He hadn't formed a sentence before Theodosia read his mind.

"Why did you say those things to me at the gallery?" She looked at him, sadness in her eyes. "Why begin something that we know cannot continue? I'm here in London for my grandfather's health only. I despise this city, a place you call home. I appreciate the extravagant day we're having and the time you're taking to escort me about, but you needn't whisper promises and lies in order to keep me entertained."

"I didn't lie. Nor do I make promises I don't intend to keep."

"You can't possibly possess strong feelings."

"Fair enough." He huffed a breath at being called out so directly. "We haven't known each other very long, but the fact that you intrigue me and I'm drawn to you remains an undeniable truth."

"It wouldn't matter anyway." She looked out the square window and her voice dropped lower. "Everyone leaves."

"I say we make no rules or decisions. What could they possibly accomplish?" He took up his walking stick and unlatched the carriage door. "Your grandfather is in capable hands at the moment. You've made your trip to the city to seek out an expert's opinion. In the meantime, we may as well enjoy what's left of day. Let's get inside."

"Distraction, you mean." She exited the carriage, her words trailing behind her. "My life is a long monotony of emotional distraction."

They climbed the steps to the amphitheater in silence, though from the corner of his eye he observed Theodosia's widening interest.

"Astley was a man with a vision far ahead of his time," Matthew shared as he gently steered her toward the bilevel stairs. "Upon his death, his son took over the family's enterprise and what you're about to see is unlike any other performance in London."

"I'm already fascinated. The building alone looks ordinary, but I've read in the London *Times* and other papers how outlandish and popular the performers are." She smiled. "I never anticipated seeing it for myself."

"The show has been labeled many things. Theater, equestrian drama, and circus extravaganza, but I attend for the unexpected enjoyment. The betters of London might look down their noses at Astley's precarious enterprise, but I'd rather peer up at the tightrope walker." He matched her grin. "Are you ready to enter? We're here in time for an afternoon show."

They'd reached the top of the stairs, where Coggs and Dora waited. Other people milled about, though none were dressed as finely. The venue was a wide wooden building with an unassuming front of limestone and plank. A railed wood fence encircled the area that met the street, and once one stepped through the gate, it appeared a world unto itself.

Theodosia's eyes rose steadily from the base of the building to the top of the roof, where a weathervane moved in the wind, featuring a man in fancy bright costume atop a white horse with a braided mane trimmed in wide ribbons. The outside of the building was covered with posters and portraits of every color and variety, all which depicted scenes of outrageous daring. There were women and men standing atop stallions, dancing dogs and ponies, as well as acrobats who appeared to be floating in the clouds.

"What will we see?" Her voice held a hint of awe. Matthew was a master at distraction, indeed.

"I haven't the slightest idea."

They ventured inside, with Coggs and Dora trailing behind them, and settled on a wooden bench near the top of the arena.

"The best view in the house I've discovered, although it nearly kills me to climb up here." Matthew pointed to a rigging of ropes and swings high above the amphitheater floor. "The swells, on the occasion they venture out to Astley's, are quick to fill the boxes below, and while it might be said one can note the color of the horses' eyes, the boxes sit so close, you can't appreciate the daring acts on the trapeze. And that is truly uncommon, isn't it?" He turned to see if she was listening and her avid expression showed her enthusiasm matched his own. "We can see horses anytime."

"Yes."

They settled at the sound of a whip cracking the air, and for a moment he appreciated the lack of conversation. He knew he'd supplied plentiful memories and distraction from anxiety today. Dr. Fletcher would likely have grim news upon the morrow. What purpose would it serve for Theodosia to be caged up in her hotel room thinking sullen thoughts and envisioning a bleak future? And while he didn't consider himself a hero or savior, whatever his role in her life, he wished to do his very best to bring her happiness if nothing else.

Theodosia folded her hands and unfolded them again in an attempt to settle her nerves. The day had proved as hectic and unpredictable as a runaway carriage wheel. What was she doing? Where was her usual composure and resolve? And how had she allowed that intimacy in the curator's alcove at the British Museum?

Ironically, it was as though she was the one no longer thinking clearly.

Yet she couldn't muster the emotion to regret one minute of the time shared with Matthew thus far. The day began with a visit to a physician who would likely relay distressing news tomorrow. But from that point forward, she'd found respite in adventure. Their visit to the apothecary alley was intriguing and interesting. The Marbles and artwork, equally so.

She'd seen the perfectly fashioned ladies at the gallery who'd given her a cursory glance and quick dismissal. Yet staring after them, she'd waited for a jolt of awareness to return her to the hurtful days at the academy, but that didn't happen. She wouldn't cling to memories or create ghosts of the present. She had a multitude of other troubles worth deliberation tomorrow. Now, she sat at the ready to enjoy a presentation of tumblers and animal tricks.

Yes, it was distraction, not a solution to the predicament. She couldn't dismiss the conflicted emotions twisting her insides tight. But coming out to see the unexpected sites as Matthew had promised, proved the right decision.

What had he to gain from all this? They'd shared an unlikely visit at Leighton House, which would always be a cherished memory. But beyond that, whether here in London or in Oxfordshire, the path forward seemed a rush into heartache. Any more kisses, embraces, and caresses would encourage her heart to become far too attached. *Truthfully, I already have sentimental feelings.* And to what end? The question pestered her brain in a relentless circle of emotion versus logic.

A single trumpet blast jolted her thoughts to the present and with no resolution except to enjoy the performance, she forced her eyes to the center stage.

Chapter Twenty-Two

It was nearly dusk when they exited Astley's Amphitheatre. They'd laughed, snacked on too many sugary treats, and lost themselves in the simplicity of the show's enjoyment. Still, reality greeted them on the other side of the door as they exited into the night. Matthew's carriage waited at the curb. It was time to return to Mivart's Hotel and claim some much needed rest. There were no more distractions to be had.

"Thank you." She hoped he heard the sincerity in her words. "I haven't worried over Grandfather's condition nearly as much as I might have. Your day of distraction has been a success." He really was a thoughtful, caring man. The remembrance of his strong, affectionate words at the British Museum rose up, but she forced them away.

"You're very welcome." He opened the carriage door and handed her inside. "With your permission I'd like to have Coggs escort Dora back to the hotel in a hansom cab. I hoped for a moment of privacy before returning you this evening."

Her pulse leapt into a faster rhythm. "Another moment of privacy?" She quirked a smile that granted him what he'd requested.

"Yes. I suppose so."

With arrangements made and Dora dispatched into Coggs's care, Matthew climbed into the carriage and they were off. But the conversation was nothing she might have anticipated.

"Tomorrow I will return to the Society for the Intellectually Advanced, where your grandfather's article has caused a high degree of conversation and speculation."

"My article, you mean."

"Yes." He cleared his throat, visibly uneasy. "There's no easy explanation for why the hypothesis set forth isn't valid. We attempted to replicate the results with little success, and then there's your grandfather's condition and inability to address the group directly. I don't wish for his reputation to be blackened."

"What are you trying to say?" She had no idea where the conversation was leading.

"Would you consider making a presentation on his behalf? I realize it's highly unusual, and for all your brilliant intelligence, those who possess a cynical, narrow-minded view might label you in an unfavorable light, but I see no other way to uphold Lord Talbot's reputation as an outstanding scientist and also provide a reason why the article is acceptable within its flawed theory. It provides an opportunity to answer questions and provide further information, despite the claims cannot be proven in the traditional manner."

"Are you suggesting Grandfather attend the presentation where I field the questions that might arise? I can't imagine a plan like that could succeed. Grandfather would interrupt, contradict, or worse, demand to be heard." She shook her head thoroughly.

"There is that."

"Meanwhile, I'm not confident in my own ability to answer questions from a room full of scholars."

"You should be. You've read every article your grandfather has written, duplicated his experiments, studied his documents and grown up at his side. That kind of tutelage is rare and unmatched. Much like you."

The compliment hung in the air between them, and while the carriage rattled over the cobbles, she wondered if he spoke the truth. Mayhap she could speak to the assembly. Would the gentlemen receive her with open-mindedness or skepticism? There was no way to know.

"Too much has happened today for me to consider this further." She wished she had a better answer. "I have Grandfather's health as my utmost priority. It's the reason I've come to London in the first place."

"Of course."

Thankfully, he let the matter drop, though the conversation didn't lag for long.

"What will you do, Theodosia?"

His question whispered across the dark interior and she wished he would turn the key on the lamp and raise the light so she could read the emotion in his eyes. She couldn't bear his pity. Or was it curiosity? Why did he care? All her emotions seemed tangled and knotted with not one thread leading to an end. "I don't know."

"You are alone."

"You needn't worry on my behalf. I need no rescuer." She told herself to believe those statements, though she remained unsure. No, that couldn't be true or else she'd have accepted Kirkman's offer.

"Of course not." His boots shuffled against the floorboards.

And then the carriage rocked to a stop.

"Good-bye, Matthew." The words held an unintentional and ominous note of finality.

"Until tomorrow, Theodosia." His were much more optimistic.

Neither of them moved.

"Kirkman will accompany me to Dr. Fletcher's office. You needn't do more. You've already inconvenienced yourself on my behalf."

"Not a chance another appointment will pull Kirkman away?" Matthew looked out the window as he answered. "I don't like the idea of you meeting with the physician without a friend nearby."

"I suppose it was a trip of dual purpose for Kirkman, but you needn't disrupt your schedule."

"That's an impossibility. You are very precious, indeed."

Words floated back and forth, though she didn't make a move toward leaving.

"I appreciate your help. I truly do." She reached across the space between them and touched her hand to his.

He clasped her fingers, folded them into his grasp and tugged her forward slightly.

Was this why she hadn't left? Had her heart insisted she wait for one more kiss?

"This isn't good-bye." His breath brushed against her temple as he leaned forward, the width between them reduced to a few inches. "We have unfinished business to attend to."

He didn't allow her the chance to answer and instead closed the remaining distance, his mouth on hers hot and demanding, a brand of sorts.

And she welcomed his kiss. Wanting his strength and reassurance. Wanting his comfort and attention. She wanted too many things and at the same time had no idea how she would ever forget him once she returned to Oxfordshire.

* * *

Matthew pulled Theodosia forward, settling her beside him on the bench. Her skirts overlapped to blanket his legs in layers of too much fabric. He shifted and angled his body so he could taste her mouth better.

He'd traveled to Oxfordshire to uncover a scientific fraud or learn an indisputable truth and instead discovered his heart. What was it about Theodosia that called to him? He couldn't label it, but this time evidence to support the hypothesis didn't matter. For too long he'd tried to squelch the fear he wouldn't find someone to suit his lifestyle, understand his personality and speak to his desire, and in an unlikely turn of events he'd arrived at the very destination he'd believed impossible.

The current location was more than he'd ever hoped for.

It took only a breath, but then with a little surrender sound, she matched his attention. Her hands crept up his chest to encircle his neck and he framed her face with his palms, anxious to keep them connected. His body reacted with a jolt of awareness, each muscle tight, while the kiss turned timeless, a symbol of what was to come, a long relationship of caring and affection, the promise of a future. He wanted to take her home with him. Feel her body against his. Skin to skin. Passion matched with curiosity and exploration. He wanted so much more than a kiss in a carriage before they parted for the evening. He had to convince her to stay. Now more than ever.

Theodosia's experience was limited. She recognized inordinate kindness, surprised by Matthew's actions and the extent of his dedication. He'd made it a point to speak to

Dr. Fletcher and then entertained her for the day so she wouldn't dwell on the inevitable truth concerning Grandfather's health. He'd been charming, handsome, generous, and lighthearted, and now . . . now he was everything a young woman could desire in a man.

Yet this kiss signified good-bye. She couldn't believe otherwise. Fear sent a pulse to her heart faster and stronger than his mouth upon hers. What if she opened her heart only to find rejection? What if she allowed herself to love and received hurt in return? Oh, she knew Matthew would never intentionally harm her, but fate had an unusual way of claiming the loved ones in her life. First her parents, and now Grandfather. She couldn't bear to fall in love and be left broken again. Loneliness didn't hurt nearly as much if nothing was at risk.

All these concerns crowded into her brain, stealing pleasure from his kiss, though she wrapped her arms around his neck and tried desperately to push the intrusive thoughts away.

But it was no use, and disappointed that she couldn't find pleasure in the moment, she broke away.

"Good-bye, Matthew." He couldn't know she meant forever. "Thank you for the day and for all you've done on my behalf. I speak for my grandfather as well."

He might have noted something telling in her expression, his eyes matched to hers with acute perspicuity. He was far too clever for his own good.

"Good night, Theodosia. It was my pleasure to share your company today."

They didn't say more and she exited, relieved to see Coggs waiting with Dora at the entry of the hotel. She went inside and didn't look back.

* * *

Matthew paced his bedchamber, his leg in mutiny of the repetitive action, but his body too restless to take ease otherwise. Something seemed amiss in Theodosia's tone when she'd bid him good night. It could be the anticipation of hearing Dr. Fletcher's observations. But then, it could be something altogether different.

He was no better the next morning. Distracted by thoughts of the news Dr. Fletcher would impart and Theodosia's reaction as she sat alone to accept the report, he called for his carriage and gladly left Coggs behind. The last thing he needed was unsolicited advice or petty gossip. Solitude and sensible thinking were his two greatest allies at the moment. And while he knew he was breaking her trust by persisting, he meant no disrespect. He cared for her. Deeply. He wasn't ready to say good-bye. She would have to accept his reason whether she liked it or not.

Arriving at the Society for the Intellectually Advanced, he accomplished the slate walkway quickly and approached the neatly bricked building with purpose in mind. He would converse with the other members present and perhaps review the schedule of planned speakers for the New Year, but by no means would he mention his trip to Oxfordshire. If Theodosia didn't care to present Lord Talbot's work, and another fascinating topic seized the interest of the members, let them forget his fact-finding mission altogether.

Pleased to see several familiar faces in attendance this morning, he moved toward his office down the hall. The library and drawing room were popular congregation areas and at the moment he wished to gather his thoughts and steal a modicum of serenity.

He glanced at the walnut longcase clock with its gleaming brass workings. His attention divided, he stared at the methodic sway of the pendulum before at last seeking the time. The hands were nearly at ten o'clock. Dr. Fletcher was due to return to his office with Lord Talbot at eleven. Kirkman was assisting Theodosia. Matthew's mood soured with the fact, but he couldn't dwell on it.

"Whittingham. What's kept you?"

Matthew turned to see Lord Rannings approach. They shook hands and proceeded farther down the corridor until he unlocked the door to his office and they entered. He placed his walking stick in the porcelain umbrella stand in the corner and claimed his chair behind the desk.

"Is there a problem that needs my attention?" He couldn't imagine what would cause Rannings to express concern over his whereabouts. He was a quiet member of the Society and rarely approached for conversation.

"No, although several members are interested in the findings from your trip to Oxfordshire. Myself, most of all. Lord Talbot couldn't possibly have achieved the results he detailed in his latest article. The chemical ratios and compounds suggested won't react and sustain existence in isolation. Dephlogisticated air is nothing more than a myth, and I challenge Talbot to prove otherwise." Rannings adjusted his spectacles as they slid down his nose, his impassioned debate having knocked them lower. "I hope you've discovered the truth and brought an explanation with you this morning. To publish an article when the experiment remains inconclusive is a misstep for the reputations of both the science community and the leading science journal in London."

"I agree." A twinge of guilt and compassion for Theodosia's situation brought his temper to the forefront. "But does it matter, Rannings? If you can prove otherwise, you should conduct contradictory research and pursue publication of your findings. Otherwise it might be in the best interest of all involved to excuse the matter as unsatisfying."

His reply stalled whatever rebuttal Rannings formulated, and the man eyed him with a trace of incredulity. "What?" He readjusted his spectacles, though this time they hadn't moved. "You left London in the harshest weather to seek out the truth and have returned with nothing more than a mild interest in the subject and a suggestion it's best left unchallenged? This isn't like you at all, Whittingham. Something strange is afoot. What did you discover? Did the old earl pay you to keep your trap shut?"

"Watch your step, Rannings. You've a suspicious mind." He mentally considered the best way to proceed. "I spoke to Talbot concerning his findings and while it might have been prudent to include a paragraph within the article that explained the results were not consistent, it matters little now. We are men of science and therefore appreciate all contributions, whether they achieve the desired result or fail miserably. It makes little sense to dwell on a past publication, however marred with error, when science is already moving forward."

Rannings appeared unconvinced, but sensing there wasn't any more discussion to be had, he nodded and moved to the door. "Perhaps, although I would like to discuss this further. Please keep this conversation in mind. If all scientific study is held to a flimsy standard, and errors are forgiven when they neither further science or enlighten the community, a grave injustice has been committed."

Rannings left and Matthew exhaled with relief. If he could convince Theodosia to stay in London, he could enact a change that would set the city on its ear. Rannings worried about inconsistent findings and the impact on modern science study, but what of society as a whole? The perception of females and their intelligence. The deflating of gossipy women or men, *Coggs came to mind*, and most of all, to the truth and proof that the workings of a woman's brain could be as powerful as the fluttering of their eyelashes.

He banged the desktop with his fist, all at once invigorated to seek out Theodosia. He needed to speak to her about a number of subjects. Of course, Dr. Fletcher's results were the most important, her well-being too, and the course for Talbot's care for the future. But then, if she was interested in the idea, he had a challenge to set before her. One which might restore her belief in the kindness of others as well as reconstitute confidence in herself. And too, he would be able to spend more time in her company and that was the sweetest reward of all.

Chapter Twenty-Three

Theodosia sat alone in Dr. Fletcher's office, her heart beating a frantic tattoo. She anticipated discouraging news and tried to prepare for the physician's opinion, but a foolish sliver of hope survived no matter how hard she attempted to squash it. Grandfather and Kirkman remained in the waiting room. Kirkman was a good man. She hoped he solved his problem, found a woman to marry and fulfilled whatever endeavor had him in a rush to the altar. *But I'm not that woman.* Last night she'd worked hard to convince herself life would be easier if she accepted his proposal and compromised her future, but the idea wouldn't take root. Now a sense of relief steadied her nerves. There was peace of mind in considering someone else's problems instead of her own.

Still, that calm was short-lived. She touched a hand to her throat to quell a threatening sob. Fear lived in her, no matter she did her best to face down every complication in her life. What would Dr. Fletcher say? She didn't want to be alone. This thought brought with it another. She missed Matthew. Already his absence caused unwanted longing as painful as an open wound. But Matthew was tied to London and London reminded her of every reason she belonged in

Oxfordshire. Her mind raced in an endless circle of confused emotion.

The office door opened, then closed, and Dr. Fletcher took a seat behind his desk, forcing her to focus on the present.

"Lady Leighton, thank you for visiting me here in London." Dr. Fletcher shuffled through a few papers atop the blotter before deciding on which one provided him the notes he needed. "It has been a pleasure to meet both you and Lord Talbot."

She leaned forward on the chair and attempted to read a few lines of his writing, albeit upside down, but he must have anticipated her interest and slanted the page upward, out of sight.

"Naturally the time I spent with your grandfather was limited and provided only a partial understanding of the difficulties he has experienced of late. The extensive information you provided combined with the hours I spent in his company yesterday proved useful in observing the interruptions pervading his otherwise typical daily life."

He paused, and Theodosia was unsure if she was meant to comment. She matched eyes with the doctor and offered a curt nod. She didn't trust herself to speak yet.

"It is my medical opinion that your grandfather suffers from dementia."

"Dementia?" Emotion raised her voice higher and she laced her fingers tight in her lap to evoke better control. "I don't understand. Please explain."

"Of course. Dementia is a state of semi-awareness, almost as if being out of one's logical thought processes while awake. Episodes of this kind range in length and may occur with no predictability. They can be long lasting, or frequent and abrupt, as well as cause drastic shifts in mood.

Otherwise good-natured people may become angry or disagreeable, and the reverse is true. At least that has been my finding as I've studied the human mind and its decline in the later years."

She forced a cleansing breath and tried to quiet her nerves. "Is there medicine to help improve his dementia or stop the episodes?"

"Unfortunately, there's nothing that will reverse the impact of the condition, but I can offer recommendations to help ease your grandfather's mind, and perhaps provide him a smoother transition into his final years."

"Will this cause his death?" She hardly whispered the question, but Dr. Fletcher answered promptly.

"Not as far as I've researched, although you should be prepared, Lady Leighton."

"Prepared?" She was having trouble breathing, every inhale a labor. "What do you mean?"

"I'm sorry, but my research has shown that the situation will not improve." Dr. Fletcher's expression became graver still. "It's always possible the dementia will not advance, but I'm aware of only a few such instances. More likely, the condition will worsen with time."

"Worse than now?" She clenched her eyes closed and opened them again. She could do this. She could care for her grandfather. She was strong and resilient. Life had forced her to be.

"Yes." He replaced the page on his desktop. "Lord Talbot may forget uses for everyday items and places he has visited many times before. He may repeat stories or forget familiar memories as the dementia progresses and his awareness declines. There may come a time when his behaviors become difficult to manage. He may act withdrawn or argumentative." The doctor paused and his voice gentled. "I'm afraid in the most serious incidents, people suffering from dementia lose a great deal of independence and need assistance to function through their basic daily routine. At its worst, Lady Leighton, your grandfather may not recognize his own family or the people who care for him every day. There may come a day when he forgets who you are."

She gasped. Spoken aloud, her greatest fear was a knife to the heart. She'd lost her parents so soon. Sharing her grandfather's company since the age of five didn't make the reality any easier to accept. She sagged against the chair and looked down at her hands, clutching her skirt so tightly her knuckles were white.

Then after what seemed a moment of unending length, she drew a shuddered breath, then another, and straightened her shoulders much the same way she'd managed all those years ago in finishing school. She would take care of the man who'd cared for her almost all her life.

"He's such an intelligent man. He's always possessed the sharpest mind. I don't understand how this can happen." Her voice sounded little more than a whisper.

"The human brain is a complex organ. I wish I had a more concrete explanation for why this occurs in some individuals and not others. I acknowledge your grandfather is an insightful, highly educated man, but in the case of dementia, education doesn't come to bear."

She looked toward the physician, beseeching him to offer her more. "What can I do? Please tell me how I can help him." Desperation laced her questions.

Dr. Fletcher cleared his throat and reached for a different piece of paper. "I have recommendations and will write a detailed report to forward to you. During the interim, try to carry on as normally as possible, with no sudden changes to disrupt your grandfather's current lifestyle or cause distress. Keep things familiar. I've found increasing evidence that participation in cognitively stimulating leisure activities that neither tax the brain nor agitate it may reduce the risk of the impairment becoming worse over time. He's an avid reader and should continue to do so. Conversation without censure is also a good idea. Don't contradict or correct him if his mistakes are unimportant. Allow him as much freedom as possible as long as he is safe."

"I understand." The doctor stopped speaking and she rose slowly from the chair, her mind numbed and her heart torn in two. "Thank you, Dr. Fletcher."

"You're welcome. I'm sorry the news wasn't more encouraging."

Forcing back her tears, she exited the office and returned to the waiting room, where Kirkman matched her attention as soon as he saw her. Grandfather stood by the window facing the street, apparently occupied by the traffic and flow of pedestrians outside.

"We should go." She eyed Kirkman and he stepped forward immediately, concern etched into his expression as soon as his eyes met hers.

"We'll go straight to the hotel. The carriage is right outside." He offered his elbow and she accepted, relieved to have someone to lean on, if only temporarily.

"Grandfather?"

He turned and smiled.

"It's time to leave." She extended her hand.

"This was a pleasant visit, wasn't it?"

"Yes." She swallowed past a lump of emotion. "It's time to collect our things and return home."

"A brilliant idea, Theodosia." Her grandfather joined

them as they approached the door. "An absolutely brilliant idea. What a fine time we've had here in London."

The skies had cleared and when they exited Dr. Fletcher's office and stepped out onto the pavement, the sunlight nearly blinded her to the bustling crowd. Lost in distraction she allowed Kirkman to lead her to his carriage and the three of them climbed inside, though her brain seemed to have ceased functioning with purposeful thought, so strong was the unbroken litany. *Soon grandfather will forget you. He will be gone and you will be alone.*

"Are you all right, Theodosia?" The soft-spoken question broke through her quietude and she looked at Kirkman with an expression of devastating loss.

"It's worse than I'd feared." She wouldn't elaborate despite Grandfather had closed his eyes, intent on a nap.

"I'm sorry." Kirkman shook his head slowly. "I'd hoped the physician delivered better news."

She didn't say anything to that.

"You don't have to be alone through this," Kirkman suggested. "I know I've presented my suit and circumstances, and you've politely refused me. *Twice.*"

"Henry." She was too tired, too sad and devoid of feeling to have this conversation.

"Hear me out." Kirkman glanced at her grandfather attempting to sleep on the bench, and back again, assured he wouldn't be overheard as he whispered, "If things are to grow more difficult, then having a husband and someone to rely on will benefit you. I need—"

"I know what you need." Her words came out razor sharp, but she couldn't stop, desperate to release some of the tension twisting her inside out. "You need a wife. Any wife. You've made that clear several times. And I'm sorry, Henry, truly I am. I don't know why you need to marry or why you need to hurry, but now isn't the time. We don't love each other. Not in the way of a husband and wife. All my life the people I've cared for have left me, through circumstances beyond my control. When I marry, when I finally find love, I want it to be everlasting. I'll do everything in my power to make that true, and forever cherish that gift."

She closed her eyes tight and forced away the ready image of Matthew. But it was too late. Envisioning him and remembering his kisses incited her anger toward Kirkman twofold. She didn't want Kirkman and she couldn't have Matthew. She wouldn't remove him from a city he loved, where everything he'd worked for was centered and thriving, and displace him to the countryside in near isolation to care for her sickly grandfather. She loved him too much to do that. Matthew would grow to despise her, and any love he declared would soon turn to resentment. "How dare you take advantage of my vulnerable mental state." The irony in the words wasn't lost on her and she blinked hard to stop the threat of tears.

"Forgive me, Theodosia." Henry pushed back on the bench to withdraw further. "I meant no harm. It was a suggestion to ease your worry. We could help each other. We need each other."

"No." She released a long-held breath. "In time we would recognize it for a rash mistake at a time of distress. We would begrudge each other for stealing away the chance at a different future, a better life. One composed of happiness instead of panic and fear." She said the words to Kirkman, but she knew they mirrored every reason she couldn't give her heart to Matthew.

Kirkman fell silent, and remained turned toward the window all the way back to the hotel. At last the carriage stopped. With only a brief word of parting, Theodosia led her grandfather upstairs where Collins waited. Once alone in her rooms, she washed her face in the basin and told herself not to cry, but the tears came anyway and she was powerless to make them stop.

Chapter Twenty-Four

"I'm going out. I'll need my coat." Matthew stopped wearing a path into the rug in his bedchamber and waited for Coggs to act.

"To your club, milord?" The valet moved toward the wardrobe. "It's rather late, almost midnight in fact."

"I didn't ask for your counsel. I asked for my coat." He had successfully resisted the urge to interfere in Theodosia's meeting with Dr. Fletcher, though he assumed the physician delivered a grim prognosis.

Had she prepared herself for such devastating news? Was she distraught? She showed the world a brave front, but he knew better. To that end, was Kirkman soothing away her despair at this very minute while Matthew battled with indecision? He wouldn't put it past the man to take advantage of Theodosia's vulnerability.

"And have Apollo saddled and brought around."

"Apollo?" Coggs censured his tone belatedly. "It's dark, and that beast of a horse is a rogue. I can have the carriage—"

"The carriage will slow me down and I'm in a hurry." He snatched his coat from his valet and started toward the door. "Why aren't you moving yet?"

"Yes, milord." This time Coggs's tone implied every unspoken word.

He would pay for his foolishness tomorrow when his leg enacted revenge. Traveling by horseback was barely manageable, but he'd wasted too much time vacillating to travel by carriage. He hadn't wanted to complicate things by showing up where he didn't belong. And yet, something inside wouldn't allow him to ignore the situation either. The bond and physical chemistry he shared with Theodosia were undeniably strong. That said, it would be a miracle if he achieved his goal and found her awake and willing to hear him out.

His valet might have considered him a nodcock, but true to his request, Apollo stood at the ready outside the town house on Cleveland Row. The horse was impressive, the strongest in the mews, and Matthew meant to capitalize on the animal's speed to deliver him to Mivart's Hotel as swiftly as possible.

Now that he'd climbed atop the Arabian he wondered why he'd hesitated, and with a knowing kick to the horse's flank they sped into the night. One luxury of such foolhardy travel was that the roadways were desolate aside from a few random coaches near Pall Mall. He made excellent time and dismounted with care, and a good thing he did. His leg already begged for relief. He ignored the pain and handed off the reins to a waiting stable hand behind the hotel. Then he moved inside with composed stealth, no matter his heart thundered in his chest. A few coins confirmed Theodosia remained a guest at the hotel, and he advanced to the stairwell, lost in concentration of what he would say when they spoke.

Upstairs the hallways were kept dark, but he strode directly to her guest room door without trouble. He refused to believe she would be asleep. If he perceived her reaction correctly, Dr. Fletcher's news would preclude the luxury of even fitful rest. He tapped lightly and waited, his effort rewarded immediately.

The door cracked open and just like the previous evening, Theodosia appeared on the other side, although tonight her lovely face portrayed sadness and defeat.

"Collins?" She widened the door a few inches more. "Is something wrong with Grandfather?"

"Bookish." He knew the one word would identify him if she didn't recognize his voice.

"Matthew."

Did he imagine he heard relief and pleasure when she'd whispered his name? He stepped closer, so much so only a few inches remained between them.

"Are you all right, Theodosia?" He gentled his tone, though he waited anxiously for her reply.

"The doctor's report . . ." She didn't finish the sentence and she didn't have to.

"Will you step into the hall?"

As expected, she was in her nightclothes and wrapper, nothing more than a scrap of white silk between him and her warm, soft skin. The wrapper clung to her body, leaving little to his overactive imagination. He forced the images away for later deliberation.

All he wanted was to offer her a shoulder of support and the knowledge that she didn't need to be strong at this moment. She wasn't alone.

She stepped across the threshold and left the door open a crack, just enough for lantern light to leak through. He noticed her hands were trembling, and when she followed his line of sight, she clasped her hands together in an effort to disguise her distress.

* * *

"You're here."

"I am."

Theodosia couldn't believe the one man she wished most to see had knocked on the door as if she'd conjured him from pure desperation and longing. How had he known she needed him?

Mayhap he didn't.

At least not for her reasons. She would ask.

"For a clandestine meeting in the hotel hallway?"

He flashed a quick grin. "To offer understanding and a shoulder to lean on."

He'd known.

"Although . . ." he continued, "I'm not opposed to the other."

Without hesitation, she fell into his arms and nestled against his coat, the wool heated despite the cold night air, the brush of his cravat a comfort against her cheek. *A strong shoulder indeed.*

She sniffled, but tears didn't come. For some reason, his being there and the knowledge he sought to ease her worry lessened her heartache. "Thank you."

He enveloped her in his arms tighter. "Your gratitude isn't necessary." He released a breath that teased the hairs on her forehead. "That's what"—he hesitated before he continued—"friends do for one another."

"Friends." She repeated the word and slid her hands inside his coat for added warmth. "I'm glad you're here."

They stayed that way for a long minute.

"Because we are friends, aren't we?" His voice was soft, though it rumbled through her as she pressed to his chest.

"Of course." She tilted her face upward as he lowered his chin, his mouth in direct line with hers. "Good friends."

"Yes, good friends." He murmured the words within his kiss.

She refused to think it wrong to seek comfort in his arms. Every minute of every day *and night* the reality of her grandfather's condition weighed heavily on her mind. A moment of respite and unexpected pleasure shouldn't cause her the slightest guilt. She needed to escape.

And his kiss became just that. An escape. An indulgence in thoughtless sensation. Pure pleasure and feeling. She allowed herself to soak up every nuance and secret them away in her heart. She pressed against his warmth, wrapping her arms tight while her hands smoothed over the muscles in his back. He groaned deep in his throat as she continued her exploration. Meanwhile, the kiss deepened, each stroke of his tongue evoking another rush of wanton desire, pulling her into his heat, wanting to be closer with no barriers in between.

"Very good friends."

He whispered across her cheek as he broke away from their kiss. She wondered if he, like she, wanted so much more but knew it was impossible.

"I wish I could change the circumstances concerning your grandfather's condition." His voice was low and husky in the darkness. She savored it, another balm to her unrest.

"I know." And she did. Unlike Kirkman, who sought to alleviate his own distress to her disadvantage, Matthew offered unselfish empathy.

She withdrew far enough to view him, but in the darkness caught the scent of his shaving soap more than the look in his eyes.

"I can't believe you've inconvenienced yourself in the middle of the night just to check on my well-being."

He didn't move, the corridor blacker than pitch. The beat of his heart against hers, strong and determined. "It's my pleasure." He shifted and separated them further, though she'd already detected the extent of his ardor. "So here we are in the hallway again, Bookish, you in your wrapper and me in my coat." There was an odd note in his voice as he spoke. "It's becoming a habit."

"I can't ask you inside. My maid is asleep."

"I know." His voice smiled with his reply and she imagined he thought better than to chuckle at her reasoning.

With that she realized how her words might have sounded. "I mean . . ." She floundered to recover but he didn't allow her the chance.

"And I can't whisk you away to my home. Alas, tonight I chose to ride out. Had I the carriage—"

"You rode? Does your leg pain you?" She wriggled in an attempt to size him up, but he wouldn't allow her to escape his hold far enough.

"I'm fit and fine." His voice held a stern note. "Most anything that matters is within my capabilities."

"I'm sure," she said at last. "I could never go with you anyway."

"I understand."

And she knew that he did. She rested her cheek against his chest, absorbing the warmth and strength he offered generously. "We leave this morning at first light."

"With Kirkman?"

"I suppose. At least, that's what we've planned."

They stood that way another moment, neither of them anxious to elaborate.

"I'm glad you're here." She angled her head upward and her lips brushed his chin. Sensation rippled through her. Desire, the intense longing to be close to him, began an incessant demand.

He lowered his mouth to hers in a kiss of infinitesimal tenderness. Her body craved a hard, claiming gesture.

Something to singe her soul and relieve her unfulfilled yearning. Instead his kiss did all that and more by way of a gentle caress, his lips upon hers, the knowing sweep of his tongue and delicious taste of his mouth.

In the morning, Theodosia greeted Henry with mixed emotions. She'd known Lord Kirkman for most of her childhood years. Only when he'd left for formal schooling and his Grand Tour did they spend long spans of time apart, and even then they'd exchanged an occasional letter. Yet despite their lengthy friendship, when she examined his familial history now, she found herself at a loss to recall anything to explain his imperative to marry as soon as possible. She'd always accepted his friendship at face value, never wishing to pry or invade his personal affairs. That said, she had scarce information to offer as evidence. The need to marry could only be a contingency to his future solvency, or why else would a gentleman willingly upset the natural course of things and sacrifice all choice and preference with insistent determination?

The return trip to Oxfordshire was quiet, and while Grandfather indulged in sporadic napping and cheerful conversation, Henry refrained altogether. His sullen expression displayed clear warning of his desire to be left alone.

With an equal desire to be ensconced in solitude, she spent the hours reliving Lord Whittingham's thoughtful consideration and midnight appearance at her guest-room door. The man was inordinately considerate. And thoughtful. *And handsome.* He possessed the gift of knowing exactly what she needed most when even she wasn't certain herself.

His kisses were another matter altogether. Passionate and reckless, they touched her soul and lived in her still, daring her to believe in the most potent magic or at least an enchanted version of physical chemistry only found in romantic literature.

The reality that her life didn't align with his, compounded how much she'd miss him, but her grandfather needed her most now. She wouldn't succumb to a foolish flight of fancy simply because Matthew's kisses melted her bones. Dr. Fletcher had advised she keep things as familiar and routine as possible. Uprooting her grandfather and transplanting him in London in a new home with different servants, away from the house he'd designed, was the most selfish act imaginable.

Additionally, his distinguished reputation would be at stake. The ton liked nothing more than the latest *on dit*, anxious to exploit news or invent information, whether it hurt those mentioned or thrust them into a poor light. She'd already learned that lesson. She couldn't foist that situation on her grandfather. One incident of public embarrassment, one sighting of his struggle, would overtake his prestigious accomplishments and label him foolish, or worse, *mad*.

Her battle of forced decision and unsettled discontent wandered down many paths in the endless hours of travel back to Oxfordshire. Christmas would be somber with the knowledge Grandfather's condition could progress until the impending outcome, when he might forget her identity altogether. That singular fact cleaved her heart most of all and weighed heavily on her mind. It stole the joy that usually accompanied the approaching festive season. She would plan for the sparsest acknowledgment of the holiday. There really wasn't anything to celebrate this year anyway.

She glanced at Kirkman, silent in the seat across from her. Feeling rejected, Kirkman would likely avoid Leighton House too. She struggled to form a convincing list of reasons to support the hypothesis that this development was for the best. She'd always found amusement in his company, at least until his recent string of proposals. Mayhap he would be forced to attend to his responsibilities, now that she'd refused him repeatedly.

Despite these grave misgivings, time passed quicker than anticipated, and a week after their return from London a delivery arrived with no explanation or card. The following days brought box after box, one and then another, all delivered by private carrier. Alberts had the cartons set in the front drawing room, and it wasn't until a fortnight into December and things had settled back into normalcy that Theodosia lent them her attention. Once examined, the packages revealed labels marked *fragile* and *perishable*. Another one was addressed specifically to her. She placed that particular carton to the side and set about the task of opening the others. They contained no cards, but it was simple to deduce who'd sent the thoughtful gifts.

There were finely crafted beeswax tapers of every variety, and stout lantern pillars with long-burning wicks in festive colors of green and white. One box contained nothing but decorative pine cones infused with the rich scent of cinnamon and cloves. The fragrance embraced the air with cheerful spirit as soon as she lifted the lid. A weighty carton contained a lovely set of silver candlesticks, their bases detailed with intricately etched snowflakes, along with several doilies of the finest blond lace, so light and gauzy they whispered against her skin as delicate as cobwebbing. She immediately recalled the sleigh ride she'd shared with Matthew and the wondrous beauty of the landscape after the snow. Her cheeks had stung from the bracing cold but his kiss heated her from the inside out.

There were foodstuffs too, sweetmeats and candied orange peels, hardbake, peppermint comfits, and caramel drops. Her teeth ached at their mouthwatering appeal, though a smile curled her lips in amusement. They'd indulged in too many treats at Astley's Amphitheatre. The memory of that day evoked a smile whenever she considered the tumblers and contortionists, the decorated ponies and jolly dogs in costume.

And still there was more. With careful diligence, she unpacked lavish ribbon-tied boxes of apricot tarts and sugary cakes in flavors of lemon, poppyseed, and currant. Gingerbread biscuits and a canvas pouch of fresh chestnuts were also included. Scented tinder was packaged with long, elegant matches in a sleek tin case, as well as wide festive ribbons in gold and red hues strewn through crystal ornaments blown from glass so fine and delicate they appeared as if no more than a child's daydream.

Overwhelmed by the gesture and immersed in the spirit, she looked about the room with tears in her eyes. She hadn't planned on decorating to a great extent but now realized she couldn't forsake Christmas. This holiday might be the last she and Grandfather shared. Once again, Matthew had proven how well he knew the secrets of her heart. Like elusive ghosts of the future, his intuition provided her memories before she anticipated how well she would regret not having them.

She touched a hand to her cheek, the thought bittersweet. Only two boxes remained. Incredibly touched by the sentiment found within each package, she approached the larger box, a heavy crate, and carefully lifted the lid to reveal four large jars of marmalade, each a different flavor. Tears stung her eyes and overflowed this time. She bit into her lower lip, her heart thudding a melancholy beat. She might have stayed that way too long if she hadn't heard the door open behind her.

"Theodosia? What's all this?"

Her grandfather approached in his nightclothes and robe, a curious expression on his face. She smiled. She would always remember this evening.

"A rather large shipment of Christmas, I believe. The holidays have arrived whether we like it or not." She wiped at her wet cheeks and turned with a broad smile.

He came to stand beside her and peered into the box she'd opened only moments before.

"Marmalade," he stated matter-of-factly. "Indeed, how your grandmother loved marmalade. She would spread it atop her bread every morning. I do miss her dearly."

Nothing was said after that. The fire crackled and Theodosia watched her grandfather, his eyes focused on the jars in the carton, his expression reminiscent and loving. Could it be his mention of marmalade, the demand for it, was really an outcry for the wife he loved so many years ago? Theodosia wondered if she'd had it all wrong.

Perhaps in his episodes of confusion, Grandfather wasn't behaving foolishly or being stubborn, but instead yearned for something else entirely. *Someone else.* For lost love. For times past. For her grandmother. His wife. Theodosia could never know.

"I think I'll retire now, Theodosia. Good night."

Did she imagine the note of longing in his voice?

She watched him go and then turned her attention to the mess she'd made in the drawing room. She'd send in a few footmen to see to the food items, but the decorations could wait until tomorrow. Matthew had thought of everything save the evergreen garland and sprigs of holly. In the morning, she'd trim the Scotch firs and decorate with their boughs to bring a little of the outdoors in.

She scanned the room again and her eyes came to rest on the box she'd placed aside. This one she would save for Christmas Day. For what it was worth, she'd like to have privacy when she unwrapped his last gift. A special moment, no matter what lay within.

Chapter Twenty-Five

"Having already traversed this distance, I'd hoped the ride would pass faster."

Coggs voiced his complaint and Matthew paid no heed. "At least you're inside the carriage this time." He couldn't help but taunt his valet for his insufferable mood. "Unless you'd rather ride with George. I'm sure he'd enjoy the company on the driver's seat."

This comment was met with a stony stare.

They'd set out at noon, and now as the hour grew later and the sun began to set, a chilling cold permeated the interior, no matter how finely made the carriage. They had several blankets for warmth, but the bricks near their feet long ago lost their warmth. Matthew stretched his leg as much as possible, the cramped confines and extensive travel not conditions conducive to comfort. But he had no complaints. In two days it would be Christmas Eve, and he'd managed to plan, prepare, and execute everything needed in just enough time.

"You know I predicted this outcome, don't you?"

"What are you talking about, Coggs?"

His valet leaned against the upholstered bench with a smug look. "Soon after the first time we journeyed out here, I mentioned you were taken with the lady."

"Lady Theodosia?" He bit back a smile. In less than an hour he would see her again. "I don't know what you're talking about."

"You're a terrible liar." Coggs let out a bark of laughter. "Besides, it doesn't suit you. At last I've discovered something of your person that isn't achieved to perfection."

"I merely wish to bring some holiday spirit to Lord Talbot and his granddaughter. There's nothing wrong with showing kinship and generosity, most especially during the Christmas season."

"I agree, although I see the way your eyes light whenever you speak of her." Coggs chuckled again. "You may as well let me in on the truth."

"I just have." Matthew pushed the curtain aside and looked out the carriage window. They were nearly there. Would Kirkman be underfoot? Matthew had poked around for details of the man's whereabouts at White's last night but come away with sparse information. Had the cad proposed again, or worse, somehow convinced Theodosia that marriage to him was a viable option?

Matthew had intended to write. To check on her welfare and inquire if Lord Talbot was settled into his daily routine again. At first, he thought to allow her time to process the news Dr. Fletcher imparted. But after a week passed and he'd put pen to paper, the words wouldn't come. He'd sat at his desk wondering how a letter that listed the words *I miss you* over and over again would be received. He didn't wish for Theodosia to have sentiments forced upon her, feelings she'd rather keep at bay, and he made no assumption she held him in high esteem. She'd pointedly deflected his confessed sentiments at the British Museum.

When letter-writing failed him, he had taken to considering the holidays. One couldn't walk about the city without some reminder that Christmas fast approached. Theodosia would be somewhat alone with the physician's recent distressing news. Before coming to London she'd likely accepted the changes in Lord Talbot and gone about life as usual, but having spoken to the doctor there would be no escaping the prognosis for the future, and that was difficult news to harbor by oneself at what was traditionally the most joyful celebration of the year. Besides, hadn't she mentioned this season was usually a cheerful time to brighten the year's end, before January and the memories of her parents' death caused heartache?

"I can't remember a time when you've enmeshed yourself in the holidays to such exacting detail. The two carriages that follow are packed to capacity."

"I'm bringing Christmas to Leighton House. Did you expect me to leave anything behind?"

"See, I told you the lady has captured your notice."

"Perhaps, but it's more than that." He smiled slightly. "I want her to notice—"

"When you're around?" Coggs asked too anxiously.

"More so, when I'm not."

"I would wager Lady Leighton will be happy to see you."

"One can hope, though we're arriving without an invitation this time. I hope the household receives us with good tidings."

He wondered now if this all wasn't a mistake. Servants and staff were already overworked and extremely busy this time of year. His arrival would add unexpected duties to their schedules. Worse, he'd invited his sister and her husband, due to arrive before the week's end. He hoped Theodosia welcomed his company. What was meant as a brilliant idea was fast becoming tarnished in his mind.

They rocked to a stop and Matthew caught his walking stick from where it fell forward. The carriage dipped as George hopped from the box, the clack and slap of the wooden steps being extended the next sound that met his ears. Then, before the door fully opened and he exited the interior, a discordant sense of foreboding and ominous tremor of distress blanketed his jovial mood.

Theodosia wiped the tears from her eyes and entered the singed skeletal remains of her childhood home. She had slipped out of the drawing room where Grandfather napped by the fire, and with only her cloak for protection, kept a brisk pace all the way to this spot. She didn't plan on staying outside long, just enough time to whisper a prayer to her parents and conjure a feeling of love and loss. It was her own melancholy holiday tradition and one she didn't share with Grandfather for fear he would worry on her behalf.

The holiday season always evoked tumultuous emotion. She had vivid memories of Christmas morning with her parents, the gift giving and delicious feast afterward, the laughter and utter happiness. But now the cold night air bit through her cloak and seeped into her bones, warning her to hurry. Too much time spent here would invite a chill from the inside out, and then who would take care of Grandfather? That dreadful thought echoed over all others.

She repeated a vow she told herself often. She could do this. She could care for the man who cared for her all her life. She didn't need help beyond the household staff. Not Kirkman, or *anyone else.* She wouldn't invite servants who might tell stories out of turn about her grandfather's decline, or commit someone, *Matthew*, to a compromised life he wasn't meant to live.

The weight of these decisions sent her pulse skittering into an erratic rhythm and she moved farther into the ruined house, careful in the dusk on the uneven ground, where overgrown clumps of roots and other debris were abandoned to nature's care. She didn't enter the old house often. Too many memories, or mayhap, useless regrets, crowded in and caused her undue pain. She'd made an impetuous decision to come out here tonight, a sudden wish to connect with her parents, despite darkness approached and she'd be better off visiting in the morning. At times she believed she could still smell the scent of firewood ash and burnt memories, but often dismissed the thoughts as vagaries. Nothing more than a mixture of poor memory and wishful thinking.

Life had settled since they'd returned from London, and while Grandfather still had a few episodes of upset, for the most part things hadn't unraveled significantly. Of course, not many days had passed and the looming reality that the dementia could advance at any time without notice remained frightening.

She cast her eyes to the sky and located a star in wait of a wish. Then she turned to hurry back to the house, careful to avoid the fallen beams and disguised footprint of the house she once knew as a child. She'd almost cleared the uneven remains when she heard an unexpected sound and crack of twigs underfoot. Her eye saw a blur of movement. She scanned the land before her though darkness fell rapidly now. The house aglow in the distance offered no light to where she stood.

A flash of light caught her attention, and too intelligent to believe in ghosts of the past, she recognized her grandfather in his nightshirt.

"Grandfather. You'll catch your death out here without a coat."

She lurched forward, anxious to reach him and usher him back to the house. She never should have left the room and slipped out in a selfish desire to spend a few minutes alone. Her grandfather looked up and smiled, seemingly proud he'd managed to elude any servant who might have kept him under watch.

Theodosia hurried. Her cloak snagged on a fallen beam and she snapped it loose, unwilling to take her eyes off her grandfather, though mindful steps would prove prudent. She'd almost reached the perimeter of the house when the earth shifted under her feet. She threw her arms out to regain her balance but it was of no use. She fell, through roots and a snow-soaked layer of soil, down into the burnt-out hole of what was once the house wine cellar. She'd known it was to be avoided, that area of the floor plan unstable and dangerous, but she hadn't given a care in her rush to reach her grandfather.

She landed with a thud on her side, in complete blackness, down at least six feet with no way to climb the walls. Drawing a quick breath, she ascertained she'd only become scared, not injured, though her hip would be sore for having taken the bulk of the impact.

How would she climb out? Who would find her? She stood, her legs wobbly at first, and called above.

"Grandfather! Help! Can you hear me?" Would he respond? She couldn't lure him to the edge of the hole for fear he would fall in too, and he would never survive the drop. But would he realize what happened? Would he return to the house and summon help? Panic gripped her but she pushed it away, unwilling to believe she was powerless to find a way out. Mrs. Mavis or Alberts would realize she'd gone missing, but would Grandfather be able to communicate what occurred? There were too many unknowns.

In a practice of science and logic, she listed the facts at the ready to form a solution. It was late, dark and cold. She had only a thin cloak for protection against the frigid temperature. She was in an unexpected location, below eye level, far enough from the house that her voice would not be heard. Grandfather was the only person who knew where she had fallen.

It was a dismal list, at best.

Hadn't her life been equally dismal? Until lately, actually. Until Matthew. Grandfather's condition might be difficult, but somehow whenever Matthew was with her, she didn't doubt her abilities. She didn't want to spend the rest of her life alone. But she also didn't want just anyone to be with her. She wanted Matthew. And that was the most important reason she needed to find a way out.

She moved toward one of the walls, smoothing her hand over the dirt in the darkness. A shower of loose soil and debris pelted her feet. There were thick roots protruding in some areas, though she couldn't determine their size and strength to know if they'd offer support. And from what she could see, they didn't reach the top of the hole, the knotty clusters not high enough to be of any help. To climb, lose purchase, and fall backward into the wine cellar again would guarantee broken bones. It was a miracle of sorts only her hip ached at present.

She closed her eyes and summoned strength. The thought of spending the entire night in the raw air on damp, charred soil, brought tears to her eyes before she could stop them, but she blinked them away. She could do this. She wouldn't die a few days before Christmas in a house that once tried to steal her life and dreams. This house had already taken too much from her.

"Lord Whittingham. Good evening."

Alberts opened the door wide and welcomed them into the foyer of Leighton House.

"It seems I have the habit of arriving at unexpected

hours. Forgive us, Alberts. We made good time despite we landed on the doorstep at this late hour." Matthew passed off his greatcoat to a waiting servant. "My driver has taken our carriage around back and two more conveyances have followed. We have, in fact, brought the holiday season with us." He scanned the interior of the hall, gladdened to see several of the decorations he'd forwarded strewn in festive display. "May I inquire as to Lady Leighton's and Lord Talbot's whereabouts?" He was anxious to see her, hardly able to contain his own enthusiasm at seeing her shock upon his arrival. He hoped it was a pleasant reception. Coggs had planted a seed of doubt that intruded on his better intentions now, and for some reason, he knew he wouldn't feel comfortable until he saw Theodosia.

"Of course, milord." Alberts crimped a stiff smile. "Right this way."

Alberts opened the double doors of the front sitting room, where a large fire burned in the box to suffuse the interior in a warm glow. He noted the crystal ornaments that adorned evergreen garland strewn across the mantel, but had no time to appreciate it further as the clap of the French doors banging against the wall pulled his attention across the room. "Alberts, what's this?"

He quickly stepped inside, the butler behind him, to examine the vacant room. "Would Lady Theodosia venture outside this late at night? The temperature's dropped considerably." Something was wrong. He knew it warranted no further discussion and moved toward the open doors without delay. "Summon the servants, Alberts. Put together a group with lanterns and blankets. Something isn't right." He didn't remain to say more and rushed through the French doors and farther out onto the property, his fancy boots little help, his limp ignored for the time being, and only the support of his walking stick in the blackness.

He stepped lively, though he was not as familiar with the terrain as he'd have liked. He recalled his explorations when using the sleigh and the pathways he'd traversed, though he didn't assume he'd find Theodosia and Lord Talbot at the stables. Something told him to explore the ruins. It was a gut feeling at best, but he wouldn't ignore the innate intuition. Science was sometimes mystery as much as fact.

He cursed repeatedly, impeded by his compromised pace, uneven terrain, and blasted darkness. He called out several times, but he only heard the echo of his own desperation. Each step reminded him of the cold, his muscles already cramped from travel. How long would Theodosia and her grandfather last in the brittle weather? Had harm come to one of them? His heart demanded he hurry.

He advanced to the end of the estate and out into the open field. In his mind's eye he could see the ruins, but without the help of moonlight, he couldn't be sure he walked in the right direction. And then a flash of white in a far field caught his attention. He hurried, ignoring the pain that shot through his calf and wrapped around his knee, and the throbbing cramps that plagued his thigh muscles. He used his walking stick more and more, the tip anxious to sink into the damp grass, but he refused to be hindered further. He could see more closely now. The flash of white was a person. Lord Talbot. In his nightclothes? Alone. The aged earl was rushing forward at a faster pace than Matthew could advance. That was a sorry fact he would put away for deliberation another time.

"Whittingham." Lord Talbot came to stand in front of him, an expression of intense distress on his face.

Matthew took the moment to catch his breath, though he waited anxiously for Talbot to speak again. "What is it? Where's Theodosia?"

"She's fallen. She needs you." Talbot turned and waved in the direction he'd come. "You must come."

Matthew had never seen the earl so lucid. In a time of crisis Talbot had managed not to diminish his focus or become overwrought. Matthew sent a prayer of thanks heavenward and continued after the earl as fast as his legs would allow.

"Careful now." Talbot beckoned him forward. "The earth is uneven and overgrown here. Theodosia fell near this spot."

"Is she well? Did she sprain an ankle?" He was out of breath, but he wouldn't stop. Not when Theodosia needed him. He loved her and he intended to tell her so and cause her to believe. He'd made dramatic changes in his life leading up to this visit, and he wasn't about to have it all for naught when their future together remained so close.

"No." Talbot stopped long enough to turn and eye him with urgency. "She's fallen through the soil. Into the underground wine cellar at the rear of the old house."

"What?" His heart paused in its beat before it lurched forward again. He couldn't move fast enough. What if the fall had broken bones or knocked her unconscious? What if the impact caused one of the dirt walls to collapse? A vision of soil and rocks tumbling in on Theodosia had him begging his legs to move faster. The human body could live only three minutes without oxygen. Brain damage, nerve impairment, and a series of awful consequences began a chain reaction as air deprivation set in. Bloody hell, he'd talked with Alberts longer than three minutes in the foyer upon his arrival. It was wasted time. He should have told her his feelings. And been more adamant, convincing her of his sincerity. Damn his prevarication. But he hadn't wanted to pressure her when she struggled with the turmoil evoked by Dr. Fletcher's news.

At last Talbot slowed and motioned to an area to the left.

"Theodosia!" he yelled, loud enough to wake the dead.

For the longest moment, there came no answer and then—

"Matthew? Matthew!"

"Bookish!"

He walked gingerly, closer to her voice. He wouldn't rush upon the hole and cause its collapse now that he'd heard her call and knew she'd survived.

"Theodosia, are you well?" Talbot called, his question filled with concern.

"Grandfather." A wealth of relief accompanied the word. "I'm fine. Thank heavens you are too."

Did he hear tears in her words?

A commotion in the distance pulled his attention toward the estate. Coggs and George appeared along with two stable hands. "Coggs, give me that lantern." He reached for the light and turned toward Talbot next. "Return Lord Talbot to the house before he catches a chill. Use George's lantern to guide you. Have these servants return here with blankets and light. In the meantime, I'll see to Lady Theodosia."

"Milord, your leg."

"Stuff it, Coggs, and do as I say." He turned away and began to move closer to the collapsed wine cellar. His valet and driver left with Lord Talbot, and in the distance he could already see the bobbing lanterns of other servants on the approach. But he'd be damned if anyone but he rescued Theodosia.

"Please tell me what happened." He needed to keep her busy talking while he surveyed the area. He set the lantern down beside his walking stick before he lowered himself to the ground at the edge of the hole. Slowly he lowered the light in an attempt to see her. It was still too dark, but at least he could make out the dusky image of her face below. "There you are."

"Here I am."

She smiled and his heart filled with relief. She was all right.

"Out for a little stargazing?" He attempted levity. "Every scientist worth his weight knows the stars are aboveground, Bookish."

"It was a foolish idea to come out here while Grandfather slept by the fire. I've been feeling . . ."

Her voice dropped away and he abandoned the task of formulating how he'd reach her. He extended his arm and moved the lantern lower. "Alone?"

"More than that. I'm quite accustomed to feeling alone. But this is more . . ."

Again her voice fell away, and when she looked upward, he saw the truth reflected in the silver glitter of her eyes.

"Incomplete?" He cleared his voice and held her gaze. "I only suggest the condition because I'm a sufferer myself." He nodded. "Since you've left London, actually."

"I'd rather not discuss London," she answered quickly.

"Of course. Now's not the time." He set the lantern down on the rim of the hole and adjusted his position.

"How's your leg? I hope you haven't punished it to hurry out here. I'm well. Just a bit cold."

He almost laughed at her self-reliance, though her inquiry supplied him the missing piece to the puzzle. "Here. Grab on."

He leaned his arm as far over the edge as possible, his walking stick extended down into the hole. She climbed upward with the help of assorted roots that stuck out from the dirt walls, but to release them and grasp onto his stick would require a leap of faith, and he wasn't sure his body could withstand the jolt of her added weight. He tightened his fingers around the ivory knob and waited.

When she made the move, his body lurched forward, the brunt of her weight almost pulling his upper body over the edge, though he held on, planted his toes in the soil, and slowly raised her up. She scrambled against the wall and climbed over the rim to lie on the cold soil next to him. It was a blessing she was such a delicate slip of a lady. His body was spent.

They were both breathing deeply, their exhales steamy clouds between them.

"Bookish, you—"

He never had the chance to finish. Her mouth sealed over his, the words lost, but he'd never complain.

Chapter Twenty-Six

Theodosia toweled dry, her body ahum with vigor and excitement. It was past midnight, but she'd lounged over-long in the hot tub, anxious to absorb the soothing warmth of her lavender bath. Matthew had come to Leighton House. She still couldn't believe his thoughtful gesture. Not just in sending the holiday decorations ahead when she might have eschewed the joys of Christmas altogether. But he'd arrived with a veritable bounty more. Foodstuffs and packages, the likes of which she'd never experienced.

Grandfather was well, safely tucked in bed. His clarity tonight when she might have come to harm lingered as a sign of hope, and she clung to it as a miracle of sorts. There was no way to predict the future, but if she interpreted the facts correctly, at least she wouldn't face those days alone.

Now, dressed in a fine linen night rail, the loveliest she possessed, with a clean silk wrapper on top, her hair un-bound, she donned her slippers and left her bedchamber, intent on a reconnaissance mission of her own. The hall-way was silent, the flickering lamplight the only glow, though she was fairly certain her anticipation shone from the inside out.

When she reached Matthew's guest room she knocked twice and waited. He answered swiftly, almost as if he'd hoped she'd come. At least, that's what she chose to believe. He was dressed in fresh clothes, his hair still damp from his bath, and while he wore no cravat and his shirtsleeves rolled up, his state of casual handsomeness caused her heart to race.

"Theodosia." He said her name as if an endearment.

"I thought I'd show at your door for a change."

He smiled with her reference to his visits at Mivart's Hotel.

"Are you in pain?" His eyes dropped to her hip and up again. "Did a bath help? I have ginger salve."

"I find this all an odd role reversal." She couldn't keep amusement from her voice.

"You look so tempting standing there in your night-clothes, as if you've just walked out of my dreams."

"Thank you for your brave rescue." She whispered the words, filled with awe and sincerity.

He leaned forward, and when she thought he might kiss her, he angled his head right and left to peer up and down the hall.

"It's into the wee hours. What are you doing?" she whispered.

"Checking to see if Kirkman is about, at the ready to drop another proposal at your feet."

She giggled at his feigned jealousy, the laughter bubbling up and out in a too loud shriek of happiness.

He didn't say more, and reached out and hooked the belt of her wrapper to gently tug her forward into his rooms. She might have gasped, she couldn't be sure, but when he reversed their position and backed her up to the door with the strength of his kiss, she went completely breathless anyway.

And heated.

Feverish, actually.

It was as though she'd been waiting, holding her breath, each beat of her heart counting the moments until she would return to his arms. Emotion, stronger than any physical desire, lodged in her chest beside the words she had longed to say ever since she left him in London. She loved him. She wanted to share her life with him. It didn't matter where, just that they were together.

Tonight, she offered more than her heart.

Tonight, they sealed their promise to each other.

He worked the knot in her belt, quick to slip the fabric free, down her shoulders in a silky puddle at her feet.

He kissed her deeply, his tongue mating with hers in a prelude to what was to come. Her pulse hitched. She wanted to touch him everywhere. Be touched by him. He traced the ribbons at her neck where her night rail was fastened, each stroke against her skin more intriguing. Her thoughts splintered in a thousand directions while heat came in a rush of sensation to arrow straight to her core. She didn't know what to expect, his kisses incendiary alone, but this—this contact was indescribable pleasure. Everywhere he touched, when he skimmed his fingertips over her shoulders, traced her spine or grazed her breast, the powerful awareness of his intimate caress reverberated to her soul.

She swallowed, at a loss for words, and placed her hand against his chest. He was all smooth muscle, his skin heated beneath her fingertips, and for the slightest moment before he moved, she felt the steady thrum of his heartbeat against his palm.

"Bookish . . ."

He murmured against her mouth and she wondered what could be so important he'd interrupt their kiss.

"You've never . . ." He nuzzled her neck, licked past

her clavicle, his hot breath against her throat an erotic invitation.

"No."

She felt his smile.

"But you want to . . ."

"Yes." She couldn't be more emphatic. "Stop talking already."

And he did, sweeping her into his arms to carry her to the four-poster bed. He set her down on the mattress with deliberate grace and the room grew so quiet she could hear each one of their breaths.

She knew the intricacies of lovemaking. She understood the physiology of human copulation. What she hadn't anticipated was her body's reaction. The desire for sensual discovery. The need for *more* that became a force like she'd never known.

Without waiting, she lay back on the mattress and watched through lowered lids as Matthew undressed beside the bed. His muscles flexed and caught a sheen from the flames in the firebox. All the while it was she who felt afire. Burning from the inside out. Heated. Flushed. Anxious. A mixture of every emotion bombarded her with restless urgency.

His body was beautiful. Strong shoulders tapered down to a trim waist, the ridges of his stomach defined in artistic detail that rivaled the Marbles they'd viewed at the British Museum. A thin line of dark hair trailed from his chest to his abdomen, where it dipped below his waistband. She followed that line as he continued to undress, his hands on the buttons of his trousers before he continued and removed his smalls. She admired his broad back that angled down to firm, muscular buttocks, indented beneath smooth skin to where his thighs were dusted with dark hair. She saw his erection as it jutted from his pelvis and shot her eyes up to his. He had the audacity to quirk a smile.

"I told you that side by side on the mattress, my bullet wound holds little significance. I'm as hot-blooded and randy as any other male."

She wanted to laugh, but nothing rose in her chest. Instead, she sat up and watched him watch her. Wanting to please, she untied the ribbons at her shoulders and slowly loosened the ties until the silky fabric fell to her waist and bared her breasts. His eyes flared, golden-brown, then went darker with wicked arousal. His expression promised unending pleasure.

He stayed her hand when she went up on her knees to remove her night rail.

"Allow me." His husky timbre sent a shiver through her but she dropped her hands to her sides and granted him permission.

He gathered the lacy fabric in his fist and swept it from her. Everywhere his hands touched her skin burned with desire. She savored how her body reacted to his in anticipation, how she grew anxious and wet, a restlessness deep inside now building with intensity.

He skimmed his knuckles down the side of her thigh, a featherlight brush against the delicate skin and across her core with the lightest touch. She trembled with want, but she said nothing, too entranced by her body's demands.

"You're so beautiful, love." He climbed atop the bed, caging her body beneath his as he kissed her firmly on the mouth. He withdrew and placed kisses down the side of her neck, the new growth of whiskers across his chin burning her skin with a delightful pain. "I want to make you mine. I need to make you mine. I can't wait any longer, Theodosia."

He moved down her body, his chest hair brushing her

breasts in the most pleasing and infuriating caress. He licked into her navel. Pressed a lingering kiss to her abdomen and then settled between her legs.

"What are you doing?" She raised up on her elbows, alarm causing her pulse to beat harder.

"I'm giving you the pleasure you deserve." His breath caused her thighs to quiver.

"I—"

She lost all interest in speech once he touched his mouth to her sex. A surge of sensation, white hot and powerful, drenched her to the core as his tongue stroked over her. She swallowed, willed herself to breathe, and dropped back to the mattress, caught between outraged objection and the greedy demand that he never stop. She closed her eyes and melted into the bedding.

Every stroke of his tongue *there*, each taste and lick, brought a wave of intense pleasure that rippled through her. Her legs trembled with need until his palms found her thighs, the press of his fingertips against her soft folds erotic as he opened her to taste her deeper.

She cried out, shocked by her inability to control emotion. Clutching the bed linens in her fists, she rocked from the purest, most blissful wave of gratification she'd ever known.

Still drifting in semi-awareness, she felt the mattress shift as he climbed above her, the damp heat of his erection against her sensitive skin causing yet another tremor of climax.

"Look at me, Theodosia."

She didn't. Sanity had returned and the realization of what she'd allowed to happen, what he'd chosen to do to her body, was too overwhelming to process. Nothing in her research had mentioned *that*.

"You're a very sensual woman." He nuzzled the side

of her neck with a string of soft kisses. "I hope you know that."

She couldn't answer, though she realized a beat later he wasn't waiting on her reply. He shifted again, and this time the subtle press of his erection against her core evoked relief most of all.

"Matthew."

His head came up. One dark lock fell over his brow, lending him a reckless, disheveled look. "Yes, love."

"I need to feel you inside me." She inched her palms up the lengths of his arms, braced with his weight on either side. She circled her fingers halfway around his muscles. "I need to feel you."

He groaned his agreement, nudging her thighs wider and angling his hips close. She knew he sought to be gentle, but she thought differently. She wrapped one leg around his hips and thrust upward, encouraging him to find her anxious and waiting.

Matthew didn't wish to scare her. He'd done that already and cursed the outcome. He didn't wish to hurt her. He'd regret that forever. But when Theodosia wrapped her thigh around his hips and opened beneath him, all wet, hot, and luscious, he knew any plan for tempering his body's commands would prove useless. He'd touched her and tasted her into sensual arousal. He hoped now she was prepared for him. He sank into her lush heat and shook with pleasure. She was tight, her muscles quick to accommodate. Did she feel any discomfort? He looked at her face, but her eyes remained closed, despite a faint smile tracing her lips. Damn kissable lips. He dipped down for another kiss and pushed himself deeper.

She moaned into his mouth, the sound and taste of her desire all the encouragement he needed. From there he began a steady rhythm.

It was an odd set of circumstances that had brought them together, and still another collection of oddities that had kept them apart, but he dismissed all logic and consideration, lost in the pleasure to be found in Theodosia beneath him.

Her skin was silky smooth, her body a wonder, and he yearned to touch her everywhere at once, if only that were possible. Her full breasts, high and firm, begged his attention, the pink tips tightened to tempting buds. He lowered to taste each one and she arched with sensual arousal. Still he measured his thrusts, determined to make their intimacy last as long as possible. She gave a little cry, one of enjoyment not discomfort, and he suddenly wished to slow time, to hold back his own pleasure if for no other reason than to watch her in the throes of climax.

Theodosia held her eyes closed, though it was more for dreaming than fear of the new experience. Everywhere Matthew touched, caressed, or kissed, felt alive with fire and sensitivity. And now that he'd entered her and she held him inside her, her heart beat so hard she could hardly catch her breath.

He'd tempered his thrusts. Their lovemaking became less demanding but equally exquisite as he withdrew slowly and then leisurely slid back within her, the sensation extremely intimate and all the more arousing. She wanted this. Needed this closeness. They fit perfectly, as if made exclusively for each other, no trial and error needed to support that conclusion.

She opened her eyes the slightest and viewed him

above her, amused to see his eyes were half closed as he continued to tease her, fill her completely and withdraw, each lovely stroke a gift of pleasure.

"Matthew."

"Yes, Bookish." He opened his eyes, though he didn't stop moving. His voice rumbled through her, low and husky, and a rush of excitement prickled her skin.

"I want—" She paused, unsure how to express exactly what she wanted.

"This?" He thrust harder, moving her upward on the mattress, her eyes wide before she grinned.

"Yes."

He didn't say more. Mindful of her hip, he lifted her leg, which allowed him to go deeper. Each stroke sent a quiver of sensation that built in her middle and radiated outward, to her arms and legs, to her fingertips. She was tied in knots and at the same time floating free. She couldn't catch her breath for the beauty of it and she chased that feeling, his sweat-slicked body above her, her own suffused with sensitivity, the heat of their bodies together another point of arousal.

"Come for me, love. Feel what I want to give you."

He angled his head down and captured her mouth in a kiss, and that's when it took her.

She climaxed hard, torn apart in a burst of hot embers, so sensitive and powerful, they seemed to explode from the inside out. She gripped his arms and embraced his weight as he came down on top of her, their mouths together still, their tongues tangled as tightly as their bodies, and nothing but sensation tremored through them both with the force of love and passion. He shook with the intensity, buried to the hilt inside her, until at the last possible moment he withdrew, his groan of release against the bedsheets echoing in her ears.

She didn't know how long they remained that way. If she dreamed or stayed awake. When at last she returned to clarity, she drowsily opened her eyes to find Matthew half across her body, one leg anchored around hers to hold her securely to his side, his hand over her heart, his face lost in the pillow of her hair.

But his eyes were open and he blinked at her as if the action would bring everything back into focus.

"Theodosia."

This time when he said her name it sounded as if a revelation.

"Bookish." His mouth climbed into a half smile. "That was incredible. That was the word that hasn't been invented yet but means better than incredible. You'll be the death of me."

"Well, we can't have that." She pushed back on the bed so she could see him more clearly, and while she attempted a serious tone she failed miserably. "Perhaps we shouldn't repeat—"

"Bite your tongue." He rose up on his elbow and peered down at her. "Never mind. I'll do that for you."

Chapter Twenty-Seven

Matthew awoke before Theodosia, but unwilling to disturb her, he lay in the bed as still as possible, despite the myriad thoughts racing through his brain. He hadn't proposed. He hadn't even declared his love. Nor presented his argument as to why they belonged together, whether that meant a residence in London, Oxfordshire, or on the damned moon. He huffed a breath of frustration and the subtle movement was enough to rouse her. Unless her mind raced too. He found she rarely escaped his thoughts, even in sleep.

"Have you been awake long?" She rolled to her side to view him, her hands tucked below her face on the pillow.

"No." He stretched an arm along the headboard so he could collect her closer to him. "Just long enough to list all the things I didn't do last evening."

"There's more?" She reared back the slightest, as if the idea was too difficult to comprehend this early.

He couldn't help but chuckle. "Not that. Although I assure you there's much more to experience." He smoothed a hand below the covers and traced a fingertip down her spine. "No, I mean *things I didn't say*. Words I meant to share with you before we made love."

She blushed prettily and he enjoyed every moment of her fluster.

"We did, didn't we?"

"Several times, indeed." He slid lower so he rested on his pillow at eye level. "Are you feeling well? Your hip doesn't pain you from the fall?"

She shook her head in the negative. "Not enough to complain. Besides, I should ask you the same. All that rocky terrain last night must have created discomfort this morning."

"I'm accustomed to aches and pains." He drew little circles along her shoulders, mesmerized with the softness of her skin. "I'm grateful I arrived when I did and your grandfather was able to lead me to you."

She perked up, her lovely gray eyes brighter. "His clear thinking of late is absolutely fascinating. I know better than to dismiss Dr. Fletcher's advice, but it's almost as if nothing's wrong now."

"Dementia is difficult to understand." He wouldn't say more, though he'd despise if she started to believe Lord Talbot's faculties were returned to normal. "You should consider each day of clarity as a gift. And that reminds me . . ." He leaned in and kissed her forehead before he rolled over and left the bed. He winced once he placed his foot to the cold floorboards, but luckily his back was to the bed. "I have something to take care of before Christmas Eve. Did I mention my sister, Amelia, and her husband, the Duke of Scarsdale, have decided to join us?"

"Here?" She shot up as if stung by a bee, her rescue of the sheet to cover herself belated at best. "You invited them here?"

"Didn't you open the box I sent you? There were several crates and cartons, but one gift was specifically intended for you. I marked it with your name." He buttoned his falls and reached for his shirt as he came to sit on the edge of the mattress. "Was it delivered with the others?"

"Yes."

She rose from the sheets and gathered her wrapper from where he'd flung it the evening before. He lost the thread of the conversation momentarily, distracted by her delectable breasts, slim legs, and pert bottom. Bookish might claim her nature quiet and reserved, but she possessed the body of a siren.

"I was saving it for Christmas Day." She looped the belt around her waist and knotted it with a vengeance. "What's inside?"

He laughed. So much had changed from the time he purchased the present until now. "I won't tell, except I included a lengthy letter in which I suggest you might come to London for the holiday season or I will bring my family to yours."

"Oh dear." A look of alarm widened her eyes. "I have so much to do. Your sister is a duchess and her husband, a duke."

"Yes, that's how it's generally arranged." He smiled at her sense of panic. No one was more unconventional than Amelia. He had no doubt his sister would fall in love with Theodosia just as he had. "But you needn't worry. Amelia is high-spirited, independent, and undaunted by societal censure. She's the last person to be concerned with public opinion, considering all the scandals and scenes she caused before she wed. She possesses an indomitable spirit similar to yours."

"But the expectations . . . I'm not the typical hostess, and Lord and Lady Scarsdale have titles of the highest nobility," she elaborated, displaying a look of genuine worry.

"You're the granddaughter of an earl."

"You don't understand." She shook her head vigorously. "The house—"

"The house looks lovely, if you don't mind me taking credit for many of the decorations. I've impeccable taste." He winked in an attempt to add levity.

"But the menu . . . Mrs. Mavis and I haven't confirmed the final courses. I couldn't decide, and now I'll have to choose, except I'll have to choose what a duke and a duchess like to eat and I don't know what a duke and duchess like to eat . . ." She sank down on the corner of the mattress and wrapped her arms around her chest, as if to console herself.

"Amelia and Scarsdale aren't picky. You're becoming overset for no reason. The house is decorated beautifully and your staff exhibits the finest decorum. There's nothing for you to worry about." He did his best to stifle his laughter at her endearing distress.

"But what if Grandfather . . ."

"Your grandfather is an engaging man with many exceptional qualities." He hoped his confidence would boost her belief.

"I don't know." Her eyes beseeched him as she stood and stepped nearer.

"I do." He came to stand beside her and gently brought her into his arms. "Once you meet Amelia, you'll understand you had nothing at all to fret about. She isn't like the petty girls you remember from the academy. Her husband is one of my closest friends. Together we will have the grandest holiday."

"I hope you're right."

She exhaled deeply and he rested his chin on the top of her head as he held her tight. "I honestly can't imagine a different outcome."

* * *

Everything was going wrong. Theodosia dictated orders to the servants, *barked them, actually*, her usual good-natured demeanor long lost. Ever since Matthew informed her Lord and Lady Scarsdale would arrive in two days' time, she couldn't hold a thought in her head. So much needed to be done, and yet all the responsibilities of daily life still existed. How could Matthew behave with nonchalance when the house was being turned inside out, rugs beaten twice, silver polished three times, and every other detail, all for the benefit of a good impression. *An important impression.*

She wasn't fooled. She suspected what lay inside that mysterious square box that she still hadn't opened. And if there was to be any hope of a future for Matthew and herself, she'd need to show she wasn't some odd bluestocking hidden away in the countryside. She needed to prove, to herself most of all, that those haunting memories from long ago were caused by nothing more than insignificant jealousy, and as the wife of an earl, she could entertain, make conversation, and charm guests as eloquently as any cultured debutante.

A clattering brought her attention to the front hall and she whirled to the right to watch footmen climb ladders to reach the highest glass panes in the entry window. They'd need to change the tapers in the chandeliers while up there too. She pivoted to the right as Mrs. Mavis waved a shopping list after two maids who hurried toward the door. She turned again, but changed her mind, swinging in a full circle, arms flailing, and that did little more than cause a rush of dizziness.

"Are you practicing a new dance step without me?"

The tap of his walking stick on the marble tiles alerted her to look to the upper landing. Matthew grinned, sly mischief in his eyes. She wondered then if all the stairs in Leighton House caused undo strain on his leg. Although her nightly ritual of rubbing ginger salve into his calf and thigh muscles proved surprisingly sensual and arousing.

"No." She managed a wobbly grin. "I just want everything to be perfect when Their Graces arrive."

"I can't imagine why." He came down the stairs and approached, and that same charming sparkle lit the depth of his eyes. "Amelia and Scarsdale are as far from perfect as the rest of us, not discounting my valet will make a solid case he deserves the label."

"How can you be so relaxed when the household is in disarray?"

"Little will come from a sense of panic."

"That's easy for you to say." Though in truth his composed attitude calmed her pulse significantly. "Thank you." She smiled a little easier.

"I'd like to speak to your grandfather. Have you seen him about?"

"I left him in his study. He was looking through correspondence left unattended."

"Thank *you* then."

He leaned in and pressed a kiss to her cheek before he left, meant to invoke further peacefulness, no doubt, but it didn't last.

Alberts bustled by with a huge bouquet of hothouse flowers, two footmen in his shadow with ornate vases that overflowed with blooms of every color. With a renewed burst of determination, she followed after them, ticking her fingers as she mentally reviewed the endless list of preparations. At least she had another two days' time.

* * *

"Lord Talbot." Matthew entered the earl's study, gladdened to have found him alone. A conversation was overdue. An important one, at that. Matthew planned to propose to Theodosia on Christmas Eve, and keeping with honor and tradition, sought to ask her grandfather's permission. He closed the double doors behind him and walked toward the earl with a smile. "Will you spare me a moment?"

"Of course." Talbot beckoned him forward with a matched expression of welcome.

The last few days had been domestic bliss without mishap or misery. Talbot seemed unusually clearheaded, no matter the estate was in a state of chaos due to Theodosia's overthinking and overplanning. It was difficult not to tease her, but Matthew respected her genuine concern even though none was warranted. Amelia would be the last person to voice a disparaging word at being considered *different*. Her husband, Scarsdale, was of like mind.

Besides, he took great pleasure in relieving Theodosia's tension each night when she snuck into his guest room.

"How can I help you, Whittingham? Your visit has spurred new life into our holiday celebration. I'm enjoying every bit of it. Thank you." Talbot gestured to the brandy decanter on the sideboard, but Matthew declined as they took opposing chairs. This was too important. Perhaps they'd toast the impending marriage when the matter was settled.

"As you already know, I'm very fond of your grand-daughter. Our friendship has grown since that first winter night when I showed up on your doorstep in acceptance of your invitation."

"Indeed." Talbot's brows flinched the slightest. "It seems like a long time ago, but I remember it clearly. At times, my mind plays tricks."

"I understand." Matthew nodded thoughtfully. "With Christmas Eve only two nights away, I'd like your permission to propose to Theodosia. I have every reason to believe she will have me." A spike of excitement shot through him as he said the words. This was something he wanted more than his next breath.

Talbot remained quiet a beat too long, and as the silence stretched a shadow of unease overrode Matthew's heightened anticipation.

"Is something wrong?" Matthew hurried on. "If you have any doubt of my solvency or ability to care for your granddaughter, I'll instruct my solicitor to forward a copy of my financial records. I love Theodosia sincerely and will protect her with my life."

Talbot stood and walked to the writing desk near the far window. He didn't say anything and his reluctance to speak unhinged Matthew's patience. He stood now too, prepared to list every reason why he'd honor and cherish Theodosia all their shared days, her happiness his singular purpose. His mouth pressed tight in a grimace of distress when Talbot shook his head in the negative.

"You're too late, Whittingham."

He mustn't have heard Talbot correctly. The words didn't make sense. "Too late? How so?"

"I signed a marriage contract last night granting Lord Kirkman permission for Theodosia's hand. He led me to believe they had an understanding and that you were for London after the holidays, committed to your Society and determined to stay in the city. Theodosia dislikes London. I remember her face from all those years ago when I persuaded her to go. I could never force her to that kind of life. She would suffer, far more than she's already suffered these years."

As each word met his ears, his heart drummed louder.

Surely Theodosia knew nothing of the contract. What did Kirkman hope to achieve with his lies, besides heartache and anger? She would never agree. Kirkman couldn't mean to steal her away, could he? The idea was laughable, the stuff of poorly written gothic novels. How had everything become so complicated, when only moments before he'd anticipated the start of his future happiness?

"Have you spoken to Theodosia about this?" His voice sounded distant, his mind at work to understand the most prudent way to proceed.

"No." Talbot huffed a deep breath. "Kirkman insisted we keep it between us. He wants to surprise her at Christmas."

"Indeed, it will be a surprise." Matthew glanced over his shoulder to the closed doors and back again.

"He told me I'd given my word and I must have forgotten. Although we did talk once in the carriage." Talbot shook his head, his expression drawn as he clasped his hands together. "I've done something wrong. I should have spoken to Theodosia first. I need to fix this. Do you think she'll be displeased with this arrangement?"

"Yes." Matthew stood and paced to the hearth, careful with his tone, not wishing to incite further upset. "This isn't as complicated as it may appear. We simply . . . I mean, *you* simply need to speak to Kirkman and explain he can spare himself the embarrassment of a refusal by tossing the contract into the firebox. Once the matter is settled, I will propose and things will continue on their intended course." He said this aloud to convince himself as much as Lord Talbot that it all could be accomplished so easily.

"Kirkman was emphatic he needed to marry."

"That may be so, but Theodosia won't be his bride."

"I will send him a message at once." Talbot returned to the writing desk and withdrew a sheet of paper and his pen.

"I'll ask him to visit us here at Leighton House tomorrow before the festivities get under way."

"The sooner, the better." Matthew curled his hands into fists at his sides, anxious to obviate even the slightest tension. "And let's not upset Theodosia with this wrinkle in the plan. She's already distracted with unnecessary worry over my sister's visit. I wouldn't wish to add to her distress."

With any luck Talbot would defuse the situation and Kirkman would acquiesce with no impact on the holidays. If not, Matthew was prepared to take the matter into his own hands. Theodosia belonged to him and him alone. He wouldn't have some half-mad dandy ruining Christmas, never mind the beginning of the rest of his life.

Chapter Twenty-Eight

It was half noon when Theodosia returned from the orangery. She'd taken Matthew's advice and sought a few minutes of respite from the chaos she'd incited with her desire to perfect every detail in preparation for the Duke and Duchess of Scarsdale. She still wanted everything neatly arranged, but appreciated the stolen peace found among the plants and animals, if only short-lived. She was exhausted, body and mind, and pushed herself to continue, conjuring an air of control as Alberts approached her in the front hall.

"Milady."

"Yes?" She hoped he had a reporting of the servants she'd sent to purchase extra essentials and menu delicacies for Cook.

"The carriages have returned and are being unloaded at the rear door of the kitchen."

"Excellent." At least something proceeded as intended. "Is there anything else, Alberts?"

He seemed reluctant to continue. "I'm afraid so."

She searched the austere butler's unusual expression for a clue to what troubled him.

"I've been informed by the house drivers that an elaborate barouche with the Scarsdale insignia emblazoned on the door was spotted at the top of the Leighton House drive."

"What?" A loud humming began in her ears. Her mind blanked before she reclaimed clarity. "There must be some mistake. Our guests aren't due to arrive until the day after tomorrow. Late. For dinner."

Alberts watched her closely, his mouth tight with a frown. "Might there have been a change of plans?"

"No." She glanced down at her yellow day gown. A long, dark smudge of *something* angled along the left side of her ribcage, her shirts wrinkled and dusty. "No." She touched her hair, not surprised to discover she'd lost several pins in her rush about the estate. "No, no, no, no." She stepped backward as if by separation she could alter reality. "This isn't supposed to happen. The house isn't ready. I'm not ready."

"Ready for what?" Matthew entered the foyer as Alberts took his leave. "Another of my kisses? Is that what has you in this agitated state?"

At the sound of his rich tenor, she lifted her head and they matched eyes. She would have appreciated his cheerful teasing and claimed the kiss he offered if the threat of disastrous disappointment hadn't crowded in with ferocity.

"Your sister and the duke are due any moment." She rubbed her temple while she hemmed her lower lip. "Alberts said their equipage was seen on the drive. Their arrival is imminent."

The rumble of carriage wheels on gravel overrode the end of her sentence.

Matthew smiled and reached for her hand.

She startled as he tugged her into the adjoining corridor for what she suspected was private reassurance or a few well-meant directions.

"You needn't worry. The house looks like a festive

tapestry. The kitchen is filled with a multitude of divine aromas, all which promise extraordinary culinary fare. Amelia and Scarsdale will adore you." He paused. "I know I do."

"You do?" She looked up into his golden-brown gaze and relaxed considerably.

"Yes." He traced the pad of his thumb across her cheek, his voice low and silky. "And so much more. Theodosia, I must tell you, I—"

"The Duke and Duchess of Scarsdale."

She gasped as Alberts's voice boomed across the entry hall. She'd never heard him sound so regal.

"I don't want to embarrass you. I'm not like the refined London ladies who usually keep your company."

"Thank heavens for that."

"But I can't—"

His mouth found hers and rendered her speechless for more than one reason. The kiss demanded her attention and effectively forced her into a lovely calm. Too soon he pulled away, his breath warm against her forehead. He squeezed her hands as he released her.

"Now let's discover what's brought my sister here early without so much as a message of warning. I've found she's best tolerated in small doses." He smiled, his eyes agleam with mirth as he placed her hand on his arm and they walked together toward the hall.

Only by strength and concentration did Matthew divide his emotions. His mind still worked through the unexpected and infuriating discovery that Lord Talbot had signed a betrothal agreement foisted on him by Kirkman. Had Kirkman manipulated Talbot and taken advantage of the earl's dementia? It would be the most heinous maneuver to advance one's goal by taking advantage of another's disability. He cast a fleeting glance at his leg, the tap of his walking stick on the tiles a constant reminder he fell into that category of vulnerability. Never would he be held back by his impairment, and damn anyone who tried to diminish him because of it.

As if that wasn't maddening enough, he'd happened upon Theodosia in the front hall, her usual confident demeanor reduced to insecurity and hesitation. It had proven too much to bear. He'd needed that kiss as much as she, albeit for different reasons. Tonight, he would confess his feelings. Too much time had passed and he no longer wished to keep his sentiments bottled inside.

The arrival of Amelia and Scarsdale proved a diversion, though it splintered his attention further. All precisely laid plans were unraveling with reckless speed, and he didn't like the disorganization.

"Welcome to Leighton House."

Theodosia fell into a deep curtsy, but Amelia clasped her hand and returned her to standing, only to pull her forward in a loose embrace.

"Please," Amelia chided. "I wish for us to share a splendid holiday. There's no need to fuss." She glanced to her husband at her side. "Scarsdale, this is Lady Theodosia."

"Scarsdale." Matthew drew the duke aside after he'd greeted Theodosia. "You caught us unaware. We expected your arrival in two days' time."

"Please pardon our early visit. It's my fault completely," Amelia interrupted. "My dearest friend, Charlotte, Lady Dearing, entered her lying-in earlier than expected. The physician advised she stay off her feet, confined to her bedchamber until the baby is due. There seemed no need to remain. I'd hoped to help with her preparations for the upcoming birth, but then everything changed. I suggested we set out apace for Leighton House instead of waiting in London. Everyone has scattered for the holidays to spend time with their loved ones and I wanted to be with my family as well. I'm still not pleased Mother and Father decided to extend their travel through the New Year."

"With Father's health much improved, they sought a change of scenery, no doubt." Matthew added. "Charlotte is doing well then?"

"Yes, quite so. Lord Dearing is beside himself with anticipation of becoming a father and has the household more than ready," Amelia continued. "Otherwise we would never impose. I hope our early arrival hasn't caused an inconvenience."

"Not at all." Theodosia managed a smile, though she snuck another look at her wrinkled dress. "We're delighted to have your company."

Matthew watched the interaction closely. Theodosia didn't appear nearly as nervous as before, although she remained too quiet for his liking, her words carefully measured. He thought to intercede.

"Well, as long as you're prepared for a bit of slapdash attention this evening, I'm sure we'll get on with no trouble at all. Lord Talbot is in his study. Perhaps I can persuade you to have a brandy, Scarsdale, and I'll make introductions."

"No persuasion needed, and please don't set the staff at odds. The duchess and I require nothing more than a roof over our heads and a hot tray of food taken in our rooms. Together in the carriage for several hours, Amelia's enthusiasm has been"—he paused and his voice acquired a teasing note—"unhampered to say the least."

They shared a laugh at Scarsdale's jest and it eased the tension another notch.

"To the study then." Matthew gestured to the right with

his walking stick before speaking to the ladies. "I trust you'll be right as rain."

"How ridiculous, Matthew," Amelia answered quickly. "You needn't worry about me."

"You? Hardly." His voice followed him as he left the foyer with Scarsdale. "I was speaking to Theodosia."

"You're not at all as I expected." Theodosia's face warmed as she imagined how her words sounded, but she hadn't a chance to consider it long.

"Did Matthew portray me in a poor light?" Amelia donned a look of sibling annoyance. "I love my brother, but he can be stubborn when he sets his mind to something. Still, he's changed of late. I'd like to believe I brought about his new view of life with my recent marriage." Her expression transformed into one of pride.

"He's spoken very highly of you both."

Nicolaus sauntered into the front hall, his whiskers and tail a-twitch in the sunlight.

"Oh, who is this fine fellow?" Amelia lowered to the tiles, her hand extended to welcome the striking feline.

"Nicolaus Catpernicus." Theodosia took a deep breath. Perhaps she'd worked herself into a state for no reason. Amelia seemed lovely and not at all as pretentious as Theodosia had assumed. "He's one of my closest companions."

"I could tell he was important as soon as I laid eyes on him. My cat, Pandora, is my dearest friend, aside from Charlotte, and Scarsdale, of course." She rubbed Nicolaus between his ears and the cat bowed his head with pleasure. "Such a handsome boy with a clever name. It sounds like something Matthew would suggest." She stood and smiled in Theodosia's direction. "You two must think alike."

Despite her lengthy travel and having crouched down

low with several layers of skirts and underskirts to pet Nicolaus, Amelia looked flawless, from the beautiful dark ringlets on her perfectly coiffed head to her silk embroidered slippers. Her eyes glinted green, with a sparkle that could only be caused by an inner glow of happiness. She resembled Matthew in hair color and height, yet Theodosia much preferred his golden-brown gaze and the way it caused all kinds of warm feelings inside her.

"If you enjoy cats, I suspect we'll get along swimmingly." She found an easy smile, much relieved from the gut-wrenching anticipation she'd tortured herself with the last few days.

"Oh." Amelia sounded genuinely surprised. "Had you worried? I knew all along we'd be wonderful friends. Matthew may be the singular most particular male on the planet, and to have chosen you, well, that speaks loudest of all."

Theodosia didn't know how to reply to that, though her cheeks surely turned crimson. He'd chosen her? What did that mean exactly? Granted, they'd become intimately involved since he'd arrived, and her heart was tightly bound to his, but so many aspects of their relationship remained uncertain. She recalled how adamantly he'd confessed his feelings when they'd visited the British Museum and how she'd refused to accept his words. Her view on that decision had altered greatly. If only he would confess those words again, she'd accept them and return her own heartfelt sentiments.

Yet if he'd shared his fondness for her with his sister, it wasn't a matter to be taken lightly. Did she dare believe? Perhaps this Christmas all her hopes and dreams would solidify. Grandfather was much improved and she'd fallen hopelessly, helplessly in love with a wonderful man. All those years of quiet holidays and dismal remembrances through January, of wishing and wondering if her life would ever be more than endless longing and unfulfilled imaginings, seemed necessary now. She wanted to embrace that fragile trust with both hands and hold on tight before it vanished. Love did that to a person. It caused one to invest in the impossible if one was brave enough to take a chance.

Chapter Twenty-Nine

Later that evening, after guest rooms were assigned and all necessary tasks settled, Theodosia stole down the hallway and knocked lightly on Matthew's door. The panel opened as if he'd waited right on the other side, and the idea pleased her in the nicest way.

"Hello." She smiled as she stepped over the threshold. How fascinating that she no longer held misgivings about entering his bedchamber after hours. What did that say about her? She shook her head and dismissed the notion. "I'm glad you're still awake."

"Of course, I'm awake." He chuckled. "I was waiting for you."

"You were?" She bit her lower lip to prevent a smile from escaping despite he had the devil's own grin upon his face. She paused beside the bureau, her hands laced. "Thank you for earlier. For helping to keep things in perspective and for inviting Amelia and Scarsdale. They're both delightful company. And too for introducing Grandfather to His Grace. Grandfather was thoroughly impressed."

"It was my pleasure." Matthew drew her forward into his arms. "Already I miss having you all to myself though. I've always been rubbish about sharing. With Amelia around we'll have scarce peace and quiet the next few days."

"You did invite her," she pointed out. "But I can come here at night." Her face heated with the bold insinuation, never mind the inadvertent double entendre.

"Indeed." He pulled back to look her in the eyes. "I agree wholeheartedly."

She slipped from his grasp and sat on the edge of the mattress, enjoying their little game. She removed the bandeau that kept her hair bound and loosened the lengths about her shoulders.

"Who is this seductress in my bed?" He advanced, a wicked gleam in his eyes. "The same woman who spouted random science facts when I attempted a kiss all those weeks ago?"

"It's cruel to tease." She hardly managed to squelch a giggle.

"Who's teasing? All that science talk made me randy. A fetching female exposing her intelligence to me in a dark library. Why, that's a scholar's naughty boyhood fantasy come to life."

"Is that so?" She slowly pulled the ribbon that kept her wrapper tied at the neck, her heart in her throat as he stopped one stride from where she sat. "The average person falls asleep in seven minutes."

"I have a feeling we'll be up all night." He widened his stance and pulled his shirt over his head, his chest and arms a feast for her eyes.

"It's impossible to sink into quicksand if one raises his legs and lies still on his back." She giggled, the picture in her mind amusing.

"Now there's an interesting position." He worked the buttons loose on his falls, exposing himself piece by piece, and her heartbeat applauded as each garment fell to the floorboards.

Anxious to keep her hands moving as her throat went dry, she slid the wrapper from her shoulders and then set to work on the tiny ivory buttons of her night rail. Her fingers trembled, but she managed, aware of his intense focus on every move she made.

Nothing was said for a breathless moment, the tick of the clock on the mantelpiece the loudest sound in the room.

"Theodosia." His voice held such gravity she sobered immediately. "I've been remiss and I wish to remedy that now." He paused with one knee bent on the bed, his body clothed in only his smalls.

"Yes?" She didn't know what he meant to say, but she knew it held great importance.

"I love you." He drew a deep breath, her eyes trained on his muscular chest. "I tried to tell you the depth of my feelings before, and like any experienced scientist, you were quick to refute my claim without evidence, but I find that impossible now."

He slowly perused her bare body. Her skin flushed under his admiring scrutiny.

"My body calls to yours, but more so my heart." He paused, a flash of emotion in his eyes. "Do you feel it too, Bookish?"

Her pulse thundered in her veins. Here stood a wonderful man, good-hearted, handsome and intelligent, who proclaimed his love for her. Only a fool would ignore this dream come to life.

"I love you, Matthew. I do." She smiled, the words alive on her tongue. Then she laughed, the relief and joy of her admittance almost too much to bear.

"Now that's settled." He leaned in and captured her mouth in a deep, openmouthed kiss.

Enjoying their playfulness, she wasn't ready to relinquish control. "The ears of a cricket are located on its front legs right below the knee."

"Right about here?"

He ran his fingertips along her calf to the soft, sensitive area just above. Her body quivered with anticipation and she promptly forgot all facts or logic, the game abandoned.

"Or here?"

He smoothed both palms to the front of her legs and slowly skimmed them upward, his thumbs tracing the delicate skin of her inner thighs. She didn't move and closed her eyes with a sigh as she nestled deeper into the bedding. His weight caused the mattress to dip, but still she lay in wait and wonder. He whispered kisses across her breasts, his tongue hot and determined against the tips, the texture of each pass echoed below, where she grew anxious and wet.

When had she become so wanton? So free? This sudden lack of inhibition was wrong, but felt so incredibly right, she couldn't deny it. It made her feel desired. *Cherished.* She wanted him to touch her. To make her experience wonder as rare and elusive as a rainbow's beauty.

His arm brushed across her hip, the hair leaving a trail of heat and expectation until he smoothed his fingers over her abdomen, then lower to her sex, where he parted her folds and rubbed the tight center with insistent strokes. Desire built rapidly, each tender caress of his attention tinder to the heat within. She clenched her eyes in order not to do the same with her legs, the pleasure partly composed of restraint, dependent on total surrender. She allowed him to lead her, begging for release, until nothing mattered aside from sensation, intense and drenching, wholly consuming.

He didn't let her drift off, drowsy and sated, but instead brought his mouth to hers, his tongue now as insistent as his fingers had been, her body open and ready. He slid between her thighs, her legs anchored on either side of his, and sunk into her deep. She shuddered with pleasure and wrapped her arms around him.

Matthew growled with satisfaction as he buried himself in Theodosia's heat. She was wet and tight and he couldn't feel her enough or have her enough. It wasn't possession that drove him. It wasn't misplaced fear or Kirkman's audacity or any other number of things that caused his fervent desire to bind himself with her.

Weeks before when he'd first met her, something ignited inside him. Something beyond an insatiable curiosity. And the more he came to know her and share her company, the more committed he became. He'd fallen hard before he knew if it was wise, and given his heart before he'd ascertained if she'd ever want his attention. It went against every ounce of logic he possessed, all thoughtful planning abandoned, but it didn't matter now.

With a murmur of approval, he welcomed her arms around him, urging him down for another openmouthed kiss as his pulse hammered an urgent beat, his body pulsing with need and want. They'd learned each other now, were familiar with each other's body, and Theodosia no longer worried about the act. Her hips undulated beneath him in invitation, her muscles pliant and giving.

He pressed into her and rocked the slightest, the blood hot in his veins as he struggled for control. Everywhere he looked she was beautiful, her hair spilled over his pillow, her smooth creamy skin and perfectly formed curves. And she was his to claim. His to love. A sense of wild longing seized his chest. He forced a long breath. Then another.

He slowed, wanting their joining to last, needing their bodies to melt together, to become one as closely as possible. When he withdrew he was bereft, eager to return, sheathed tight within her heat, but his cock throbbed, hard and thick, too anxious for release and the sensual pleasure it promised. He'd always pulled away from her at the last moment and spilled himself on the sheets, but he couldn't tonight. Not after the words they'd shared. He could no longer bear that separation either.

He began an instinctive rhythm, their bodies in perfect synchronicity, and measured his strokes though the battle was lost, a sheen of perspiration on his forehead, his muscles flexed against the inevitable. In less than a few heartbeats, her body went rigid beneath his, her breath fast and ragged, a keening cry on her lips, and so he thrust into her again, her body holding his in velvet heat, keeping him as he climaxed with such intensity he nearly collapsed atop her from the force.

"I suppose I've become shameless." Theodosia smiled broadly with this announcement, her expression in contradiction to the censure of her words.

"Are you proud of that quality?" He couldn't help but tease her.

"And what if I am?" She turned on her side beneath the covers and propped up on her elbow.

"You won't hear a complaint out of me." He chuckled. What time was it anyway? No doubt they would need to play attentive host and hostess tomorrow during breakfast. He really shouldn't keep her awake any longer. "We should get some rest."

"We should," she confirmed, though she placed her

hand atop his chest and fanned her fingers through the soft mat of hair. "You've changed my life in the best way."

Her shy admittance touched his heart, and he angled his head on the pillow so he could see her more clearly. "As you did mine."

"I know I've been adamant about where I'd like to live, including thoughts of Grandfather's well-being, of course, but I've also come to realize that as long as we're together I needn't fear the future. It's not a matter of where we choose to live as much as how we lead our lives and the love we share between us."

She didn't say anything further, and thinking they would seek sleep, he closed his eyes with her words replaying in his head. She would offer him the world, and the sentiment warmed him from the inside out. And he would do likewise.

Turning to her, he brushed his hand across her cheek. "And I know I've tried to convince you London is not so bad, but the truth is I'd relocate to a remote island in the Aegean Sea if it meant we would spend our future together."

The sheets shifted as she repositioned herself. The room fell quiet.

When she traced a line down his chest and lower to his abdomen, he sucked in a sharp breath, forbidding his brain to go to the place it wanted to go; still, his cock twitched in concurrence of that hope. He didn't need to wonder long.

She brushed her hand across his hip and settled her palm on his arousal. Blood rushed to fulfill her request, simultaneously vanquishing logic and thought. Still he didn't open his eyes. It heightened the sensuality of her innocent exploration. He told himself to breathe and willed his pulse to calm as she lowered the sheet from his waist.

She circled her fingers around his erection timidly at first, though after the first stroke she handled him with swift mastery. He still held his eyes closed, though he wondered if she watched him or concentrated on the task. He imagined her silken hair falling forward, her lovely gray eyes intense with desire. He didn't expect what came next.

The first touch of her mouth on him caused him to jerk in surprise. Clever of her to make him believe in one thing when she'd planned quite another. He doubted he would last more than a few seconds, the soft, smooth caress of her inquisitive tongue an excruciating delight. She took him into her mouth and he groaned with pleasure, his body rock hard while his mind melted to liquid.

She didn't linger and returned to cuddle at his side a moment later. He forced his eyes open, the blood pounding in his veins.

"Good night then."

He could hear the smile in her voice, the minx.

"If that's your idea of a good night kiss, then I suggest you prepare for mine." The words rasped out, his body caught in a state of agonizing pleasure.

She didn't move at first, but then when she went to roll away and escape, he caught her around the waist, pulled her under him, and said good night properly.

Chapter Thirty

Theodosia hummed a cheerful tune as she watered the lemon trees in the orangery and cared for her menagerie of pets. Outside, the first rays of dawn stretched toward the sky. She wanted to complete her responsibilities before changing clothes and greeting the duke and duchess at breakfast.

Tomorrow was Christmas Eve. Despite her worry and speculation of disaster, things had proceeded with considerable ease and the house was prepared for a spectacular holiday. Every time she recalled Matthew's sincere declaration of love, an ethereal tingle reminded her she wasn't dreaming. And when she dared reflect on their shared intimacy afterward, she knew from her body's pleasant aches that indeed her happiness was real.

She replaced the watering can and dusted off her hands with a nearby rag. Best she stopped lingering among the plants with her daydreams and focus on entertaining her guests. Grandfather's attention remained clear and his temperament congenial; still, she wouldn't risk upsetting him in any manner that could cause a disruption to their holiday.

A shadow passed the front glass, near William and Isaac's glass bowls, and she turned swiftly to question what caused it. It wasn't often she had company here, but it could be any number of groundsmen who thought to get an early start on their tasks outside. Seeing no one, she shook her head in dismissal and turned to leave. It was then that Lord Kirkman appeared in the doorway.

"Henry. It's so early. What are you doing here?" She approached as she questioned him. It was odd for him to have arrived at this hour. "Is everything all right?" His mouth was drawn tight and she recognized an intensity in his eyes.

"I've come to talk to you." He cleared his throat and closed the distance between them. "The matter couldn't wait."

"Are you unwell?" Her voice dropped, concern coloring the words.

"No. Not in the sense you might think." He cleared his throat a second time. "I've tried to convince you of how serious my situation. I've proposed several times and presented my best arguments."

He paused and she rushed to curtail what she assumed would come next. "Henry, I thought we'd decided that any notion of our being married is foolish. It isn't easy for me to see you like this and refuse your repeated requests, but marrying you is not something I can do as a favor or good turn. I don't love you, nor do you love me in that manner." Why did he persist? Sadly, their relationship had transformed from comfortable friendship to the worst awkwardness.

"Love doesn't matter at this point. I'm in a desperate fix with no way to see myself out."

"But you've refused to share your problem with me. How can I possibly empathize with your trouble if you won't tell me a word? I will help you any way possible if you explain the circumstances fully." She didn't wish to be hurtful, but no amount of polite refusal seemed to suffice.

"I can't." He ran his fingers through his hair in an act of frustration. "The most I can reveal is that I need to be married as soon as possible. The why of it doesn't matter. I've always held you in high regard. We get along well enough. I may have unwisely narrowed my choices to one, but hindsight can't solve the issue now." He came closer and placed his hand on her shoulder, his voice low as his eyes found hers in a penetrating stare. "We need to wed, Theodosia. I don't mean to frighten you, but I must insist we get married."

"What?" Her mind spun with confusion. She stared at his hand on her shoulder, his grip having tightened. Now his fingers bit through the fabric of her gown and caused bruising pain.

And then he was removed.

Shoved to the side of the orangery, where he struck a shelf of newly potted nightshade plants in a collision of glass, soil, and greenery. She moved back in shock and Matthew stepped forward, his fist meeting Kirkman's jaw in a jolting connection of flesh upon flesh.

"Matthew!" She watched as Henry reeled backward, his arms flung out to break his fall, though she feared he might continue straight through the greenhouse window. "What are you doing?"

"Step aside, Theodosia."

She didn't move. She had no idea what had happened. "Henry was talking to me."

"No." Matthew peered over Kirkman's collapsed form, his voice low and menacing. "He was touching you."

"I don't understand." She looked at Henry on the floor, his eyes open though he didn't make a move to rise.

"Kirkman can't be trusted." Matthew assessed her person, up and down, as if to confirm she was well before he returned his watch to Henry on the dirt floor.

"That's absurd." She tried to comprehend. "I've known

Henry nearly two decades. He would never do anything to harm me."

"Convincing your grandfather to sign a betrothal contract and grant your hand in marriage should suffice. I suspect trickery, but you need to ask the fool yourself." He jerked his head in Kirkman's direction and released her from the demand in his eyes.

"That's ridiculous." She began to move closer, but Matthew stayed her with a raised hand. She shook her head at the inanity but stilled nonetheless. "Henry, tell me this is all a misunderstanding."

"Everything was proceeding smoothly until you came along, Whittingham. You've proven an irritating nuisance." Henry slowly rose from the ground, his clothing covered with soil and pieces of broken pottery. Thankfully, the greenhouse panes had taken the impact of his weight without complaint. "I would have had Theodosia's hand one way or the other."

"But I don't want to marry you." She said the words softly to buffer their impact. "I've told you several times." Matthew stepped closer, at the ready to act if necessary.

"We would have found our way to an agreement," Kirkman insisted. "And you would have come to care for me."

"I do care for you." She ignored the abrupt grunt of objection from Matthew beside her. "All this time while I've been consumed with my grandfather's condition, I've neglected my duties as your friend. You're so troubled, Henry. I want to help, but I can't marry you to do that. I'm so sorry."

Silence enveloped them.

Kirkman rubbed his jaw and looked at her a long time. His emotionless stare sent a sense of disquiet skittering up her spine. "It's inconvenient we couldn't settle matters more easily. I never intended for it to end this way."

"It didn't have to," Theodosia replied, her voice soft. "I

wish you would tell me why you're so insistent we marry. What could possibly cause this impetuous behavior?"

"My father." Kirkman spat the words as if the taste of them was poison on his tongue.

"Your father died last year. Was it something in his will?" Theodosia shook her head. "Are you saying his will stated you must marry *me*?"

Kirkman drew a deep breath. "I cannot say more than I must marry. Anyone. But you would have done nicely. Your nose is always buried in a book. I would have my funds and you would have your independence."

The air stilled to what seemed an endless moment.

"You insult my honor." She lifted her chin and stared at the man she once called friend. "You should go now."

Kirkman's eyes lit with anger, though he remained silent.

"Aren't you forgetting something?" Matthew advanced and blocked the man's path within an arm's reach, no matter how Kirkman attempted to pass. "I'll have that marriage agreement before you leave."

"Matthew." She tried to harness her patience, wanting nothing more than to be rid of Henry. She'd always shown him kindness, and his words were hurtful. "He can't do anything with it if I don't agree." She understood Matthew's reasoning and felt a loss for Kirkman's desperation. She'd known despair and a keen sense of loneliness in her short lifetime.

"I'll have it anyway."

"I came here for Theodosia, but I see the real problem more clearly now." A sad, sinister thread wove through his words. Kirkman reached into his coat pocket to retrieve the document and withdrew a long knife. "Perhaps a little persuasion is necessary."

The glint of the silver blade snared their attention immediately, but Kirkman lunged forward, the knife held high as he leapt. Things blurred as she was shoved out of the way. She scrambled aside, unwilling to be a nuisance underfoot as both men grappled for control.

"Henry, what are you doing?" Her voice sounded shrill, her pulse on the run. "You can't mean to hurt someone."

She watched in horror as the struggle played on. Caught unaware, Matthew was unsteady. He took several strides backward to compensate, but Kirkman pushed on with fervor, backing him closer to the large glass window on the opposite side of the orangery. The force of two men together would definitely break the panes, and an image of Matthew's bloody body, cut by the broken shards, brought her to her feet, ready to act.

She had few resources within her reach. A trenching spade leaned near the potting bench, but she might hit Matthew as easily as Henry, wielding its cumbersome weight. Instead she grabbed a hand trowel and launched at Henry's shoulders, striking him repeatedly. He jolted one shoulder back, able to deflect her easily, but she would not be deterred. The men had advanced within a stride of the same window where she'd cried her good-bye to Matthew after he'd left Leighton House all those weeks ago. Where she'd noticed his fingerprints and realized her heart was given, despite her brain refusing to hear reason.

She ran forward in a chase she feared she wouldn't win, and she didn't. A scream broke free as the men crashed through the glass wall, out into the cold and onto the hard ground. Sobbing with anger and fear, she swung her arm with all her strength and brought the trowel down on the side of Henry's head, putting an end to his unrelenting attack.

He slumped over and Matthew quickly reversed their

positions, on guard should Kirkman continue his challenge, but the man was as motionless as a buried rock.

"You've knocked him into the New Year," Matthew quipped, his chest heaving hard from exertion. "Well done of you."

"How can you jest at a time like this?" Emotion raised her voice to a higher note, tears of fear and frustration flowing freely now. "I don't swoon. I don't swoon," she chanted after another gulp of air. "I thought you would . . . I didn't know if he . . . I—" She stopped any further attempts at coherent speech and pressed her face into her trembling fingers.

"I, on the other hand, am remarkably unscathed."

He stood and turned full circle. She opened her eyes to examine him and noticed nothing more than dirt stains on his clothing and a few specks of blood on his back and shoulders. Wiping away her tears, she dragged in a ragged breath.

"Now for a few remaining details." Matthew retrieved the knife and placed it behind him on the gardening table. Then he bent over Kirkman and rifled his pockets until he came away with the folded betrothal agreement.

"Was that truly necessary?" She needed to be held, and every minute he made her wait left her bereft and wanting.

"Yes." He tugged her into his arms and flush against his body, the paper clenched in his fist. "I'll not have a man walking the planet with a document that grants him permission to take you from me."

"You're absurd." She drew back to offer him an incredulous stare but he was having none of it, and before she could think otherwise, he leaned in and claimed her mouth. His kiss immediately restored her clarity. Would she always feel this way within his embrace? As if she belonged nowhere else other than the circle of his arms? She hoped so.

When at last they brought the kiss to an end, she rested her head upon his chest, her ear over his heart. "Why did you think to come to the orangery?"

"I woke up and knew something was wrong as soon as I saw you weren't beside me." He stroked his palm down her back and squeezed her tighter. "I inquired of Lord Talbot first, but Collins assured me the earl slept still. From then it wasn't a matter of knowing where you'd be. It was more the distinct awareness of ill ease that drove me out here."

"Do you believe Henry would have stolen me away?" She liked listening to his heartbeat. By far it was her favorite sound.

"I'm not sure. But desperation changes one's personality and often rationalizes what otherwise might be unconscionable. I've experienced something similar in my recent past during my sister's difficulties and my installment as chief officer."

"I'm sorry." She wanted to know more about that time in his life, but her questions would have to wait until later.

"In the end it all proved a learning experience and ultimately brought me to you." He pressed a brief kiss to her temple. "I wouldn't have guessed Kirkman had the audacity. He must be in a terrible fix." He cut a swift glance to the ground where the man remained unconscious, his breathing measured by a stray elderberry leaf that fluttered atop his chest with each exhale. "When I realized you might need help, no matter the urgency, I worried whether I could move fast enough through the house to reach you in time."

"You don't have your walking stick." Her words came out troubled. "Does your leg pain you?"

"Not as much as seeing you in distress."

She didn't say anything for a moment, content to be held in his arms until a whistle of cold air rushed through the open panes and invited reality to intrude.

"Why didn't he just ask if he needed funds?"

"I suspect much more was at stake than a loan between friends. Pride, humiliation, and reputation, no doubt." Matthew paused. "Would it have changed your mind if he'd confessed from the start?"

"No." She couldn't reply fast enough. "Of course not, but I might have helped."

"He doesn't deserve your kindness."

"It doesn't matter now." She dismissed his comment out of hand. "I'll assign two footmen to return Kirkman home and require them to advise his household to keep him under watch until the physician arrives." She shook her head at the surprising turn of events. "I must have hit him a lot harder than necessary."

Matthew gave a slight smile despite the severity of the subject. "That outcome is too good for him, a true holiday gift, though I suspect you'll spare him further embarrassment and won't pursue actions more detrimental to his character. You should go into the house so you don't catch a chill. If you'll arrange for Kirkman's disposal, I'll stay until the footmen arrive and then we'll contend with closing up these broken panes." He looked at the mess of shattered pottery, glass, and plant debris strewn inside and out. "I'm sorry, Theodosia. I know this is your special place and now it will hold unpleasant memories."

"It's all in our ability to repair." She offered him a reassuring nod and smoothed her hands up and down her arms to ward off the cold. "As long as you're well and Kirkman leaves, I haven't a complaint. I never wish to see him again.

Let the consequences of his rash display and dishonorable behavior sever any friendship that remained between us." And then, as if only just remembering, her eyes flew wide and she added, "Lord, the duke and duchess will believe me the worst hostess."

Chapter Thirty-One

Christmas Eve proved to be as enchanting as Theodosia dreamed it could be. The house hummed with holiday cheer, each window, hearth, and doorway decorated with generous evergreen garland, the greenery adorned with apples and clove-studded oranges, red satin ribbons, and ornate silver charms. Wreaths made from pine boughs with holly, rosemary, and hawthorn graced the newel posts where the decorations cascaded upward, interwoven in the baluster spindles to carry the adornments to the second floor.

The kitchen rejoiced with the scents of gingerbread and marzipan, and the cookies were consumed as quickly as they cooled, while spiced wassail simmered in a pot over the fire to lend a cinnamon-sweet fragrance throughout the ground floor.

Having just finished an elaborate holiday dinner of roasted goose with chestnut stuffing, mackerel with fennel, fried oysters, pickled asparagus, and side dishes too decadent for second helpings, Theodosia led her grandfather, Matthew, and Their Graces into the formal drawing room for conversation before they planned to partake in a dessert course of almond cream trifle and plum pudding. As a sign of prosperity and good fortune, a yule log burned in the firebox, but Theodosia couldn't imagine a wish she needed to make. One glance around the room proved she had everything her heart desired.

Grandfather still struggled at times, his dementia more pronounced later in the day than early in the morning, and she wondered with the mind of a scientist if she shouldn't record his patterns and focus her attention on what the information revealed. He still demanded marmalade occasionally, and often lost the end of his sentence or story, but she reveled in his spans of clarity when things appeared almost normal again. She treasured those shared times most of all.

The Duke and Duchess of Scarsdale were exactly as Matthew described them. Accepting and affectionate, not just with each other, but in every situation. They were patient and understanding concerning Grandfather's condition and more fascinated with her unique qualities and unusual interests than in censuring her personality. She'd managed to keep her nerves under control *mostly*, and with that ease of comfortability, found friendship and camaraderie with Amelia and her husband. The hope lived that she would be able to consider them her family, a new sister and friend, at the least.

Matthew and his ability to charm seemed most pronounced as Christmas fell upon them. Or mayhap it was the limitless love that grew in her heart that made it seem so. His presence caused her to smile, his knowing touch heated her soul. She couldn't imagine a life without him in it, as her friend and ally, her lover, *her husband*. Again, her eyes settled on the yule log aflame in the hearth. Mayhap she did have something to wish for after all.

"I propose a toast." Scarsdale raised his glass of port and they all took their drinks in hand. "To the unexpected delight of this holiday. To Lord Talbot and his gracious hospitality. To Leighton House, and its diverse and intriguing dedication to science. To the fine company of my wife and brother-in-law, but most of all, to our lovely hostess, Lady Theodosia."

"To many more years and many more Christmases," Grandfather added before he took a sip of wine.

"To family, most of all," Amelia countered, a knowing smile on her face as she turned to look at her husband. "And what is to come." She placed her hand delicately on her abdomen as they matched eyes.

"To love," Matthew continued. "To finding the person with whom you're most meant to share life. To understanding and caring. To protecting and cherishing." His voice dropped lower as he walked closer. "To knowing you will never be complete nor happy without the returned affection of your soul's match."

All eyes turned in her direction and her pulse hitched. How could she possibly follow all the heartfelt sentiments already expressed? She blushed in spite of herself. From the corner of her eye she saw Grandfather wink, his expression bright with pride. At her extended silence, Matthew provided yet another rescue. He moved beside her and promptly placed her hand in his.

"A few months ago, I came to Leighton House on a mission of discovery and investigation." He glanced briefly at her before he eyed the others, who sipped their wine and listened attentively. "I had no idea what I would find, but I was after the truth in the most elemental form." He turned to face her now, and she nervously hemmed her lower lip.

He looked absolutely dashing, his formal wear cut to perfection, those same golden-brown eyes that warmed her from the inside out, alive with merriment and mischief. Her heart beat heavily but only because it was near overflowing with love.

"My journey was successful. I identified the truth readily, but what I discovered during the process proved more valuable than any mission of knowledge and fact." He raised his wineglass in her direction and for all her past insecurities of being picked apart and analyzed, dissected and measured by public opinion and scrutiny, a confident smile broke through. "Instead I found my heart."

"Cheers."

"Merry Christmas."

"Well said, Whittingham."

Conversation and gaiety extended into the late hours, and it wasn't until half eleven that Theodosia found herself alone with Matthew in the drawing room. Amelia and Scarsdale had scurried upstairs long before, while Grandfather had been the first to say good night.

Now, with only minutes left before Christmas Day was upon them, she walked to the mantel and retrieved the gift Matthew had sent, which she'd never opened.

"At last, a few moments of quiet and privacy." He joined her on the settee where she held the box atop her lap.

It wasn't heavy and she couldn't imagine what was inside. A letter, of course. The one she was supposed to read, which announced her current guests' arrival. But the box was too big for a betrothal ring, and secretly that's what Theodosia desired most of all.

To know she was loved as thoroughly as she loved him.

To spend the rest of her life with this man beside her.

"You really should open it," he prodded. "I'm no longer certain the condition of the gift will be what I intended, considering how long you've kept it wrapped up tight." He grinned, his eyes aglitter beneath those long, dark lashes.

"Should I have opened it at once?"

"Secretly I hoped my instincts proved correct and you would save it for Christmas Day so I'd be here beside you."

"Oh." She didn't know what to say to that and hurriedly untied the white velvet ribbon. "I have no idea what's inside." She carefully removed the paper and lifted the lid of the box. The scent of rosemary, bay, and laurel quickly flooded her senses. "How beautiful."

"Like you, Theodosia." He reached into the box and removed the kissing bough, a tight ball of mistletoe sprigs, evergreen, and herbs, decorated with a bright red ribbon at the top, though he didn't hold it high enough for them to move beneath and kiss, instead keeping the bottom portion and ribbon settled in the box. "I have the tack here for hanging. I put it in the bottom of the box."

"It's lovely. Thank you." She smiled and slid to the side of the settee so she could stand and usher him to the doorway threshold. "We'll hang it here and pass through often. Since every time you claim a kiss we must remove a berry, I think we should enter this room as often as possible."

"Fond of my kisses, are you?" He approached the doorway, though he still held the decoration at his side.

"It's a wonderful holiday tradition," she rebuffed, her voice a little dreamy, her body already anxious for their first kiss claimed.

"Indeed. I do enjoy traditions. Christmas Eve is also the night for stockings, isn't it?"

"Yes." She shuffled her slippers in a restless dance.

"In your case I look forward to taking them down, not putting them up."

He winked and she released a breath of impatience. What was taking him so long with the kissing bough? Her lips tingled with anticipation as she stood in the doorframe waiting.

Finally, he reached above her and pressed the tack into

the wood. The kissing bough fell gracefully down the ribbon and settled with a sway right above their heads. She didn't give it another look, her sole focus on him before her. She stood so close, the white starched linen of his cravat nearly brushed her nose and the fragrance of his shaving soap mingled with the scented sprigs of herbs. She inhaled deeply and allowed her lids to fall closed.

Still he didn't kiss her.

After an awkward pause, she snapped her eyes open and tried to control her pique. What was the sense of having a kissing bough if the man she loved wouldn't offer her kisses beneath it?

Matthew stared into Theodosia's crystalline gray gaze and wondered for the hundredth time how he'd become so lucky. All night he couldn't keep his eyes from her. Her evening gown was a resplendent confection of dark green satin shot through with silver thread, as pretty as a present. One he couldn't wait to unwrap later. Her ebony hair was arranged in a braided coronet interwoven with ribbons, but a few stray strands dusted over one cheek, drawing his attention to her graceful neck and lower to the creamy display of skin all the way to the swells of her breasts. It tempted him to hurry along the process, but no. He would regret that decision and refused to rush.

He hadn't shared yet how he'd relinquished his position at the Society. He was no longer bound to London. The Whittingham residence remained there if needed, otherwise he had no objection to spending his days at Leighton House. So much had occurred since his arrival, it seemed prudent to wait until things calmed before springing all these changes on Theodosia. He didn't wish to cause her an ounce of concern.

Besides, something much more important remained up in the air.

Literally.

"I'm glad you like my gift." He smiled down at her up-turned face and his heart expanded by degree. "I wanted to give you something memorable, something everlasting."

"It's lovely." She nodded the slightest. "I'll be disappointed to discard it after the holidays, the herbs are so fragrant. Perhaps I can dry it in the apothecary and create a keepsake."

"I wasn't speaking of the kissing bough, Bookish." His pulse hammered in his veins. At last, the moment was here. "Although you may want to look at it more closely."

Her brows dipped delicately at his unusual request as she dragged her attention from him and slowly raised her head to view the kissing bough suspended from the wooden doorframe.

Her eyes narrowed before they shot open wide.

Dangling from a thin gold ribbon at the bottom of the bough was a glittering diamond betrothal ring. He'd tied it there himself all those weeks ago before he'd sent the gifts to Leighton House, and it had proved hellish to see the box sitting on the mantelpiece, all the while aware of the treasure within.

"Matthew?" She darted her gaze from the ring to his face and back again, as if she questioned whether or not her eyes deceived her.

"You didn't have any doubt, did you?" He reached above them and pulled one end of the ribbon to unfurl the bow and release the ring into his palm. Then he held the bottom of the band so the diamond on top glinted and reflected every gleam of candlelight from the hallway chandelier.

"It's beautiful." She searched his face, her expression priceless. "I've never seen such a breathtaking gem."

"It's a paragon stone. Completely flawless in color and clarity. Here." He held it aloft slightly and allowed the nearest candle flame to refract light through it. A sparkling prism of rainbow flashes showered the closest wall. "The dispersion of white light into spectral colors is unmatched."

Her breath caught.

"Just as you are."

She shifted her attention to him instead of the ring.

"You do like it, don't you? I thought anything larger than three carats might interfere with your work."

She laughed, softly at first. Then louder. "There's so much joy inside me right now I'll combust if I don't let it out."

He took her hand, noting how it trembled, and slipped the ring on her finger. "You will marry me, won't you, Bookish?"

"Yes." She breathed deeply, her smile tremulous as she stared down at her hand and splayed her fingers. The ring glittered light in myriad directions. "It's magnificent, although I would have been happy with a stone from the drive if it signified our promise to each other."

"I have no doubt, but I wanted to give you a reminder to carry with you always."

She laughed again, this time more softly as her words whispered out. "I don't need a ring or anything to remind me how much I love you."

"Of course not. That's not what I meant." He tilted her chin up, his mouth almost lowered to hers. "A diamond is a symbol of everything you are, Theodosia, strong and brilliant and rare."

She didn't say a word and blinked several times, her struggle to hold back tears almost successful. The clock on the mantelpiece chimed midnight as if on cue.

"Merry Christmas, my love."

And then, because he couldn't wait any longer, he gave in to his heart's desire and sealed their vow with a long, lingering kiss.

Epilogue

A rousing burst of applause filled the lecture hall at the Society for the Intellectually Advanced, and Matthew beamed with pride alongside Lord Talbot as they assessed the invigored crowd. Theodosia's presentation had gone smoothly, all questions fielded with intelligence and good humor, and the cordial reception she was offered as the first woman speaker ever to take to the podium was well worth the risk.

"I daresay my granddaughter is brilliant." Talbot turned to him with a prideful expression. "She effectively quieted any naysayers in the crowd with her exactitude for detail pertaining to that suspect article about the isolation of dephlogisticated air."

"Suspect, indeed." Matthew couldn't contain his smile. Lord Rannings seemed to have lost all interest in pursuing any further explanation, now that he'd assumed the role of chief officer at the Society. Matthew's ringing endorsement fulfilled Rannings's pining and reminded of a time not long ago when he himself had desired the very same outcome. Of course, that was all before he'd found his way to Oxfordshire and his greatest discovery of all, *Theodosia*.

"I suggest we celebrate," Talbot added.

"Capital idea." Matthew's eyes shot to Theodosia, who approached, her path intersected frequently by well-wishing members who complimented her speech and sought an introduction.

"I've heard the restaurant at Mivart's Hotel sets an excellent table," Talbot continued, his attention drawn to Theodosia now too.

"Then Mivart's it will be." Matthew nodded, accustomed to addressing old topics as new ones, the earl's ability to recall past experiences better at some times than at others. But traveling and living a full life had become easier for all of them. Theodosia had hired more staff to assist, discreet and respectful people who wished to serve and didn't speak out of turn, a sense of loyalty their greatest quality.

At last, Theodosia managed to reach the area where they'd waited on the side of the presentation room. "I think that went rather well."

She appeared proud of herself, as she should be. Her lovely gray gaze met his and held. Blast, if he wasn't the luckiest man in England. Not only was his new wife beautiful in every way, but her intelligence made her incredibly rare indeed.

"More so," he agreed as he reached for her, tugging her closer to nestle her hand in the crook of his elbow. "Your grandfather would like to dine out this evening instead of returning to the town house on Cleveland Row."

"Truly?" She wrinkled her nose at the suggestion as they began to walk toward the door. "All day I've dreamed of nothing else but a quiet evening."

"Perhaps we can compromise."

"In what way?" She seemed genuinely disappointed, and he didn't wish to put a damper on the evening. Besides, he had a plan in mind.

They left the building and advanced down the stairs

to their carriage waiting at the curb. Moving aside, they allowed Grandfather to climb in first. Then Matthew clasped Theodosia's fingers, at the ready to assist her up the steps.

"A celebratory dinner out with everyone, and then . . ." He winked and pulled her closer. "A private dessert course at home later."

"In that case, I'm famished. By all means, let's proceed to Mivart's."

Her face heated to a lovely shade of pink, though a beguiling look of invitation sparked her eyes. He climbed up into the interior behind her and settled on the squabs. A sharp knock on the roof with the knob of his walking stick set the carriage to a roll.

"I can't imagine a better ending to this evening," she whispered for his ears only as she set her head against his shoulder.

He laced their fingers together, his heart thudding a heavy beat as he murmured right back. "Imagination has no limits, love. Our dreams can only come true from now on."

Connect with U s

Visit us online at
KensingtonBooks.com
to read more from your favorite authors, see books
by series, view reading group guides, and more.

for sneak peeks, chances to win books and prize packs,
and to share your thoughts with other readers.

facebook.com/kensingtonpublishing
twitter.com/kensingtonbooks

Tell us what you think!

To share your thoughts, submit a review,
or sign up for our eNewsletters, please visit:
KensingtonBooks.com/TellUs.

Books by Bestselling Author
Fern Michaels

___The Jury	0-8217-7878-1	$6.99US/$9.99CAN
___Sweet Revenge	0-8217-7879-X	$6.99US/$9.99CAN
___Lethal Justice	0-8217-7880-3	$6.99US/$9.99CAN
___Free Fall	0-8217-7881-1	$6.99US/$9.99CAN
___Fool Me Once	0-8217-8071-9	$7.99US/$10.99CAN
___Vegas Rich	0-8217-8112-X	$7.99US/$10.99CAN
___Hide and Seek	1-4201-0184-6	$6.99US/$9.99CAN
___Hokus Pokus	1-4201-0185-4	$6.99US/$9.99CAN
___Fast Track	1-4201-0186-2	$6.99US/$9.99CAN
___Collateral Damage	1-4201-0187-0	$6.99US/$9.99CAN
___Final Justice	1-4201-0188-9	$6.99US/$9.99CAN
___Up Close and Personal	0-8217-7956-7	$7.99US/$9.99CAN
___Under the Radar	1-4201-0683-X	$6.99US/$9.99CAN
___Razor Sharp	1-4201-0684-8	$7.99US/$10.99CAN
___Yesterday	1-4201-1494-8	$5.99US/$6.99CAN
___Vanishing Act	1-4201-0685-6	$7.99US/$10.99CAN
___Sara's Song	1-4201-1493-X	$5.99US/$6.99CAN
___Deadly Deals	1-4201-0686-4	$7.99US/$10.99CAN
___Game Over	1-4201-0687-2	$7.99US/$10.99CAN
___Sins of Omission	1-4201-1153-1	$7.99US/$10.99CAN
___Sins of the Flesh	1-4201-1154-X	$7.99US/$10.99CAN
___Cross Roads	1-4201-1192-2	$7.99US/$10.99CAN

Available Wherever Books Are Sold!
Check out our website at **www.kensingtonbooks.com**

Books by Lisa Jackson

TREASURES

INTIMACIES

WISHES

WHISPERS

TWICE KISSED

UNSPOKEN

IF SHE ONLY KNEW

HOT BLOODED

COLD BLOODED

THE NIGHT BEFORE

THE MORNING AFTER

Published by Zebra Books